W9-BXL-104

IN SHINING WHATEVER

A Three Magic Words Romance

Other Books by Carolyn Brown

The Dove
The PMS Club
Trouble in Paradise
The Wager
That Way Again
The Ladies' Room
Lily's White Lace
The Ivy Tree
The Yard Rose
All the Way from Texas
A Falling Star
Love Is

The Angels & Outlaws Historical Romance Series:
From Wine to Water
Walkin' on Clouds
A Trick of the Light

The Black Swan Historical Romance Series:
From Thin Air
Pushin' Up Daisies
Come High Water

The Broken Roads Romance Series:
To Hope
To Dream
To Believe
To Trust
To Commit

The Drifters and Dreamers Romance Series:
Morning Glory
Sweet Tilly
Evening Star

The Three Magic Words Romance Series:
A Forever Thing

IN SHINING
WHATEVER

•

Carolyn Brown

AVALON BOOKS
NEW YORK

This book is dedicated to Willie and Jana who've been the best neighbors ever for more than thirty years!

Published by Avalon Books,
an imprint of Thomas Bouregy & Co., Inc.
New York, NY

Library of Congress Cataloging-in-Publication Data

Brown, Carolyn, 1948-
    In shining whatever : a three magic words romance /
Carolyn Brown.
    p.   cm.
    ISBN 978-0-8034-7467-3 (hardcover : acid-free paper)
    I. Title.
    PS3552.R685275I5 2012
    813'.54—dc23
                                        2011040251

PRINTED IN THE UNITED STATES OF AMERICA
ON ACID-FREE PAPER
BY RR DONNELLEY, HARRISONBURG, VIRGINIA

Chapter One

Being a smart detective didn't keep Kate from making the biggest mistake of her life. She wasn't fifteen anymore; she was thirty. She wasn't a high school sophomore in love with the quarterback of the football team. She was a detective, albeit only a relief policewoman in Breckenridge, Texas, at that time. There was no excuse for falling asleep next to Hart Ducaine—granted, that's all they'd done; but if anyone saw her leaving the motel, she'd have a devil of a time convincing them of that.

She knew where she was and what she'd done before she opened her eyes, but it didn't keep her from wishing it were a dream like all the others. His snores from the other side of the king-size bed in the Ridge Motel in Breckenridge told her it had been very real.

She gently rose up on one elbow.

It was Jethro Hart Ducaine, all right. Blond curls lay on his neck, a testimony that his father had no say-so anymore about Hart's haircuts. Soft tendrils fanned out across his cheeks, thick but by no means feminine. His face was a study in angles, with a scar running from below the left earlobe to just under the eye, a souvenir of a bull ride he didn't win. His jeans were tight, his shirttail untucked; his boots were sitting beside a chair with his hat hanging on the back of it. He slept on his side, with one hand up under the pillow and the other wrapped around the extra pillow.

She held her breath and eased off the bed. She hadn't meant to fall asleep in his room, hadn't even meant to go to his room; but he'd wanted to talk and she wasn't about to take him home. Her momma would have shot him.

The clock on the desk clicked: 5:10. She slipped her feet into the bright red high heels, picked up her fancy little red satin purse, and tiptoed across the floor. The door creaked slightly when she opened it, and a cold blast of winter air rushed in, but he slept on. She waited until she was outside to don her coat. In five minutes she'd started her truck and was pulling out of the Ridge Motel parking lot, headed east into town.

At least she'd gotten away clean. She wouldn't even tell Sophie and Fancy, her two best friends, about where she and Hart had gone after Fancy Lynn's wedding.

Hart awoke to the noise of someone beating on the motel door. He sat up and combed back his blond curls with his fingers, wished for a breath mint, and went to let Kate back inside. She'd probably gone to McDonald's for breakfast and didn't take the key.

He slung open the door. "What took you so—"

It wasn't Kate.

Two uniformed police officers each had a pistol pointed at him.

"Jethro Hart Ducaine?"

He nodded.

The younger of the two, a fresh-faced kid barely old enough to buy liquor, cleared his throat nervously and said, "Jethro Hart Ducaine, you are under arrest."

He tugged the sheet tighter around his body. "For what?"

"For the murder of Stephanie O'Malley. Hands behind your back."

"Can I put on my boots and get my hat?"

The older partner, balding with a gray rim over his ears, nodded. "With the door open and us standing here with guns. If you try to run, we will shoot. Makes no difference to us if you stand trial or not."

Hart hurriedly crammed his feet down into his boots. Stephanie was dead? How did that happen? He'd just seen her the night before, right before he went to Theron and Fancy's wedding. How did she get dead in that length of time? And, more important, who did it?

"Hands behind your back now," Fresh Face said.

"No funny stuff, either. You have the right to remain silent." Gray Rim read him his rights.

"I did not kill Stephanie," he said through gritted teeth.

"And I'm the Pope," Gray Rim chuckled.

Fifteen minutes later he was in an interrogation room at the police station. He laid his head on the table and tried to get his wits together. He'd seen Stephanie the evening before. He'd passed the lobby on his way out of her room and waved at the night desk attendant. Surely if he'd been there to murder his high school girlfriend, he would have been a little more discreet than that.

In a few minutes Gray Rim came into the room. "Where were you last night between midnight and one o'clock?"

"I want a lawyer. Call Allie Morton over at the courthouse. She takes care of my business," he said.

"Have it your way. Only the guilty lawyer up," Gray Rim said.

Hart didn't answer.

Kate showered and dressed in her Breckenridge police uniform, strapped on her Glock, tied her shoes, and drove to the police department. She yawned and looked forward to a long, boring day. She'd had enough excitement.

From kindergarten through her freshman year in Albany, twenty-four miles west of Breckenridge, she'd had two best friends. They'd all moved away and never thought they'd be back in central Texas again. But the fall before, Kate quit her job in Louisiana and moved back with her mother, Sophie's Aunt Maud needed help down in Baird and Sophie was going through a tough time with a divorce, and Fancy Lynn's grandma fell and broke her hip.

And they'd all come home. Fancy Lynn had gotten married the night before, and it had been a whirlwind week. Kate had been infatuated with Hart Ducaine that summer before she moved away, and there he was at the wedding. They had a history that made her so mad she could cuss, but she couldn't stay away from him.

He'd wanted to talk, and that's why they'd wound up in his

motel room. Now she wondered why he'd rented a room when he lived just south of Breckenridge. Nothing Hart Ducaine had done since she left Breckenridge had escaped Kate's eyes. She knew when he graduated college, when he went on the rodeo rounds, when he won the prizes for bull riding, and when he'd moved back to Stephens County a few months before.

She drove to the police station and parked her truck in a space reserved for officers, adjusted all her gear, and braced herself for the cold. Barbwire fences and mesquite bushes do not provide much of a windbreak for Texas blue northers. She ducked her head and rushed into the building.

"Mornin', Belle," Kate said, shivering.

Belle had been the dispatcher at the station for so long that some folks wondered if she'd pulled a lawn chair up onto the lot a hundred years before and they'd simply built the building around her. Her hair, dyed stovepipe black, was ratted into a gravity-defying hairdo that required enough hair spray to pollute the air in all of Stephens County. Her voice had the gravel texture of decades of cigarette smoke and her face the wrinkles of oxygen deprivation.

"Already got us an exciting day brewin' up, girl," Belle said.

Kate moaned. "Thought it might be a nice quiet Saturday."

"Not hardly. Not when some girl named Stephanie O'Malley is over in the morgue and the killer is already in the room hollerin' for his lawyer. And here the lawyer comes across the courthouse lawn right now. Allie Morton in the flesh and a tight black skirt. I'd give up my Virginia Slims for them legs."

Kate gasped. "Stephanie O'Malley is dead? In Breckenridge? What happened?"

Belle nodded. "Why'd I have to mention cigarettes? Now I want one and it's not break time. I remember back before they caused health problems and I had a cute little ashtray right there." She pointed to a place on her desk.

"Belle! Stephanie?" Kate said.

"Oh, that! Found her in her room at the America's Best. One shot to the heart. Through and through. Found fingerprints all over the room. Dumb fool didn't even try to wipe down the place. Prints on the wineglasses. We're lucky. Ran them through the machine and up popped his picture. Go on back to the room and take a peek. It'll shock you when you see who Allie is going to represent. Wouldn't be surprised if it's not on television this evening. There's other prints on a beer bottle that's running through the program. Probably his too."

Stephanie O'Malley had been Hart Ducaine's girlfriend in high school. Head cheerleader and football quarterback. All that stuff that is written in the stars, only evidently they'd gone their separate ways after graduation, because Kate knew for a fact that Hart had never married.

Allie followed her to the interrogation room without saying much more than a simple good morning. Kate stopped at the window and literally stopped breathing. There was Hart Ducaine sitting behind the table.

Allie sashayed into the room and took a seat on the other side. "Okay, talk to me. I hear you are being held for the murder of Stephanie O'Malley. Your fingerprints are all over a wineglass they found in the room."

"I was there at six o'clock in the evening. We had a glass of wine together. I was gone by six fifteen and at a wedding in Albany until a little after ten."

"You were taken into custody at the Ridge Motel. The lady there said you checked in at ten thirty and a dark-haired woman followed you into the room."

Hart's jaw worked in anger. He couldn't implicate Kate. She worked at the station and hoped to get a full-time job there eventually. Breckenridge was a small town of less than six thousand people. Nothing could kill a career like gossip.

Kate couldn't leave him out to dry, not even if it meant she'd be doing waitress work at her mother and aunt's Mexican restaurant until doomsday. She opened the door and stepped inside.

"Allie, I need to talk to you," she said.

Allie looked her up and down. "Why, Officer Miller? I have the right to talk to my client."

"Kate, don't do it," Hart said. "It'll all come out in the wash. Don't say a word."

Kate slowly shook her head. "I was with Hart all night last night. I followed him to the Ridge from that wedding and spent the rest of the night with him. I left at exactly five ten this morning, less than two hours ago. What time was Stephanie killed?"

"Sometime between eleven and midnight, the doctor says."

"Then Hart couldn't have killed her. I was with him. We talked until almost three this morning."

Allie's face lit up. "Willing to put that on paper or testify to it?"

"Yes, ma'am. I surely am. My truck was parked right beside his. We were together all night. He didn't leave the motel; neither did I."

"Thank you," Allie said. "Hart, give me ten minutes. I'll be back."

She and Kate left together.

Allie almost humming.

Kate seething.

"So what's the history between you and Hart?" Allie asked.

"Your business is taking care of your client. The history between us is mine. They don't mix," Kate snapped.

"Honey, there was more chemistry back there than in a NASA lab. You've known each other for years, haven't you? You're not giving a guilty man an alibi, are you?"

"Honey," Kate drew out the words into several syllables. "If I could have done it with a clear conscience, I'd have kept my mouth shut."

"Good old honest girl, are you? Guilt will eat canker sores in your soul if you don't tell the truth, huh?"

"That's right, and it takes one to know one," Kate said as they reached the captain's office.

"You got it. Through and through. Church on Sunday morning since I was born. That's one reason I wasn't so sure about Hart Ducaine. He looks like a bad boy that would be a lot of fun, but I'm ready to settle down with a good boy, not just have a good time with a bad boy."

"Good morning, Chief," Kate said. "You got the wrong man for that murder." She went on to tell her story.

"Okay, Kate, but in light of all this you better go on home today," said the chief of police, Lucas Elliott.

"And the future?" she asked, already knowing the answer.

"Like always. We'll call when we need a fill-in. Okay, Allie, let's go turn him loose. Bet that's the quickest you've ever made an hour's salary."

"I've never handled a murder trial. Maybe when you bring in the real killer I'll get the case," she said.

Disappointment was written all over the chief's face. Too bad he couldn't use Kate Miller's detective experience on the case. She had the experience and the reputation as a crackerjack detective. Her superior officer had given her such a rave review that the chief had wished he had a full-time opening. Now he was glad he didn't. When today's news hit the gossip lines, Kate's name would be mud in Stephens County. She might as well turn in her uniform, because she'd never need it again in his department, especially in an election year.

For Hart, it was the longest ten minutes he had spent in his entire life. Finally the door opened and Allie walked inside with Chief Elliott. "You are free to go. We need you to be available later for information, since you could be the last person to see Stephanie alive before she was killed," Lucas said.

"Yes, sir," Hart said.

"I'll bill you later," Allie said.

"Where's Kate?" Hart asked.

"She's gone home for the day," Lucas told him.

"This isn't going to affect her job, is it?" Hart asked.

"She is a relief officer. We'll call her when we need her, but since she's implicated in this case, she won't be working it." Lucas was walking out the door when he said the last few words.

"Let's go," Allie said.

They were on the sidewalk outside the station when Allie asked, "Is Kate telling the truth?"

Hart nodded. As bad as he hated to admit it, yes, Kate was telling the truth. He hadn't even kissed her, not last night. If they wanted to ask him about fifteen years before, he'd have to admit that the few kisses they'd shared that summer still haunted him.

A smile tickled the corners of Allie's narrow mouth. Her hazel eyes twinkled. "You are a lucky man, Hart Ducaine. That woman probably just shot her career in the heart for you. I'm not so sure I wouldn't have left you out there to rot with those odds."

"I didn't kill Stephanie, Allie. We had a glass of wine, talked, and I left. She said she was in big trouble and I told her to call the police. She said she might. We left it at that and I went to the wedding."

"It's going to be a circus," she said.

"I'm just glad I'm not the center attraction."

"No, Kate's got that billboard in Technicolor." Allie smiled.

"Think you could give me a ride back to the motel? My truck is there," Hart asked.

She motioned across the street where Kate waited. "I could, but I've got a feeling that dark-haired, steaming-hot-mad lady over there in her truck is waiting to do that. Call me if you need me."

"Thanks for coming so quick," Hart said.

His stomach growled as he headed toward her. Eight o'clock in the morning. Chores to be done at the ranch. He was starving. Terrible way to start the morning after attending the wedding of his good friend Theron. He opened the passenger door and hefted two hundred pounds of pure muscle into the seat. He grabbed the handle on the right side and pushed the seat back as far it would go to accommodate the long legs on his six-foot-plus frame.

"Want some breakfast?" he asked.

Kate glared at him.

"I guess that's a no. Then would you please take me to the motel so I can get my truck?"

She fired up the engine and drove around the block until she hit Highway 180, which was the town's main street, turned right, and headed west. She passed the Mexican restaurant her aunt and mother owned, passed Allsup's C Store, Lawrence IGA, with a sign out front advertising hunting and fishing licenses, which were sold at the grocery store.

Words and sentences formed in her brain, but somehow every time she opened her mouth nothing came out. When she pulled into the parking spot in front of the motel, she found her voice, and the volume button was on high.

"Talk!" She screamed the one word so loudly, it echoed around the truck like a marble in an oil drum.

"You've got a right to be angry with me, but hear me out. I did not kill Stephanie. Trust me or not, that's your privilege. Thank you for being honest and giving me an alibi. I wouldn't have told them. I'd have sat in that jail forever but I wouldn't have jeopardized your job."

Kate squeezed the steering wheel until her knuckles turned white. "Just get out, Hart. I never want to see you again."

"I'm sorry," he said.

He stood beside his truck, watching as she backed out and headed west toward Albany. He wondered if she still lived in that little frame house not far from the elementary school. He unlocked the door to his truck, leaned his head back on the seat, and tried to get his bearings. Finally, he drove a couple of blocks west to McDonald's and ordered breakfast from the drive-through. He ate it on the way back through town and down south to his ranch.

Kate shuffled through her purse and found the cell phone. She called her mother at the restaurant. Courthouse employees and policemen often walked across the street to the Three Amigos for lunch, and she didn't want her mother to hear the news via the gossip vine.

"Talk fast, I'm making tamales," Mary said when she answered the phone.

"Stephanie O'Malley was killed out at the America's Best last night. They hauled Hart Ducaine in for it since they found his prints. We had gone to his motel room, but just drank coffee and talked. I fell asleep fully clothed, and so did he, but no one will believe that. I was his alibi. Is that fast enough?"

"I'd say it's fast enough. Hart Ducaine! After all these years? I thought I'd knocked that boy out of your mind years ago." Exasperation filled Mary's voice.

"It'll be all over town by noon, when the courthouse crew hits the restaurant," Kate said.

"Your job?" Mary sighed.

"Probably swirling around the toilet bowl even as we speak," Kate said.

"Where are you?"

"On my way to Fancy's place."

Mary's voice went up two octaves. "No, you are not! Turn

that truck around and come right back here. You're not running
from your bad decision. Might as well face it rather than run
like a scalded dog. You'll be here in fifteen, right?"

"No, Momma, I'm going to talk to the girls," she said.

"You are not going to Fancy's. She's only got a two-day honeymoon, and you are not going to ruin it," Mary said.

"But . . ." Kate slowed down and pulled over onto the side of
the road.

"You go there, and I swear I will invent a reason for her to
need you the day after you get married," Mary threatened.

"I'll be there in thirty minutes. I have to go home and change.
And, Momma, I'm not ever getting married, so you can't scare
me with that," Kate said.

"Leave the gun at home. I won't have blood shed in my business if Hart comes in here for lunch," Mary said.

"Has he been in there?" Kate asked.

"Couple of times."

"And you didn't tell me?"

"He's old news and bad history. See what happened when you
didn't know. What would have happened if you did?" Mary asked.

"I'm turning around. I'll be there," Kate said through gritted
teeth.

"Don't use that tone with me. I didn't tell you to fall for that
bad boy when you were fifteen, and I sure didn't tell you to talk
to him all night."

"How did you know?"

"You just told me."

"When I was fifteen?" Kate asked.

"Oh, that. A mother knows these things. Why did you think I
didn't fight your father to stay in Texas when he wanted to go to
Louisiana back to the sugar plantation? Now I've got tamales to
make. You've got a job to get to. We'll talk later," her mother
said.

Silence filled the car and Kate flipped the phone shut. She
slapped the steering wheel a dozen times, but it didn't help. She
dialed Sophie's number and said a prayer that she wouldn't be
out in the pasture doing chores. When her friend answered, she
almost wept.

"You're supposed to be working. Boring day on the force?" Sophie asked, without saying hello.

"Far from it. You got a minute?"

"I'm on my way to the barn. Cold today, isn't it?"

"Remember when Fancy came back to Albany that first night and we were all talking about K. T. Oslin's song "80's Ladies," and how we decided you were smart and Fancy was pretty and I was the borderline fool?"

"We decided no such thing. You said you were the borderline fool, and you're beating around the bush. Spit it out," Sophie said.

"I spent the night with Hart Ducaine last night. Spent the night with him at the Ridge Motel, and all we did was talk, Sophie, I swear," Kate said.

"Well, you spat it out, all right. I agree. You are the borderline fool for today. Maybe tomorrow I'll get the dunce hat, but today, girl, it belongs to you. Why did you do such a dumb thing?"

"Oh, it gets better," Kate said, and then repeated the whole story to her.

"Need a place to hide out until it blows over?" Sophie asked.

"Momma says I have to work at the restaurant today."

"Whew!" Sophie giggled.

"I'm thirty years old and I want to run away from home. I know she's right. That's what makes me so mad. She even knew about me liking him when I was fifteen," Kate said.

"Go on home and face the music, my friend. Might as well bite the bullet and get it over with," Sophie said.

"Some friend you are," Kate snapped.

"Does that mean you want me to come support you today?" Sophie said.

"God, what was I thinking? Even when things are innocent, he's trouble," Kate moaned.

"Quit whining. Life isn't fair," Sophie said. "I'll call Fancy. If Theron brings home the news from school, she'll be ready to string us both up."

"It won't travel as far as Albany," Kate said.

"If you believe that, you really are the borderline fool. Good-bye and good luck. Call me tonight."

The phone went dead in Kate's hand for the second time. She

stared at it for a long time before she made a U-turn and headed back to town.

She parked in the backyard and went in through the kitchen. She fished cold tamales from the refrigerator and ate them with her fingers on the way to the bedroom. She locked her gun in a small safe sitting on the dresser, spun the combination dial a few times, and yanked on the door to make sure it was secure.

Her starched uniform went back into the closet, all the way to the back. She wasn't so much the fool as to think she'd be called again. That job was finished. She slipped a pair of jeans up over her slim hips and chose a bright red, long-sleeved T-shirt to go with them. She tucked the shirt in and laced a black leather belt with silver conchos through the loops. She added loopy silver earrings and her favorite silver cross necklace. She put on a pair of comfortable Nikes and headed out the door.

By the time she got to the restaurant, the first of the coffee-break crew were already there. Her mother handed her an apron, which she tied below her belt, and an order pad to slip into the pocket.

"So was he worth it?" Mary asked.

"Momma!" Kate blushed.

"You've let a lot of good men slip through your fingers because you had Hart Ducaine on a pedestal above the angels, so was he worth losing your chance at a career with the police department? You know they'll never call you now," she said.

Talk stopped and silence filled the restaurant dining room when she stepped out of the kitchen with a coffeepot in her hand. A few hushed whispers and a few stares, and then it went right back to normal. She filled orders and thought she'd gotten past the rough part until the lunch crowd appeared, and Slim and Bobby, the two officers who had arrested Hart, rushed in out of the cold.

"What're you havin' today, guys? Special is taco salad and a drink for four ninety-five," she said, pad in her hand and pencil ready.

She took their orders and was halfway back to the kitchen when Hart pushed the front door open. She bristled but didn't stop her long stride. "The special is taco salad and a drink for four ninety-five," she repeated, without looking into his pale-green eyes.

He hung his black cowboy hat on the row of hooks just inside the door and took a seat next to the window. "That's fine. Sweet tea."

She took the order to the back and brought out two red plastic bowls of chips and two of salsa on a tray. She stopped at Slim and Bobby's table first and unloaded one of each.

"You be careful with that one, kid. Hart Ducaine has a reputation as a playboy," Slim whispered.

"I'm a big girl. I can take care of myself," she said.

She set the chips and salsa in front of Hart.

He reached out and gently touched her hand. "I want to talk to you," he said.

"You may be wanting a long time, Jethro."

His brows drew together in a frown. "You know how much I hate that name."

"And I'm not real fond of the name that I have in this town this morning, so it's only fair that you be Jethro."

His mouth set in a firm line. That woman could rattle his cage. She'd been able to make him mad enough to spit tacks when they weren't anything but kids, and she hadn't changed a bit since then.

"Can we talk?" he asked through gritted teeth.

"When St. Peter trades in his white robes for a devil's pitchfork."

"I'll talk to him about that tonight. Call me when you are ready to talk," he said.

"Don't hold your breath," she snapped.

Chapter Two

Kate tugged the jacket of her basic go-everywhere black suit tightly around her chest and shivered, as she trotted as fast as her three-inch heels would allow into the church. She signed her name on the register and opened the doors into the sanctuary to find no one there. It was at two o'clock, wasn't it? She checked her watch: a quarter to the hour. When Momma Lita, her Mexican grandmother, was alive, she'd preached that a person always showed up at a wedding or a funeral fifteen minutes before the hour. It showed respect for the living or the marrying. Being late was not an option in Momma Lita's world.

Flowers surrounded the white casket at the front of the church: roses, tulips, carnations, lilies, gladioli, and every kind of green plant available at the florists' shops. A huge arrangement of pink roses lay in a bed of fern on the bottom half of the casket. Evidently Stephanie was well remembered, but where were the people?

Kate checked her watch again. Ten minutes to the hour. She looked at the memorial folder in her hand. Pink with a spray of lilies printed on the front. The Twenty-third Psalm on the back. The information about Stephanie and the schedule for the service on the inside. Time: two thirty. That explained it.

She didn't have enough time to go back home or even run to McDonald's for a cup of coffee, so she settled in the back pew and waited. Stephanie's photo sat on a pedestal at the head of the casket. She'd been a vivacious, petite blond. The one who was always at the top of the pyramid of cheerleaders. The one who walked Hart Ducaine off the field after every football game.

Kate stood up and went to the front of the church for a better look at the picture sitting on an easel beside the casket. It was taken when Stephanie was a senior in high school, and she wore a pink sweater and had perfectly styled blond hair, with makeup done by a professional just for the picture.

In death, she wore a pink suit with a white rose corsage pinned to the lapel. Her blond hair had been styled and fanned around her face just right. Her hands were folded across her waist and she wore an enormous diamond wedding ring on her left hand. So she'd been married? Why had she asked Hart Ducaine to her hotel room?

Kate's detective mind went into overdrive. What had she been doing, and who really killed her? She wished this were all taking place back in New Iberia, Louisiana, where she'd been a detective for the police force. But despite a degree in criminal justice and several years on the force in Louisiana, these days she was a waitress at the Three Amigos and had no badge to give her the rights to ask anyone anything.

She returned to her pew, sat down, and let her mind go back in time.

It had all started fifteen years before. She'd been infatuated with Hart from grade school, but he was way out of her league. Then that summer when she was fifteen and he was seventeen, he broke up with Stephanie for a few weeks . . .

She'd met Sophie and Fancy at the elementary school playground late one evening. Fancy was seeing a worthless boy, Chris Miller, against her mother's wishes, and when he showed up, they went off hand-in-hand to the other side of the building. A pickup skidded to a stop, and Hart appeared from the twilight cloud of dust. He sat down on the merry-go-round beside her.

He'd barely said hello when Sophie's mother had driven up and taken her home. But Kate and Hart had talked for another thirty minutes. Her flip-flops had barely touched the ground when she'd walked home. They'd met on the playground a few more times, shared a few kisses, and then the night had come when he had told her that he and Stephanie had made up and were getting back together.

When she got home that evening, her mother gave her the

news that they were moving to New Iberia, Louisiana. Her father had the promise of a foreman's job on a sugar plantation. The next night, she met her two best friends at the playground again. Sophie's dad was an oil well driller and his job was taking him to northern Oklahoma. Then Fancy moved to someplace in Florida.

The three friends were split up for the first time in their lives but stayed in touch. Then Sophie moved back to Baird to live with her Aunt Maud, while she figured out what she wanted to do with the rest of her life after her husband's death. Kate's father died in Louisiana, and her mother, Mary, wanted to come home to Breckenridge to be around her large Mexican family. Fancy's grandmother, Hattie, fell and broke her hip, so Fancy offered to move to Albany for a year and teach school there so she could see after Hattie.

Sophie slid into the pew beside Kate. "You are early."

Sophie wore a dark green suit with a lighter green silk shirt, a leftover from her preacher's-wife days. Her kinky, strawberry-blond hair had been tamed into an updo and roped down with a big clip. Her eyes were the color of heavy fog, smoky gray.

"Got the time wrong," Kate said.

Fancy joined them from the other end of the pew. "I'm here! Thought I was going to be late. Thought it was at two, but then I called Theron and he said it was two-thirty."

Her navy blue dress and matching jacket fit snugly. At barely five feet tall, she looked more like a little girl playing dress up in her mother's clothes than a bona fide thirty-year-old former schoolteacher.

People began to filter in by twos and threes until the church was almost full. At 2:25 goose bumps tingled on the back of Kate's neck. She'd worn her long black hair twisted up in a severe knot on the top of her head, secured with two wooden picks that resembled chopsticks. She wished she'd worn it down to cover the crimson rash already making her itch.

No doubt about it, Hart had arrived.

He stood for a few minutes at the back of the church, then sat down on the end of the pew right in front of Kate. She took a deep breath and let it out slowly.

"I'd forgotten how handsome he is," Fancy whispered behind the memorial folder.

His blond curls lay on the back of a black Western-cut suit collar, and the aroma of his shaving lotion wafted to the pew behind him.

"You got your forever thing, lady. That fulfilled the three magic words. Me and Sophie don't get ours," Kate whispered back.

Fancy had always said that she would never marry anyone but a Greek god. Blond hair. Six feet tall and built like a . . . well, a Greek god. When they asked her if she hadn't married because she hadn't found her Greek god, she'd told them she'd grown up since then and now she wanted someone to fulfill the three magic words. They figured the words were "I love you."

But Fancy said they were the promise of a forever thing. Sophie had laughed and said her magic words would be "life after wife." She wanted to know that someone could be true and faithful after the wedding, someone who could give her a life after she became a wife.

Kate remembered her own words well. She wanted a knight in shining . . . and that was where she got stuck and couldn't remember *armor.* She was a detective and couldn't remember a simple word like that. So she'd waved it off with a giggle and said, "a knight in shining . . . whatever." They'd teased her about it ever since.

"Please stand for the family," the preacher said.

Hart turned his head slightly when the family started down the aisle. He nodded ever so slightly at Kate but didn't smile. His light green eyes were serious and his angular face noncommittal. She couldn't tell what he was thinking. Was he hurting because of what could have been and wasn't? Was he wishing that he'd married Stephanie?

The preacher said a prayer, and there was a rustling as everyone settled into the pews and got ready for the service. The president of Stephanie's senior class gave the obituary. She was born on this date and died at the age of so many years, months, days, and hours old. She left behind a grandmother, her parents, and a loving husband.

Then the cheerleading squad from high school all took their places in the choir section behind the podium, and Stephanie's best friend spoke a few words. Kate wiggled in her seat. It was the most preposterous funeral she'd ever attended. Stephanie had been thirty-two years old. The church looked as if it was putting a senior in high school to rest.

Sophie poked her in the ribs and whispered, "Be still. It'll be over soon."

She waited for Hart to take his turn at the podium and relive his days with her, but when the cheerleader finished, they played Stephanie's favorite song from high school. Kate thought it was the only thing about the funeral that seemed fitting.

Then the procession began at the back pew. Sophie was first in the long line to walk past the casket and view Stephanie one last time. Kate was behind her, and Fancy came next. Hart was the next one. They all four glanced and kept moving to the back of the church and out to the parking lot, where friends waited respectfully for the family.

"Kate," Hart nodded when they were outside.

"Afternoon, Hart," she said.

"Fancy and Sophie. It's good to see you," Hart said.

"You okay with this?" Fancy asked.

"What we had was over long ago. It was a high school thing and finished fifteen years ago."

"But you went to college together," Sophie said.

"One semester, then I transferred to A&M. We'd broken up long before the semester ended," he said.

"We're going to the Eagle's Nest. Want to join us?" Sophie asked.

Kate almost swallowed her tongue.

"I'd love to," he said.

"Then we'll all meet there. We're in different vehicles," Fancy said.

Hart headed toward an older-model white truck minus the tailgate.

Kate looped her arm through Sophie's and led her toward their vehicles, whispering the whole time into her ear, "I will hide your body where no one can find it. When you get home, make out a will and leave everything to Fancy, because you are a dead woman."

Sophie giggled. "Oh, hush! I can see the way that man looks at you. Same way Theron looks at Fancy. He's your knight in shining whatever."

Kate shook her head. "You've got rocks for brains. Y'all go on and have coffee with him. I'm going home."

"Just shows I'm right. You can't even sit at the same table with him," Sophie said.

Kate had no choice but to follow them to the café after that remark. Hart was already there and had claimed one of the tables with four chairs surrounding it. Eagles were on everything from the clock on the wall to the billboard that held last year's Albany Lions football team pictures. Hart's photo had been among them years before, right along with Stephanie's who had been the pretty cheerleader at the top of the pyramid.

White vinyl covered the twelve tables in the dining room. A small washtub of condiments, along with a sugar shaker, clear plastic paper-napkin holder, and a red bottle of ketchup were arranged in the middle. The salt shaker had bits of saltine crackers in it to keep the salt from clumping. Red-and-white-checkered valances hung on the windows.

"What're y'all havin'?" the waitress asked.

"Coffee for me. Ladies?" Hart asked.

"Sweet tea and an order of French fries," Fancy said.

"Coffee," Kate said.

"Same," Sophie said.

Fifteen years earlier, Kate would have done backflips off a lightning bolt if she could have gone to the Eagle's Nest with Hart. To sit with him at the table would have been right up there next to kissing the Pope's ring. Right then, she just wanted to gulp down the coffee and make an excuse to leave.

"What'd you think of that service?" Hart asked.

"I figured you'd speak," Sophie said.

"Not me. I don't want to be a part of that. She wasn't a high school kid anymore. She was a grown woman," he said.

"Well, thank you," Kate said. "Who on earth planned such a thing?"

"Her mother. Who else? She was in her glory when Steph was a cheerleader. When she went to college and things went south, her mother never forgave her."

"I'm in the dark. As you know, we left that summer you and Stephanie went off to college. What went south?" Fancy asked.

Kate was all ears.

"Everything. That summer, we had a big argument. Stephanie wanted an engagement ring before we left, and I was too young to be that serious," Hart admitted.

"But you made up. Did you give her a ring?" Sophie asked.

Hart shook his head. "We made up for about two weeks. During the time we were apart." He stopped and sipped his coffee.

Sophie touched his hand. "You don't owe us an explanation. Let's talk about something else."

He looked into Kate's pecan-colored eyes without blinking. "I think it would help if I talked about this now.

"We were apart for a little over a month, and during that time she was seeing Billy Joe Miller. We got back together and went to college. That's when it went south. He rented a trailer not far from campus, and she spent most of her time over there. Her mother didn't know until Christmas that we weren't dating."

"Billy Joe Miller. Chris Miller's older brother?" Kate couldn't believe her ears. Billy Joe was the real resident bad boy in a three-county area. Chris Miller was an innocent babe compared to Billy Joe—and Chris was a womanizer, drunk, and general skunk. He was the reason Gwen jerked Fancy Lynn off to Florida so quickly.

"That's him. He was twenty-five. Her mother almost died when she married him at the courthouse. No big white wedding. No gift registry. I was in my first semester at A&M when that happened," Hart said.

"So why didn't they call her Stephanie Miller at the funeral?" Sophie asked.

"They divorced about a year after the wedding. I guess she finally got enough of his lifestyle. She was high maintenance, and her father cut her credit cards off when she married him. It took a year before she looked around and figured she'd had enough.

Her mother had big notions about the two of us even then, but Stephanie didn't want me."

"So what happened?" Fancy shot ketchup over a platter of fries and began to eat them with her fingers.

"She changed schools. Went off somewhere and wound up married to her psychiatrist. That's when she got the big wedding. Billy Joe got swept under the rug. My momma went to the wedding and said it was the biggest thing in Albany. Stephanie opted to keep her maiden name."

"So that's the story?" Sophie asked.

"It is the bare-bones facts far as I know them," Hart answered, but he was looking at Kate the whole time.

"Poor Stephanie," Sophie said.

"Why? She made her choices and lived with the consequences," Hart said.

Fancy shook her head. "I don't think she did. She was everything her mother wanted her to be. She got her rebellious streak too late. It should have come along when she was about fifteen, and then her mother and father could have taken care of it. As it was, they didn't know until it was too late, because she was out from under their thumb. She couldn't handle her life when it went south, as you say."

The conversation stalled, everyone thinking about what Fancy had said.

"I've got to go." Kate used the lull in conversation to escape. She picked up her purse and laid a dollar on the table.

Hart handed the dollar back to her, brushing her fingertips. "I'll get this. Thanks for asking me to sit with y'all."

She willed herself to not let his touch affect her. It did not work.

"Thank you," she said and looked at Kate and Fancy. "I'll see you two later."

Sophie downed the last of the coffee. "Got to run also. I've got chores, and Aunt Maud is failing fast."

"So how's the first week of marriage?" Hart asked Fancy when they were alone.

"Wonderful!"

"Theron's little girl adjusting?"

"Tina is great. She and I were friends long before Theron asked me to marry him. He says the only reason I said yes was to get a daughter." Fancy smiled.

"Theron is a great person. I'm glad he's going to go into full-time ranching. He was born to it as much as I was," Hart said. "It's what brought me home off the rodeo rounds. Grandpa died and left me his spread over south of Breckenridge."

"When was that?"

"Actually a month ago, but I already had my money up for the Professional Bull Riding, so I went on ahead and made one last ride."

"How long have you known Theron?" Fancy asked.

"Ever since he came to this area and bought his Uncle Joe's ranch. His uncle and my granddad were friends. I visited Granddad as often as I could and met Uncle Joe years ago. When Theron came to live on the ranch, I was one of the first people he got to know."

"And Kate?"

"I don't have to tell you about any of that, I'm sure. You three were best friends in high school, and it's evident you've kept in touch. I couldn't believe my eyes when I saw her at Theron's wedding. Well, I expect I'd best be getting on home to do chores too. Again, thank you for the invitation to sit with you ladies for coffee."

"You are very welcome. Come see us. Maybe we'll plan a dinner party," Fancy said.

"Just call me. Theron has the number."

Chapter Three

Kate was bored nigh unto death. She hadn't realized how much she would miss the uniform. Back in New Iberia, when she first made detective and didn't have to put on a uniform every day, she thought she'd plumb died and gone to heaven. Now she wished she had it back. She'd been trained to be a cop and worked at it until she made detective—the youngest female ever to have that honor in New Iberia.

She carried a tray of chips and salsa to a table of four early tourists. They had their little maps out and were planning to go on over to Albany and do the walking tour, check out the antique shops, and stay at that quaint little Hereford Motel. She answered a few questions about Breckenridge, told them where they could find the Chamber of Commerce, and headed back to the kitchen with the tray and their orders.

"Busy day, isn't it?" the other full-time waitress said in passing.

"It'll make the time go faster," Kate said.

She stacked the tray on the table and picked up the coffeepot with one hand and the tea pitcher with the other. Bobby and Slim were seated at the nearest table when she came out of the kitchen. They both motioned for her to join them. She checked the other customers and slid into one of the two vacant chairs.

"What're y'all doin' today?" she asked.

"Needin' your help, but we'd be in trouble if the captain found out we were even talking to you. It's small-town Texas, darlin'. You're not going to change it. But we need a good detective. This case is eating our lunch," Bobby said.

Kate cocked her head to one side.

"We don't solve this Stephanie case, we'll be marked for the town where gangsters can bring their bodies and dump them in hotels and never get caught," he said.

Kate laughed. "That's a little on the dramatic side there, Bobby. I can't play detective. I was only part-time relief anyway, and I didn't make the grade to even get a full-time position, so I can't be detective. So how could I ever help?"

"Under the table," Slim said.

"Captain would fire you," Kate said.

Bobby nodded. "We'll take the chance. It's been two weeks, and we got nothing."

"Okay, then what have you got that I don't already know?"

"You know about the fingerprints that Hart Ducaine left. That was around six, before he went to the wedding and hooked up with you," Slim said.

Kate opened her order pad to a back page.

"Report came in this morning. The other fingerprints in the room belonged to Billy Joe Miller. He's got a jacket but not murder. It's mainly drunk driving, drugs, that kind of thing. So he's staying over in Albany with his brother, and we go over there to talk to him. He's got a rock-solid alibi. He was there but he left at eight, got picked up on a DUI just as he was going into Albany, and spent the rest of the night in jail before his brother could make bail and spring him. Booked in at eight thirty," Slim said.

She took notes while he talked.

"Anything more?"

"Past that we are empty-handed."

Cookie Mannford waved at Kate from the door. "Texas ain't supposed to be cold. It's supposed to be hot even in the winter, so what's going on?"

Kate left the officers and followed Cookie to a back booth. "What are you doing in town? This isn't the second Friday in the month."

"No, me and Gloria had to switch some days. Why aren't you at the police station?" Cookie slid into the booth.

"They won't be calling on me for relief work anymore." Kate joined her.

When her mother was diagnosed with cancer, Cookie took a

sabbatical from her truck-driving job. As the only unmarried sibling among five children, she left the lush mountains of Luray, Virginia, where she had been living, and returned to the mesquite and mosquitoes of Texas. Her only request was that her sister take care of their mother once a month, so Cookie could have a night to herself. She usually checked into a motel and read a big thick romance book.

"I heard some junk like that, but I didn't believe it. Those fools really aren't going to give you any more work? Why? Is that the two that caused you a problem, sittin' right there?"

"No, it's not Slim and Bobby. They are actually the good guys." Kate told her the whole story.

Cookie threw back her head and laughed. A natural redhead, complete with a face full of light freckles, she had sparkling green eyes and delicate features and was almost six feet tall. She didn't fit the stereotype of a female truck driver at all. Give her a professional makeup artist and put her in a designer gown, and she could easily walk the models' runway in New York City.

She wiped at her eyes. "Now if that ain't the pot calling the kettle black, I don't know what is. Woman has a right to talk to her boyfriend wherever she wants to talk to him. If that had been a male officer talking to a woman, nobody would've thought a thing about it."

"He's not my boyfriend, Cookie."

"Well, he ought to be. He was the handsomest one that went into that room that night. I'm just nosy, but hey, I only get out twice a month. Lady got there at five o'clock, saw her in the office when I paid for my room. She was a bottle blond and looked hard. We walked out at the same time, and she took a little bag from her car. License plate right here. White Escalade. Showed me right quick that she come from money and I'd been wrong."

"How'd you know all that?" Kate asked.

"That's the motel I was staying at, and I couldn't get interested in my book, so I was sittin' out there in the shadows, smoking a cigarette. Only room they had that night was a nonsmoking one. Anyway, I was sittin' out by the door in a chair I pulled out there, all wrapped up in a blanket, telling myself that with what goes on in a small-town motel, I could write my own romance book if I knew how to put the words together."

"No one mentioned her car," Kate said.

"I don't imagine they did. It left later on that night. I'll have a tamale dinner with extra refried beans on the side," Cookie said. "Put in my order and come back, and we'll give those two officers something to chew on."

Kate went to the kitchen and returned with two tall glasses of iced tea.

Cookie went on. "After the good-lookin' cowboy left, some seedy-looking guy drove up in a ratty old pickup truck. Blue and white. Squared-off-looking, not rounded like the first feller's new truck. He stayed about an hour and came staggering out. Took about three times to get his truck started, and he was already weaving all over the road by the time he turned back to the west toward Albany."

Kate nodded. "That would've been Billy Joe Miller."

"It was quiet for a while. I watched a couple of other folks but nothing that interested me, so I went on back in the room. Ate a candy bar and drank a Coke and decided I wanted another cigarette. So I wrapped up in the blanket and went back outside."

Kate held her breath. "What happened next?"

"Big old black Tahoe SUV pulled in beside the white Escalade. Three people inside, a woman and two men. Woman went inside the room. Men got out of the truck and leaned on the back. I decided to be a detective like you, so I wrote down their license numbers. Here they are on the back of this matchbook, with the ones from those first two trucks, if you want them."

"Would you tell this to those officers?"

Cookie's eyes narrowed. "I reckon I would. Let's go visit with them."

She crossed the café in a few long strides, Kate right behind her. Cookie laid the matchbook on the table between Slim and Bobby and pulled up a chair.

Bobby looked up at Kate.

"Listen to her. She's about to break your case wide open," Kate said. She told them what Cookie had just told her.

"Those are the numbers right there," put in Cookie. "Didn't

think they'd ever be needed. I was just entertaining myself. The woman was dressed in black and real skinny. She had on a hooded sweatshirt. She was only in there a minute, and when she came out she threw the hood back. Her hair was that fake red—the burgundy kind that comes out of a bottle. Long and straight, cut in one of those choppy styles. She went to the Escalade toward one of the men, who had on fancy pleated slacks and a sports jacket. Other man had on a long black trench coat.

"The one in black pleated slacks and a sports jacket opened the car door with a key from his pocket. He and the woman kissed a long time before he opened the door, and then she took a big silver gun out of her pocket and they put it in the glove compartment."

"You sure it was a gun?" Slim asked.

Cookie shot him a dirty look. "Honey, I know a gun when I see it. The barrel was real long, so I reckon it had a silencer on it. The kissy-kissy man got into the Escalade and drove away with the woman beside him. Mr. Black Coat got into the Tahoe and followed them. I didn't think about them killin' nobody, or I would've called the police right then. I figured she'd gone in there to scare that blond away from her husband or to buy drugs. I went on to bed. Was out of there early the next day.

"Luck would have it that Momma had a bad day and we were in the hospital a few days, so I didn't even pick up the paper until yesterday. Figured I'd tell Kate what I saw and the plate numbers today."

"You willing to tell all that on the stand if they catch the killers?" Bobby asked.

"Sure I will. I reckon it was the bottle redhead that did her in, wasn't it? Nobody should die like that no matter who they are."

"Thank you, Cookie," Slim said.

"Order should be ready. Let's go on back to the booth and catch up on everything else been going on," Cookie said.

She was in the booth waiting when Kate made a run through the kitchen and brought her plate. The officers were on their way out the door. Cookie pointed toward them.

"You ever have a hankering for that young one? He's not too bad looking."

Carolyn Brown

Kate shook her head. "He's just a baby."

"Get him young and train him up the way you want."

Kate smiled and changed the subject. "The district attorney is going to dance a jig on his desktop with the news they're about to bring him."

Chapter Four

Kate was up early the next morning and took a box of donuts to the police station. Belle met her with a hug and picked out the chocolate-iced one. She poured two cups of coffee and motioned for Kate to sit in the chair in front of her desk.

"Big doin's in the precinct this morning and last night. Caught the men that killed that girl. DA has them over at the courthouse. Something about the good doctor's affiliation with Big Boy Termide. That's of course all confidential, and if you breathe a word of it I'll put a curse on your love life." Belle laughed.

"Big Boy Termide?" Kate's eyebrows drew downward.

Belle reached for another donut. "That'd be like *termite* only with a *D*. He's just what his name says. A big boy—and he's mixed up with every illegal operation in Taylor County. Drugs mainly. I hear that Stephanie's husband's friend, Mr. Sanders, was Termide's lawyer, and that the dead girl overheard some talk about a hit on a prominent business man in Abilene last year. The assassin was the woman Stephanie's husband was seeing on the side. What a tangled-up mess."

"The DA will sort it all out, I'm sure. Who sang first? You know?"

Belle clapped her hands like a child. "You bet I know. I made twenty dollars on the bet. Stephanie's sorry husband talked first for a deal, but he'll have to give back all that insurance money. Bobby told how you helped. I raked the chief over the coals and told him to give you your job back," Belle said.

"I don't want to work for him."

"Maybe someday he'll be gone." Belle winked.

"Maybe by then I'll be doing something else."

"Like maybe something to do with Mr. Ducaine?" Belle's eyes twinkled.

Kate blushed. "That's not even an option."

"Then you are stupid. If I was thirty years younger, I'd flirt with him."

Kate finished her donut and stood up. "Gotta run. Café opens in five minutes. Momma doesn't like it when I'm late."

"You stay away two weeks again, and I'll hunt you down," Belle said.

"I'll remember that," Kate said.

She drove around to the back of the restaurant, parking her truck beside her mother's old Caddy. Fifteen years old and still running like it did when it was brand-new and transported the three of them to Jeanerette, Louisiana.

She grabbed her apron and wrapped the ties around the front. She was cleaning off a table when Hart pushed the front door open. He hung his hat on the rack and pulled out a chair.

"Mornin', Kate," he said.

"Little early for lunch, but the special is right there. What'll you have?"

"Got a minute?" he asked.

She put her order pad back in the pocket of her apron and sat down. "Case has been solved and it had nothing to do with you. I've got a friend named Cookie, and she had the good sense to write down numbers."

"Do I get the full explanation?" Hart asked.

"It'll be all over town in a matter of hours, anyway. Besides, I'm not bound to secrecy," she said. She gave him a rundown of what she knew.

"I wouldn't want to sit on that trial," he said when she finished.

"I doubt it will ever go to trial. Prescott talked first, so he'll get a deal. Spend a few years in prison but not the max."

"And the woman who killed Stephanie?" Hart asked.

"If she tells everything she knows and gets in the witness program, she might wind up in Idaho growing potatoes," Kate said.

And how is all this really affecting you down deep, Hart? Do you have feelings in your heart that you don't even want to face?

"I feel responsible. If I hadn't been in a hurry that night, she might have told me more, but I just wanted out of there," he said.

"Can't blame yourself."

"Will you have dinner with me tonight?" Hart asked.

Kate was speechless. "That was an abrupt change of subject."

"Frankly, Kate . . ."

" 'I don't give a damn'?" she finished.

"I wasn't going to be Clark Gable here. I was going to say that I'm glad it's over and the courts are sorting out the whole mess. But I really do want to go out with you."

"No, Hart, I will not. I'm still Kate Miller. You are still Hart Ducaine. You can't mix oil and water."

She shook her head at him, and then nodded at Slim and Bobby, who had just walked through the door. "Hey, guys!"

Bobby pointed to the special written on the board. "I'll have two of them with extra cheese."

"I won't just go away," Hart whispered.

She pretended she didn't hear him.

Chapter Five

Kate threw open the door of her closet and stared at the contents. There was an impromptu backyard barbecue to celebrate Fancy's pregnancy. She flipped hangers, and finally decided on a red tank with a denim overshirt that could be removed and tied around her waist if it got too hot.

It was a lovely spring day, the second week in March, and Easter was early, so maybe the last of the cold weather had passed. She looked forward to an evening with Fancy and Sophie.

She pulled on skintight hip-slung jeans and stomped her feet down into cowboy boots. She fluffed at her hair but it still hung straight down her back. She envied women who could do that thing with their hands, and their hair would frame their faces in volumes of waves. Not Kate. She'd gotten her mother's straight dark hair and her father's light brown eyes. She'd wished for her grandmother Miller's blue eyes her whole life and had often considered blue contacts, but she didn't even need glasses, so it seemed a waste of money.

She touched up her makeup and grabbed the denim overshirt. It had clear sparkly stones set in the shape of a heart on the breast pocket. She opened her bedroom door to find her mother coming out of the bathroom, wrapped in a white bathrobe, with a towel around her head.

"I'm going to a barbecue at Fancy's house. I could be late."

"I'm watching a movie and going to bed early," Mary said.

Kate nodded and went out to her little pickup truck. She crawled inside and turned the key. Music filled the cab, and she kept time with her fingers on the steering wheel to an old Clint Black tune that let a memory of Hart at seventeen sneak into her mind.

The second song, "Somebody's Knockin'," by Terri Gibbs, brought a vivid picture of Hart to mind—only he was the grown man of today, not the teenager of yesterday. The lyrics talked about the devil wearing blue jeans, and described Hart Ducaine to a tee.

With Hart still on her mind, Kenny Rogers started singing "Lady," a song about the man being her knight in shining armor.

Kenny continued to sing about her being his lady, and she thought back about her own three magic words. Kate smiled when Kenny finished his soft ballad. She'd said that she had to have a knight in shining whatever. It would be nice to be that damsel in distress and have that knight ride up on a white horse and carry her away into happy-ever-after.

Ronnie Milsap sang about being lost in the fifties. Kate could still see her father offering his hand to her mother after a long day, and the two of them slow-dancing around the kitchen floor to the song. They had to be middle-aged by then, and still the way he looked at his wife left no doubt he loved her. That's what Kate wanted. She wanted all of the magic words. She wanted her knight in shining whatever. She wanted a forever thing. She wanted life after wife. Her mother had gotten it all, and there had to be men out there who still had it to offer.

She pulled her truck into the driveway at Theron's ranch and listened to the rest of the song before she got out and headed toward the front door. Tina had her nose pressed to the glass and waved when Kate stepped up on the porch.

"I'm here," Kate yelled, as she opened the door.

"In the kitchen," Fancy hollered back.

Fancy was dressed in jeans and a baggy T-shirt. Not quite five feet tall and with her blond hair pulled back into a ponytail, she looked like a kid. It was no wonder Theron hadn't believed she was thirty when she crawled out of that little Camaro the first time they met.

"Hey, your blue eyes are bright. You really didn't upchuck all morning, did you?" Kate said.

"I told you when I called, this is a celebration that the morning sickness is over. Now I can just get fat and cranky," Fancy said.

Tina ran out the back door, slamming it behind her, yelling that she was going to help her daddy.

"I like that," Kate said.

"What? Fat, cranky, or Tina?"

"No, that wooden screen door. These modern-day storm doors don't slam like that. I remember a door like that when we were kids. Remember how Hattie used to threaten us with a switch if we slammed it one more time?" Kate said.

"Oh, yeah!" Fancy finished cutting up a tomato and added it to the salad.

Kate handed her a cucumber, and she sliced it thinly over the top of the lettuce.

"Momma Fanny, Momma Fanny, Sophie is here!" Tina yelled through the screen door.

Sophie just appeared in the kitchen, in all her red-haired glory. She towered above Fancy and topped Kate's five-foot-six by two or three more inches. Sophie's kinky-curly red hair had given her fits in high school, but now that she was a ranching woman, she lived with the curls with a minimum of swearing. That evening she had pulled her hair up in a ponytail that defied the band; some of it lay in ringlets down to her shoulders, the rest crept out to frame her face. Her eyes were the color of dense fog; Kate swore, even as a child, that she'd been kissed by a witch and could see straight into a person's soul.

"So you aren't sick anymore? Hallelujah!" Sophie bent to give Fancy a quick hug.

"No, thank goodness. How's Aunt Maud?"

"Failing. If she makes it through summer, I'll be surprised." Sophie picked up a bunch of green onions and washed them for the salad. "You are living dangerous," she said.

"And I intend to do so. I haven't eaten real food in two months. I'm ready for the good stuff. Steaks. Baked potatoes. Salad with onions. And I even made pecan pies for dessert . . . or I made part of them. Dessa rolled the crust for me. I swear I don't know what I'd do without her," Fancy said.

"A daughter, a maid who can cook, a Greek god. I'd say you got it all in one big ball of wax," Sophie said.

"I told Theron after the morning sickness he could let Dessa go, but he says no. He's thinking of hiring her oldest son as fore-man for the ranch and putting a trailer somewhere out there on the two sections of land. No more school after this year is fin-ished. I'll be married to a full-time rancher. I never said any-thing about cows and muddy boots when we were fifteen, so don't give me grief." Fancy shook a spoon at Sophie.

Sophie pointed out the window to the backyard. "Who is that?"

"That would be the good Reverend Marcus Broadwell. But not to worry, darlin'. Tonight he's just plain old Marc. He's hung up his wings and halo for the evening."

"You invited him for Kate, didn't you? No way you'd bring a preacher into the mix for me." Sophie continued to stare at the handsome preacher man.

He was tall and on first appearance rather lanky, but his three-button knit shirt stretched over his biceps. He wore wire-rimmed glasses and had a round face and light brown hair combed straight back. Not bad, but a preacher? Fancy was goofy as an outhouse rat if she had matchmaking on her mind.

"He's not for me," Kate said, after a moment's glance out the window.

Then Hart Ducaine rounded the end of the house and joined Theron and Marc at the barbecue grill.

"You said you were only inviting us girls," she stammered and stuttered.

"I did. You didn't ask me who Theron was inviting," Fancy said, blue eyes all wide with innocence.

"You did this on purpose. I never one time pulled something like this when you were running from Theron."

"No, you didn't, but I'm more devious than you are," Fancy giggled.

Kate started for the door. "I'm going home."

"I'll tell him that you are so in love with him you can't be in the same room with him," Fancy threatened.

"Well, at least he's not a preacher. I'll flip you." Sophie pulled a quarter from the pocket of her tight jeans. "Heads, you get Hart. Tails, I don't get the preacher."

"That don't sound fair to me," Kate said.

"It isn't. Five minutes with a preacher and I swear I'll slap the righteousness right out of him." Sophie flipped the coin and slapped it down on the back of her hand. "Heads. Hart is yours and the preacher goes home alone."

"Five minutes with you and he'd spend the night on his knees begging God to forgive him for lusting," Fancy told Sophie.

Kate reached for the salad. "Looks like we are eating on the picnic table. But, girls, Hart is off-limits. I don't want to get hurt again."

She stiffened her backbone and carried the big glass bowl out to the table.

"Kate, come and meet my friend and minister of our church," Theron said.

"I met him at the wedding reception," Kate said.

"Yes, I believe we were introduced at the wedding," Marc said.

Hart touched her elbow. "Kate?"

The warmth of his touch didn't even surprise her. Not anymore. "Hello, Hart. Haven't seen you at the café in a while."

"Miss me, did you?"

"Not at all," she said.

"I've been busy with springtime ranching. I'll be in next week. Hey, you want a job? I'm thinking about hiring a cook and housekeeper."

"I have a job, and you don't want me to be your cook and housekeeper. I hate to cook and I'm a terrible housekeeper."

"That's not what your momma says," Hart said.

"When did you talk to my momma?"

"We all have our little secrets," he said.

She let him have the last word and plowed back into the house, slamming the screen door behind her.

"He's insufferable. I'm sorry I helped put that assassin behind bars. I could use her services," Kate snapped.

"If Hart Ducaine died, you'd be the one in the black veil weeping and throwing yourself in the grave with him, so don't be talking like that," Sophie said.

"Who died and made you God?"

"No one yet. If you hate him so much, then you sit by Marc.

That ought to be a hoot," Sophie said, glancing out the back window again. Neither of the men appealed to her.

"Are we fighting, ladies?" Fancy asked.

"No, but we might be before the night is over. Why did you invite us and a preacher and Hart?" Kate asked.

"I bet they are asking Theron the same thing: Why did you invite those two hussies? We all run in the same circles. You'll have to get over him, Kate, or else learn to trust your heart," Fancy said.

"And Sophie? Does she have to get over her business with preacher men and learn to trust her heart?"

Fancy nodded. "Yep, she does."

"You are crazy," Sophie said. "But your intentions are good. I'll admit that much. Look, Theron is taking steaks off the grill."

Kate headed for the door. "I'm starving. Hart Ducaine better eat fast, or I'll lay claim to part of his. When I'm nervous I eat, remember. And if one of you mention that at the table, I will lay a Cajun curse upon you."

Fancy carried a platter piled high with foil-covered baked potatoes. Kate followed her with the butter, sour cream, bacon bits, and a bowl of cheese on a tray. Sophie brought up the rear with a pecan pie in each hand.

"And here comes the rest of the supper, along with the three prettiest women in all of Texas," Theron said.

Kate passed close to him and whispered out of the side of her mouth, "They will never find your body if you do this again."

"You'd never make Fancy cry," he chuckled.

"What are you two whispering about?" Fancy asked.

"She wants me to say I'll name the baby Katherine," Theron said quickly.

"Sophia Katherine." Fancy let the name roll off her tongue. "Are we going to dress him in pink lace and put his hair in dog ears? What do you think, Tina?"

Tina giggled and rolled her dark brown eyes. "No. We're going to name him Tiger Rufus if he's a boy."

Hart guffawed.

"Don't sound much worse than Jethro Hart, does it?" Kate said.

"Hey, don't start arguing before grace is even said. Marc, would you do the honors?" Theron asked.

Marc shifted his weight to one side during grace, and his knee brushed Kate's. Not one single tingle shot through her leg and into her heart. On the other side, however, was a different story. Hart's leg and shoulder were six inches from hers, and the heat of the sparks threatened to set the backyard on fire.

"Amen," Marc said, and they all looked up.

Theron passed the platter of steaks first.

"Rare on this side?" Kate pointed to the steaks on the left side.

"You got it. Well-done in the middle. Medium on the other side," Theron said.

She plopped a huge rare T-bone onto her plate.

"You going to eat that whole thing?" Hart asked.

"Yes, and a potato. And the reason Fancy made two pecan pies is that I eat a whole one," she said. "You got a problem with that?"

"No, ma'am." Hart chuckled.

"How do you stay so thin?" Marc asked.

"Talk burns calories. Fightin' words burn more than nice words. I like to eat, so I'm not nice."

"Is that for my benefit?" Hart asked, as he passed the salad her way.

She gave him a big fake smile. "You make it so easy for me to scarf down the calories."

"I've got an announcement," Theron said.

"Is it twins?" Kate looked his way.

"No, it's just one baby. Announcement is that you have to pay for your supper tonight. There's a reason you are all here."

Sophie groaned. She wasn't going to a revival and listening to that preacher. Not even if she had to cough up the most delicious steak she'd ever put in her mouth.

"How much?" Kate figured it was a fund-raiser for school equipment. She'd hand over a twenty without batting an eye for her supper.

"We have career day for our fifth-grade students next week. The cost of this supper is that you are all coming to the school Tuesday afternoon and giving a ten-minute speech about your careers."

"I'm a waitress. You want me to encourage the children to put on an apron and carry salsa and corn chips to tables?" Kate said.

"You are a detective. Maybe not a working one, but a detective and, from what Fancy says, a very good one. That's what you are going to talk about," Theron said.

"And me?" Sophie looked up.

"You are a ranchwoman. That will appeal to the girls in the group who are in 4-H and looking at FFA when they are in high school. It will show them that ranching isn't just for men anymore, that women can run a ranch too," Theron said.

"She's covered ranching. I guess you won't need me," Hart said.

"Not so quick, partner. You're going to talk about rodeos and riding bulls. Bring your buckles and get ready to brag. We're proud of our royalty in this part of the world. And Fancy is going to talk about being a teacher, even though she's not working at that anymore. They see their teachers every day, so it will be good for them to see someone else who did that job too."

"Expensive steak," Kate muttered.

Theron laughed. "Enjoy. And don't think you are off the hook either, Marc. You are going to talk about going into the ministry."

"I'd be glad to," Marc said.

Hart looked at Kate. "So give me your practice speech. What's it like to be a female detective?"

"You can hear it on Tuesday with the rest of the speeches," she said.

When they'd finished eating, Theron put a CD on the small player on a table beside one of the Adirondack chairs out under the shade trees. When George Strait started singing a slow ballad, Theron held out his hand and Fancy took it gracefully, melting into his arms to dance with him. Kate turned green with envy at the way they looked at each other and fit so well together.

"What about you?" Hart asked.

"What?" Kate asked.

"Want to dance, or you a chicken?"

Nobody dared Kate or called her a chicken. She stood up at the same time he did and walked right into his arms. She listened to the words of the song as they danced around on the grass.

"This feels good," Hart whispered in her ear.

"You only want what you can't have. You wouldn't want it if you got it," she said.

"I don't know about that. Why don't you give me a chance?"

The song ended, and the next CD started on a Zac Brown Band tune that had a Zydeco sound to it. Kate grinned. She raised an eyebrow and stepped back to do some Cajun dancing. Hart folded his arms over his chest while she danced all around him.

When the song ended, Fancy's and Sophie's eyes were wide with surprise.

"Where did that come from?" Fancy asked.

"Bayou dancing. That song sounded Cajun," Kate said.

"You miss it?" Hart asked when the fiddle music started on the next song.

"I'd be proper and ask you to dance, but I'm afraid I don't have any idea how to do any of that," Marc said to Sophie.

"Me, either. But I'm going to make Kate teach me. That looked like fun."

Theron turned down the music and pulled Fancy into his lap on a lawn chair.

Hart would have liked to do the same to Kate, but it was way too early. She hadn't even agreed to go to dinner with him. But with the dance, he'd laid claim to her that evening, and the preacher man wouldn't be stepping in on his territory. Hart wasn't blind. He'd seen Marc eyeing both of the women, and his pick had been Kate.

Chapter Six

Kate arrived early and chose one of the second-row seats that had paper signs taped to them, with CAREER SPECIALIST written in bright red marker. Would someone in her eleven-year-old audience turn out to be Stephens County's first major detective?

It happened to you, only you weren't eleven, you were sixteen. Remember the first time you got a whiff of the courthouse in New Iberia?

Hart slipped into the seat beside her, his arm brushing against hers. "You're not much of a detective. I just slipped up on you. Could've been a bad cowboy wearing a black hat instead of a white one and about to kidnap you."

She moved her arm, but it still tingled.

"I figured you'd come all decked out in uniform," he said.

The air around her sizzled. Kate wasn't sure what that meant, but she was sure she'd never felt it anywhere but in Hart's presence.

"Detectives wear plain clothes," she said. She'd chosen black slacks, comfortable shoes, a mustard-colored button-down shirt, and a black leather blazer. It was pretty close to what she wore every day on the job in New Iberia.

The kids filed in, and with them several other members of the career specialists. Sophie sat on the other side of Hart. Fancy slipped in beside Kate. A nurse in white, a judge in a black robe, and a man in a suit that Kate recognized as the fellow who owned the local newspaper. She almost groaned. It was going to be a long afternoon. No way could she deliver her little speech and escape. Out of respect, she'd have to sit there until every last person spoke.

Fancy had been right last fall when she said that Theron Warren had looked like a little boy playing dress-up in his police uniform. Kate thought that he should have an orange pumpkin half full of candy in his hands when he took his place behind the podium on the stage in the school auditorium.

"Good afternoon, boys and girls. We have some very distinguished guests in our presence today, so I expect you to be on your best behavior. I'm your principal, but I've also worked as a relief police officer for several years. Today I am going to talk to you about the duties of a police officer and what kind of training you would have to take to be one. I'll talk to you for a few minutes and let you ask questions. They will be asked in an orderly fashion, and each career specialist speaking to you today will only take questions pertaining to their job, not personal questions. Raise your hand and wait until I nod at you . . ."

Kate listened with one ear and chanced a glance toward Hart, who winked at her. She lost it all—concentration, what she was going to talk about, all of it! Then Theron was introducing her. She stood up, hoping she'd have a few intelligent words when she got to the podium.

"I'd like to introduce you all to Kate Miller. She used to live in Albany when she was a little girl. She even went to school right here in our elementary school. But then she moved to Louisiana and became the youngest woman detective ever to work in New Iberia. When she's finished, she will introduce Hart Ducaine, who is sitting beside her."

Kate took her place, and surprisingly enough, her voice sounded normal. "Hi, kids. Thank you for inviting me to your career day. I lived in Albany until I was fifteen. It was during a career day when I was a junior in high school that I decided I wanted to be a detective," she said.

When she finished she asked if there were any questions.

The first one came from a little black-haired girl in the front row. "Do you carry a gun like in *Law & Order*?"

Kate had anticipated that question. She took off her jacket to reveal a black leather shoulder holster and her Glock. "Yes, I do. And I respect it very much. I don't draw it out of the holster unless it is absolutely necessary."

Next question was, "Did you ever kick down a door?"

She bit the inside of her lip. These kids spent too much time in front of a television or with a Game Boy in their hands. "No, I never had to do that. Most of my work is a little boring, to be very honest. It's a lot of asking questions, following up on leads, taking notes. So if you think you want to be a detective, learn how to pay attention and take very good notes in your classes. And it also helps to be able to write well enough that you can read it when you go back later, so good penmanship is important."

There were several hands in the air, but her time was up. "Sorry kids, but that's it. Now it's Hart Ducaine's turn to talk to you about the rodeo circuit and bull riding. Be sure and ask him about that belt buckle he's wearing. He won it a few months ago at the Professional Rodeo in Las Vegas."

Her gun was soon forgotten when Hart took the stage. The emergency room would probably have a run on twisted ankles and broken wrists that weekend, when the kids mounted the rangy old bulls in their pastures. Hart talked about staying on the bull's back for eight seconds, and the way the judges gave points for the bull and the rider. The kids asked questions about his vest with all the logos on it, how bad it hurt to fall off, and if he was ever a rodeo clown.

Then it was Sophie's turn.

Theron had judged their time well; the last career specialist finished two minutes before the final bell rang. Theron thanked everyone for coming, did a quick poll of how many kids were going to be a detective, a teacher, a rancher, a nurse, a bull rider, a doctor, or a fireman. The bull rider got most of the boys' votes, which made Hart grin. The girls were split between nursing and teaching.

"Girls are more mature than boys," Kate said, as they left the auditorium.

"Why's that?" Hart asked.

"Boys see the glory and excitement in life. Girls recognize reality. Momma's right; the only difference in men and boys is the price of their toys."

Theron came up behind them. "Hey, now."

"She's just mad because the little girls didn't want to be a detective and carry a fancy gun," Hart said.

"Be careful. I can beat you to death with the gun even if it isn't loaded," she said.

"I saw a couple of kids raise their hands for detective," Theron said.

"But they were boys," Hart said.

"That's because girls are more realistic. Point proven," she said.

"Then why are you a detective?" Hart asked.

"I liked the pretty gun," she said, and picked up her pace to catch up to Sophie and Fancy.

"Got time for a cup of coffee down at the Eagle's Nest?" she asked her friends.

"Sure we do," Fancy said.

Sophie pointed to the holster. "Is that thing loaded?"

Kate shook her head. "No, but maybe if it were, I could just shoot him and put myself out of this misery. I'll meet y'all there."

She got into her truck and drove west. Suddenly she was tired of talking about him, thinking about him, dreaming about him. Very few waking minutes didn't involve something that would bring him to her mind. Maybe she needed to call Captain Trudeau in New Iberia and beg for her old job back. He said he'd hold it a little while until she was absolutely sure she wanted to go back to the Texas heat.

She got caught by a red light, so the others were already at a table when she walked into the place. She pulled out a chair and sat down. "I'm hungry. Let's share a great big order of fries."

"Sounds wonderful," Sophie said.

"What can I get you ladies?" the waitress asked.

"A triple order of fries, and I'll have sweet tea," Kate said.

"Diet Coke or Pepsi, whichever one you have," Sophie said.

"Sweet tea for me too," Fancy said.

"Why are you ordering diet, Sophie? You don't have an ounce of spare fat," Kate asked.

"Marc didn't say that he liked skinny broads, did he?" Fancy asked.

"I'm ordering diet because I like the taste of it better than the real stuff. Now I want to know about all those vibes that light up a room when you and Hart are in it together," Sophie said.

Kate hated to be in the hot spot, especially when she had to be truthful.

"Okay, I admit it! I was flirty when I did that Cajun dance at the cookout the other night. It was spur-of-the-moment, and I shouldn't have done it."

Fancy took a long sip of the tea. "Fifteen years ago you moped around, and we handed you tissues to blow your nose with while you cried over Hart Ducaine dropping you for Stephanie. Now you've got a chance to go with him, and you're turning it down. Why?"

"I'm afraid that if I let my guard down, he'll just hurt me again," she said.

Fancy's cell phone ringtone made her smile. "That's Theron. Sorry, girls, I've got to take it. Hello, darlin'," she said, and all the color left her face. "Oh, no! Are you sure it was him?"

Sophie and Kate both stared.

"We'll go right on over there."

"What?" Sophie asked. "Is something wrong with Theron?"

Fancy shook her head. "No, it's Hart. He's been hurt bad, and they've taken him to the hospital."

Kate's heart fell out of her chest to the floor and stopped beating. She stared at Fancy with blank eyes. Hart couldn't be hurt. He'd stayed on the back of a bucking bull for eight seconds multiple times and only had one little scar. He was invincible. She'd just left him and made that joke about shooting him. She was only teasing. Why were they looking at her like that? Didn't they know she could never shoot Hart Ducaine? She couldn't harm a hair on his head.

"Kate, did you hear me? Get up. Hart's been hurt."

"What happened?" she asked hoarsely.

Sophie reached down and pulled her up by her arm, picked up her purse, and tugged her out the door. "You are riding with me. You can't drive."

"Please tell me this is a joke," Kate whispered, when Sophie started up her truck.

Sophie started up the truck and said, "Theron wouldn't pull a sick joke like that on us."

"What happened?" She was still whispering, but her words boomed in her ears.

"I don't know, but we'll find out when we get there," Sophie said.

She turned back toward town and made a right turn on Gregg Street. Kate was out of the truck and running toward the emergency-room doors before Sophie turned off the engine.

"Hart Ducaine," she said breathlessly to the first lady in scrubs that she saw.

"Stitching him up now. Are you family?"

"No."

"Then have a seat."

"I'm going back there. You tell me where he is," Kate said.

"If you aren't family . . ." the woman said.

"Then I'm family," Kate said. "I'm his wife."

The woman smiled. "I don't believe you, but I'm not going to argue."

Hart lay on a table that looked too small and much too narrow for his big body.

The doctor looked up.

"She says she's his wife, but I don't believe her. Hart Ducaine isn't married," the woman said.

"Old work truck didn't have airbags. If it had, it could have saved these fifteen stitches in his hairline," the doctor said.

Tiny black dots went from one side of Hart's forehead to the other, and they'd shaved his hair back about two inches. He was going to love that when he looked in a mirror.

"Anything else?" Kate asked.

"He's a lucky man, Mrs. Ducaine. Lots of bruises. He was wearing a seat belt, and that saved him. No broken bones. Truck driver wasn't so lucky. He had a heart attack and was dead before his big rig hit Hart's truck.

"We will be keeping him overnight. He was agitated a while ago and kept fighting us, saying your name over and over. I assume you are Kate."

"That's right," Kate said.

"We had to cut off his chaps and that vest. You can explain it all to him when he wakes up. Okay, guys, put him in a room." The doctor snapped off rubber gloves and tossed them in a trash can.

"Kate?" Hart reached out and grabbed her hand but didn't open his eyes.

"I'm right here," she said.

"Don't leave me."

"I won't."

His grip relaxed and he slept again.

"Is that normal?" she asked.

"Very. He's had a trauma. We'd give him something for the pain, but he'll need to be awakened every hour."

"I'll take care of that. I'm going out to tell my friends what's going on, and then I'll be right back," she said.

Kate literally plopped down in the chair between Sophie and Fancy. "They've stitched up his head, but there are no broken bones. Y'all can go on home. Sophie, you need to do chores. Fancy, Theron is going to be waiting."

"You sure? I'll stay until he's in a room," Sophie offered.

"Theron is a big boy, and Dessa is there," Fancy said.

"He's not dead or dying, and they're only keeping him to-night. I just lied to that woman over there behind the glass and told her I was his wife. I won't hear a word from either of you!" Kate said.

Fancy giggled nervously, and Sophie guffawed. Kate couldn't help but join in the infectious laughter. Three friends giggling and one woman staring at them as if they were crazy. That's how Mr. and Mrs. Ducaine, Hart's parents, found them.

"Kate?" Mrs. Ducaine stopped in the middle of the room. She was a tall woman with gray shot through her short blond hair. She had a round face that defied wrinkles. She wore jeans and a button-up pink shirt with a zippered pink sweatshirt over it.

"Yes, ma'am. That's me. I'm sorry we were laughing. It's not funny that Theron was hurt but . . . anyway, he's only got a few stitches, and I'm staying with him tonight to wake him up if he falls asleep. . . . I'm sorry we were laughing," Kate talked too much and too fast.

"You don't have to explain. And please call me Elisa," she said.

"And you can call me Patrick." Mr. Ducaine extended his hand before asking, "Where is he?"

Hart had inherited his genes from his father. The man was over six feet tall, broadly built, thirty pounds heavier than Hart with the weight carried around his middle; he had light brown hair and hazel eyes. It was evident he'd just come in from doing chores, because he still wore overalls, a buff-colored work jacket, and scuffed work boots.

To save Kate from replying to Patrick's question, a nurse popped his head out of the emergency-room doors at that moment. "I'm Steve. We've got him settled in. I'll take you to his room."

Fancy hugged Kate. "See you tomorrow."

Sophie hugged her. "Good luck."

Steve led.

They followed.

Hart was flat on his back. His eyes opened when he heard them in the room.

"Hello. Are we having a party?"

"What happened?" Elisa went to his side and lightly touched the bandage across his forehead.

"Big truck was sideways in the road. I tried to swerve, but it caught me broadside and flipped the truck. I hate to lose that old work truck. Grandpa would cry if he could see it now."

"Always told your momma that if you had to go hit something, it ought to be your head. Always been hardheaded. Hardest thing on your body." Patrick spoke gruffly, but his eyes said he was teasing.

Elisa touched Kate's arm. "Don't be paying these two no never mind. They both go on like that when they're nervous. Too big in their manhood to admit they're worried, so they tease about it."

Kate nodded. "I'll go and . . ."

Hart reached out from the blanket and grabbed her hand. "You said you'd stay with me. You promised that doctor. Momma and Daddy, y'all can go home. Kate's already said she'd stay. She told that woman that she was my wife so she could come back into the room."

"But . . ." she stammered.

"That thing under the bandage any worse than the one on your cheek where the bull gored you?" Patrick ignored the remark about Kate.

"Only hurts when I frown," Hart said.

"Well, that's simple enough. Don't frown. Don't know why you would anyway, with a pretty girl like this to keep you company all night."

"Maybe I'm keeping her company, and maybe she'll need an alibi come daylight," Hart said.

Kate blushed deep scarlet.

"Call me if anything changes," Elisa whispered to Kate.

"I will. I promise."

"I was hoping the stitches would be on the back of his head so they'd cut those sissy curls off," Patrick said.

"I like them," Kate said, then wished she could reach out and suck the words back into her mouth.

Patrick laughed out loud. "She's got spunk, son. Let's go, Momma."

They were barely out of the room when Hart pushed the button to raise the head of the hospital bed to a sitting position. "So you like my curls, do you?"

"That just slipped out."

He drew his eyebrows down. "Ouch!"

"Your dad told you not to do that," she said.

"I should have listened. I'm hungry. Did you have supper? Call the Dairy Queen and go get us some food."

"Is that an order or a request? I'm sure they can brew up some instant chicken broth and Jell-O in the kitchen if you are starving," she said.

He changed his tune. "Would you please go get me food? I'll be dead by morning of starvation if I don't eat."

"I'll check with Steve."

"Who in the devil is Steve?" Hart was careful not to frown.

"He's the nurse who took care of you. I figured you'd remember the fellow who cut that fancy vest and your chaps off for you," she said.

"You let them destroy my vest and chaps?" His eyes bulged.

"I wasn't here or I would have said, 'Hey, y'all, don't hurt the vest and chaps. Let him die but don't lay a finger on his precious toys.' Just goes to prove I was right all along. The only difference in men and boys is the price of their toys."

"I get testy when I'm hungry," Hart said, by way of explanation.

"So do I," Kate said.

"They aren't going to let me drive to the Dairy Queen. It's your call. We eating out or staying in for Jell-O and broth?"

She stood up and walked out to the nurse's desk where Steve was doing paperwork. She asked him about food for the patient, and he said Hart could eat whatever he wanted, but if it nauseated him, to ring the call button.

She stuck her head back inside the room and said, "Steve says you can eat. What's the order?"

"Double cheeseburger, two large fries, and a chocolate malt. That might get me by until midnight when I'll need a snack, so stop by the convenience store or the grocery store and get us some junk food. Pretzels and chocolate cupcakes and a six-pack of soda. Surely they have ice here. Take my wallet. It's in the drawer, and there's money in it."

"No thanks. I'll pay for it. You can get it next time." *Mercy!* Why did crazy words keep coming out of her mouth? There wasn't going to be a next time.

He smiled. "I'll hold you to that. Dinner on Saturday night, then?"

"Hamburgers when I'm laid up in a hospital bed overnight," she shot back as she disappeared out the door.

Not until she was outside did she realize she was several blocks from the Eagle's Nest, where her truck was parked. Hart would have to go hungry a little longer, but a walk would work the tension knots out of her body. She would have run if she had on the right shoes, but since she'd opted for black flats that afternoon for the career thing at school, she set off at a brisk pace. Two blocks up Gregg Street she made a turn onto Fisher, and kept going the better part of five more blocks until she reached the Eagle's Nest, where her truck sat waiting.

She fished around in her purse for her keys and almost panicked when she thought she'd lost them. But there they were, tangled up in the center zippered pocket, the very place she never put them. Leave it to Hart to tie her up in knots so tight she couldn't even put her keys in the right place. She unlocked the truck and slid inside, moaning aloud when she saw her holster and gun lying right out in plain sight. It was a wonder someone hadn't bashed in a window to steal it.

Before starting the engine, she put the weapon into the glove box and locked it. Then she drove to the Dairy Queen, ordered from the drive-through, and waited in line for takeout. She stopped at a convenience store on the way back to the hospital and picked up two small bags of pretzels, several candy bars, and four packages of chocolate cupcakes.

She locked the truck when she got back to the hospital and went in through the front doors. She carried three bags of food in one hand and a cardboard drink holder in the other.

Hart was sitting up in bed, eating Jell-O. "Don't give me that dirty look. It's barely enough for an appetizer."

Steve pushed a machine into the room. "Time for vitals." He checked Hart's blood pressure; it was slightly elevated. "Little higher than it was this afternoon."

"With good reason." Hart waggled his eyebrows at Kate.

Steve chuckled. He was a short, round man with a spare tire around his middle.

"My wife does the same thing to me. Any time she gets all dolled up to go out on the town with me, my blood pressure hikes up twenty points."

Kate fought the blush, but she lost the battle. "We're not married. I just said that to get into the emergency room with him."

"You fight like you are," Steve said, as he pushed the machine out into the hallway.

Chapter Seven

Thank goodness for that rule about not talking with food in your mouth. At least while they ate supper, Kate didn't have to think about conversation. She carried the empty containers to a trash can outside, so the room wouldn't smell like burgers and grease all night. She checked the big clock on the wall behind the nurse's station: seven o'clock.

She fished her cell phone from the pocket of her jacket, leaned against the wall a few doors down from Hart's room, and called Fancy.

"Is he all right?" Fancy answered.

"He's fine, but the doctor would still like him to stay awake through the night if possible. I've got a problem," Kate said.

"Spit it out."

"When you rode all the way to Decatur with Theron and then got iced-in all those days, what in the hell did you talk about?"

Fancy giggled. "We had a little kid with us. You want to borrow Tina?"

"It's not funny," Kate snapped.

"Sorry, but it is funny. When I called you to get in touch with my mother and the beauty-shop ladies when I was iced-in at that cabin, you thought my predicament was pretty humorous. It's my turn to laugh," Fancy said.

"Well, get it over with and tell me what to do," Kate said.

In November of the previous year, Theron called Fancy one night and asked her to drive to Decatur with him to get his daughter. It was supposed to be a quick trip to Decatur to pick up Tina and then return to Albany, but the weather turned bad. They spent the better part of a week stuck in the cabin.

"Well?" Kate said after a few seconds.

"Pretend you are on a stakeout in Louisiana. What did you talk about with your partner?" Fancy said.

"That was my partner. He was bald and married and had four kids and grandkids to boot."

"Pretend Hart is bald and married. What would you talk about now?"

"You're no help at all," Kate said.

"Neither were you when I was running from Theron," Fancy reminded her.

"But everyone could see that you and Theron were in love," Kate protested.

"I rest my case. Enjoy the night. I remember a time about fifteen years ago when you would have kissed the devil's spiked tail to get a whole night with Hart Ducaine with no one around."

"I'm a grown-up now, not a kid," Kate said.

"Call me tomorrow and tell me the details. Bye now," Fancy said.

Kate stared at the phone. Should she call Sophie? She shook her head. Sophie wouldn't be any better at the advice than Fancy. She headed toward Hart's room, but her step wasn't springy nor her mood one whit better.

Hart looked up from a magazine when she entered the room. "What took you so long?"

"I told Fancy I'd call when they got you in your room. Everyone is worried," she said.

"About me?"

"Well, they danged sure ain't worried about me," she said.

He loved her slow Southern accent. She hadn't had that when they were younger. She must have acquired it in Louisiana, the same place she'd learned to do that bayou dancing. He laid the magazine down and looked at her. Why was he so drawn to her? She was lovely, with those Marilyn Monroe lips and that lightly toasted skin. Her voice was soft and smooth with the Cajun accent; something akin to warm honey with a splash of Kentucky bourbon to cut the sweet.

Hart took a long swig from the water on his table to wet the sudden dry mouth. "So tell me about yourself," he said, when he could sound normal.

She took off her jacket and hung it on the back of the reclining chair and sat down. It didn't feel so very different from the passenger's seat in the car the force issued to her and Rudy.

I'm on a stakeout, she thought.

"What do you want to know?" she said.

"Everything. All of it."

"We've only got one night," she said. *And if we had a lifetime, I wouldn't tell you everything. Some things a woman never tells, not even to her best girlfriends.*

"Okay then, what was it like growing up in Louisiana? It sure changed your accent," he said.

"It's a whole different world. Cypress and oak trees as old as God with moss drooping down, blowing in the breeze like it's calling your name to come and sit beneath the trees and listen to the stories. The oaks are so ancient they could tell the tales of battles fought around them during the Civil War, and sorrows and loves on a personal level."

"I'd like to visit there sometime. You make it sound beautiful. I was in Lafayette for a rodeo once, but all I saw was the fairgrounds and a pretty good place to eat Cajun food," Hart said.

"The Bayou Teche has a city park bordering it. When you visit, don't forget to go there. Sitting on a bench and feeding the ducks beside the bayou brings a peace you can't find anywhere else."

"I've heard that name before. Bayou Teche." He frowned and grimaced.

"Don't do that with your eyes when you are thinking. It pulls at the stitches," she said.

"Dave . . . my favorite author, James Lee Burke, writes about him . . . Dave Robicheaux. Hey, did you know they made a movie a while back called *In the Electric Mist* and it's filmed down there? I bought it as soon as it came out, and went back and re-read the book while I waited for it to arrive. Tommy Lee Jones does a bang-up job of creating the character of Dave in the book. So that's where you lived. I thought I recognized the name of that place when you mentioned it," he said.

"I only lived there after I graduated from college and got a job with the force. Before that we lived a few miles away in a little town called Jeanerette. That's where the sugarcane planta- tion that Daddy worked on is located. We had a little two-bedroom house on the back side of the plantation. The foundation was probably put in when the folks in the big house had slaves, but it burned years and years ago, and they built a small house for the foreman."

"You ever meet Mr. Burke?" Hart asked.

"Couple of times."

"I'm impressed," he said.

"It don't take much to impress a man with his head shaved and nothing to do all night but stay awake," she said.

Hart moaned. "Don't remind me. It'll take years for my hair to grow out, won't it?"

"Oh, don't be a sissy. It'll look fine in six weeks."

"Don't call me a sissy. I'm a bull rider," he said.

"So does that make you all tough and mean?"

"It makes me not a sissy."

"Touchy spot there, is it? Who called you a sissy?" she asked.

He turned his head and looked out the window.

That was fine by Kate. Lots of times she or Rudy, her partner, riled each other to the point that neither of them spoke for hours, and they got over it. Of course, they had no other recourse. When the shift ended and they went home, it wasn't the end of the mat- ter. They still had to face each other the next morning at eight o'clock. So they learned to argue and forget it. Hart could do the same or sit there and pout all night. Actually, that would at least keep her from having to talk, even if the seconds did take an eter- nity to tick off on the clock on the far wall beside the television.

"Stephanie," he said, after five full minutes of silence.

"What?" Kate was thinking about the hot bread at LeJeune's French bakery in Jeanerette. Nothing a person could buy at Wal- Mart could compare to the texture of that bread. Her mother often bought it and sliced it thick to go with jambalaya or clam chowder.

"Stephanie called me a sissy," Hart said.

"Why would she do a fool thing like that? You were a hunky

football player all through high school. There wasn't anything sissy about you." Kate's temper flared. The woman never did deserve Hart. It didn't matter that she was dead at much too young an age. That was just plain cruel to hurt him like that.

"It was when we broke up. She said I was a big sissy, afraid of what the guys would think of me if I gave her an engagement ring and let her start planning her dream wedding. She said we didn't have to get married until the second year of college. I said no, and she said I was a sissy because I didn't want the guys to rib me about letting her have her way."

He went on. "And then when she wanted us to get back together at the end of the summer, she said I was a sissy because I didn't want to hurt your feelings."

Kate was instantly angry with Stephanie and thought, *Okay, lady, be glad you are already sitting on whatever cloud you've been assigned because if you were still walking around in the flesh, I'd be sorely tempted to order a gris-gris bag and put a hex on your sorry hide.*

"You going to say anything?" Hart said.

"Not much. Just that I'm sorry I wasted a single minute feeling sorry for her. It's a good thing she's not able to walk through the door, because I'd yank her bald-headed and enjoy doing it. She was a witch when she was young, and . . ."

Hart chuckled. "I unleashed a monster."

"You took the chains off my temper, Jethro Hart Ducaine."

He winced. "Why won't you go out with me?"

"I'm not going there tonight, Hart. Tell me about bull riding."

She checked the clock. It wasn't even eight o'clock. This was turning into the longest stakeout of her life.

He looked at the clock. How could he slow it down and make the night last longer? He'd barely gotten her to talk about herself, and the time was racing.

"Bull riding is bull riding. Stay on eight seconds. Get the most points. Win the prize. Now tell me about your last two years of high school in New Iberia," he said.

"High school in Jeanerette, not New Iberia. I lived out on a sugar plantation. It took thirty minutes by bus every morning to get to school."

"So were you a cheerleader?" He pictured her long legs in a short pleated skirt.

"I was a geek. I studied hard so I could get a good scholarship to LSU. It paid off. I got a four-year ride on academics. Left home at eighteen and moved into the dorm," she said.

"And partied or kept studying?" he asked.

"I studied. It was ninety miles from Jeanerette to Baton Rouge, but I only went home on holiday breaks. Weekends I worked on campus. Summers I went to school. Graduated in three and a half years. Went to work at the New Iberia force right after my twenty-first birthday. Made detective when I was twenty-five."

"That's the bare bones. Did you miss your family?" he asked.

"Like the devil. I cried every night that first year. I missed Momma's cooking and I missed Daddy's big old booming voice when he came home at night. I still miss Daddy. It's been a year, and sometimes I swear I can hear his footsteps on Momma Lita's porch when the sun goes down and it's time for him to come home."

"Y'all living in your grandma's house?" Hart asked.

"Momma and I are. That's an adjustment. When I got on with the force I rented my own apartment. Momma and I saw each other every week, and that was a treat after months of being apart at college. But when Daddy died, she wanted to come back to Texas to be around her own folks. I was at a bad place in my career, so I came with her. The rest you know."

"Still bare bones. I got a confession: I looked you up on the Internet and knew you were a Louisiana detective," he said.

"Why did you do that?"

"We broke up, and I went to college the next week. When I came home after the fiasco with Stephanie, I went to your house in Albany. It was empty, and no one knew where you went. Just that you and Sophie and Fancy had all left about the same time. They thought one of you went up to the Panhandle and one south, but no one was sure."

"All goes to show what an impression we made on the class-mates. Bet if I'd been asking about Hart Ducaine instead of the other way around, they'd have told me everything about you, including what you ate for supper and what fraternity you pledged.

Want to watch television?" She picked up the remote and pushed the power button.

"I'd rather talk," he said.

"We can talk while we watch television," she said. Hopefully, he'd get involved in a show and quit asking questions.

The second channel was a movie with the credits only beginning to roll. When she saw Jennifer Aniston's name she paused. The old sitcom *Friends* had been her favorite the whole ten seasons it aired, and she still watched anything one of the stars played in.

Picture Perfect was a romantic comedy about a young advertising whiz who was a good girl. A picture had been taken at her friend's wedding of the guy who caught the garter and the girl who caught the bouquet; that being one cute blond-haired fellow and Jennifer. She used the picture to convince her boss that she was engaged so she could get a promotion, and then had to produce the fiancé. Two hours later, at ten thirty, the movie ended.

"So who was your Sam, the person you thought you loved, only you didn't?" Hart asked, referring to a character in the movie.

"Who was yours?" she asked right back.

"Kevin Bacon isn't my type."

"He's not mine either."

"Did you have a Sam?" he asked.

She fidgeted while she collected her thoughts. Yes, she had a Sam, but his name was Zac Verret. He played fiddle for a Cajun band. He had jet black hair he wore too long and ebony eyes.

"So what was your Sam's name?" Hart asked.

"What makes you think there was a Sam?"

"The look on your face. Did you love him?"

"No, I didn't love him. His spirit wasn't stable, and we'll leave it at that."

"Good God, Kate. Was he a convict?" Hart asked.

"Don't you judge me. You were dating Stephanie. Look where she ended up. As far as I know, my Sam is still playing the Cajun joints in southern Louisiana."

"He's in a band? I never pictured you as liking that kind of fellow." Hart almost pouted. He'd wanted to hear that she'd pined away for him and never had another man in her life.

"He was pretty, and it was a hot night. I mean, really hot. My sundress stuck to my body and we'd been dancing for hours, so when the band took a break and he asked me to dance with him to the jukebox, I did."

Hart didn't want to hear any more. The thought of Kate doing that dance she'd performed at the barbecue with someone else didn't sit well at all.

"Want to hear more?" she asked.

"I get the picture. What else is on television?"

"Nothing but reruns."

"You said, 'We' had been dancing for hours. Who was with you?"

"My cousins. I've got a whole beaucoup of cousins down there yet. Daddy came from a big family. We worked hard all week and we danced hard on the weekends. I wish I could bring that lifestyle to Texas. We'd all gather up at Maw Maw Miller's place out by the bayou. It didn't take much for a *cochon de lait*. That's where someone roasts a big hog, and there's music. Someone's birthday, a child's birth, a death in the family, an anniversary, the first sugar crop, anything to celebrate and have a good time."

"You missed that when you went to college?"

"I lived for the days when I could go home for the holidays. There'd always be one to celebrate my coming home. I was important to those people. I was getting an education. I was going places," she said.

"So you got the best of both worlds. Your momma's good looks and your father's Cajun parties."

"I did, but Momma is also a good Cajun cook," Kate said.

"Why doesn't she start a Cajun restaurant of her own?"

"Because Aunt Ilene needs her at the Amigos. Momma doesn't need the money, but she needs the schedule. Daddy was her life. She has to have something to fill her days since he's gone," Kate explained.

"And since you are the only child, you had to give up your job and come back to hellish Texas?"

She glared at him. That he knew so little about her when she'd lived in the same town as he did for the first fifteen years of her life proved what she'd been trying to say for weeks. He didn't know her at all.

"I have four older brothers born right after Momma and Daddy got married. Four boys in as many years. Raymond, John, Azore, and Paul. They almost had them all raised, and here I came along. Paul graduated before I even started school."

"Where are they now?"

"Raymond is in Nashville. He's a baseball coach for a high school. John is in Florida, an inspector for the government in the fruit market. Azore is in California, retired military and working for the postal service. Paul is Father Paul in Savannah, Georgia."

"I never knew any of them. Don't know that I heard them mentioned," Hart said.

"Why would you? Raymond got a scholarship to play ball at the university in Tennessee right out of high school. He married a Tennessee girl and they settled down right there. John hated school. He got a job at one of those T-shirt shops on the strip near Panama City Beach. But he found out real quick that wouldn't pay the rent and support any kind of lifestyle, so he wound up taking classes in science. Azore wanted to be an actor, so he went to California. That lasted about one summer, and he enlisted in the Navy. Paul was born a priest. Momma said Daddy marked him when he named him after the parish priest back in Louisiana. Anyway, they all left right after high school. You weren't old enough to remember them. They weren't important enough in Albany to be remembered by anyone other than our church and friends, neither of which you fit into."

Hart looked hurt. "I'm not your friend?"

"Oh, *bon ami,* stop your *bobbin',*" she said, in a slow Southern drawl.

"What did you just call me? I'm not so sure I like this Cajun talk."

"I said *bon ami,* or good friend, stop your *bobbin',* or pouting."

A smile split his face from side to side. "So I'm not only your friend, I'm your good friend."

"Maybe, but not my *cher.*"

"And that would be?"

"Anything more than a friend."

"Why can't I be a *cher*?"

"*Cher* means dear. *Chere* means my sweet. Both sound a little sissy, don't they? And I wouldn't want to be calling you a sissy."

"I could show you right here that I'm not one bit sissified," he teased.

"Not going to happen, Jethro Hart."

He almost winced, but caught himself before he actually frowned. That hurt like the devil, but he was learning.

He yawned. "Let's take just a thirty-minute nap. I've got an alarm on my watch in the drawer there."

She shook her head. "You are going to stay awake."

"Did he say I have to stay in this bed all night?"

She pushed the nurse's call button. "I'll ask Steve."

In less than a minute, Steve pushed his machinery back into the room. "I saw your button and I'm going off duty in about fifteen minutes, so I'll get your vitals one more time. What did you need?"

"He wants to know if he can take a stroll in the hospital to stay awake. He's getting sleepy," Kate said.

Steve wrapped a cuff around Hart's arm, pushed a button, and then registered his pressure on a pad. "I don't see what it would hurt. You're not attached to an IV. I'll get you another hospital gown to use for a robe. You're going to have to call someone for clothing to wear home tomorrow morning if the doc releases you."

"Didn't think about that," Hart said gruffly, remembering the price of that vest and chaps as well as the freshly laundered, starched jeans.

Kate stood up and stretched. She reminded Hart of a sleek panther, flexing her muscles like that. No wonder that band fellow was attracted to her. Jealousy flared up at even the thought of another man dancing with his Kate.

Now where did that come from? My Kate indeed. She won't even go out with me.

"I'll go with you and bring back the robe," she said as Steve left.

In a few minutes they were prowling through the halls. There weren't many patients in the hospital. The county needed it desperately for acute care, but most patients were treated and sent on to outlying larger hospitals if they needed further help.

"Let's go outside," he said.

"It's pretty cool, and you're dressed scantily," she said.

"Then let's sit in the emergency waiting room where I can at least see out. I hate this cooped-up feeling," he said. "Let's sit in your truck."

"Little cold wind might wake you up," she mused.

"Just an hour in your truck, where we can listen to some music. What you got out there?"

"Not much. Little bit of country music on a mix tape. Some Kenny Rogers and Dolly on it. Got the new Zac Brown Band. Bought it yesterday after we heard the music at Theron and Fancy's place. Oh, and that one of Trent Tomlinson that's got 'One Wing in the Fire' on it. It reminds me of Daddy. He liked his Saturday night *cochons de lait*."

"So your daddy didn't have a halo?"

"Momma says he was the bad boy of her dreams. He says that when he crawled off that bus in Albany, Texas, back when she was seventeen, she knew that minute she wasn't letting him go another mile."

He gasped when the cold March wind shot up under his gown, but kept walking beside her until they got to the truck.

"Oops, the keys are in my purse," she said.

"Hurry. I'll wait right here," he said.

She took off in a trot.

He shivered until she got back.

She started the engine and warmed the cab of the truck.

"Warm enough, *cher*?" she asked, a wicked gleam in her brown eyes.

"You calling me a sissy?"

"Take it any way you want." She pulled a CD case from under the seat and flipped through the discs until she found "Country Is My Rock" by Trent Tomlinson. She put it in the player and turned the volume up high enough that she wouldn't have to talk to Hart for half an hour. She poked the Next button until "One

Wing in the Fire" started and sang along with it, remembering her father and mother dancing on the green grass at one of the *cochons de lait* at Maw Maw Miller's place.

Tears gathered behind her thick lashes as she listened to the singer talking about his father going to church on Sunday morning, with Saturday night on his breath. Her father did love a good time but mostly, looking back, it was showing off Mary and dancing with her that he liked the most.

He'd been there for Kate from the time she was born until the day he died, giving her unconditional love. That's the kind of husband she wanted to father her own children. How on earth did Mary Miller ever survive without him? Her memories must be the stuff that romance books were written about.

The tears brimmed and fell when the singer talked about trading a thousand prayers if just one prayer would come true: that God would believe in his father. Kate knew her father had gotten a free pass through the pearly gates, because no one could make it if he couldn't.

When the song ended, Hart pressed the pause button and cupped her chin in his hand. "What is it, Kate?"

"It was written to Trent's daddy but it's about mine. I miss him, Hart. Sometimes I wish I hadn't been so anxious to leave home and get my own place."

"Hindsight is twenty/twenty. But think of it this way. They had all those years with just the two of them, like a honeymoon. What was it, about ten or eleven?"

She nodded.

He wiped her tears with the back of his hand and gently kissed her cheek.

"I like that idea. They deserved a few years without a kid underfoot. I was an accident. No question about it. My youngest brother was already in high school. Thank you for that thought," she whispered.

"I'm good for something, *chere,*" he said in a perfect Cajun drawl.

"You calling me a sissy?"

"No, ma'am. Not in my weakened state. I wouldn't dare."

She removed the CD and put the Zac Brown in. She turned

down the music when the first song started. "This reminds me of Theron and Fancy. She and Theron had a fight and she went home to her beaches that she loved as much as I do the Bayou Teche. Theron figured out he couldn't live without her, so he went down there and proposed on the beach. She was sitting in the sand and her toes were in the water, so to speak."

"He let her go after a fight?" Hart asked.

"She . . . well . . . we all said that before we ever got married, the feller we were interested in would have to say the three magic words," she explained.

He looked at her quizzically. "What?"

"Three magic words. Theron had to say them."

"I love you?" he asked.

"That's a given. They aren't magic. Everyone has their own magic words, Hart. Fancy's were 'a forever thing.' Theron had to promise her that or she would never marry him, and he didn't think he had it to give, not after that first wife of his. Anyway, he finally figured out he did have the magic words, because he'd never given them to Maria in the first place."

"You aren't making much sense."

"Not to you, but it made perfect sense to me and Sophie," Kate said.

"So what are your three magic words if 'I love you' isn't enough?"

"'I love you' won't ever be enough," Kate said softly.

"You going to tell me your magic ones?"

"Not tonight."

They listened to the whole CD and were into the third or fourth song on the mixed tape when a nurse knocked on the window. She motioned that they had to go back inside and led the way.

"Walking in the halls does not mean going outside. You are going back to your room, Mr. Ducaine," she fussed. She had a gray bun on top of her head, and her voice left no room for arguments.

She checked his blood pressure and his heart, took his temperature, and huffed out of the room once she had him safely back in bed with the rails up. She tried to run Kate off by telling her that he needed his rest, but Hart was quick to inform her that he'd check himself out of the hospital if Kate couldn't stay with him.

"I feel like I'm back in grade school and she's the wicked principal," Hart whispered.

"Shhh," Kate giggled. "She'll call your momma and give you a detention slip. She'll tell the doctor not to let you go home when it gets light."

Hart shuddered.

"See, *cher*, it could be much worse."

"So I'm more than a friend now?" he asked.

"Honey, I'm slap silly. By the time we get you home tomorrow morning, you may be more than you want to be."

Chapter Eight

The doctor made his rounds before eight the next morning and released Hart, with instructions to go to his attending physician on Friday to have the wound checked and redressed. If everything went well, the stitches would be removed in seven to ten days.

When he left, Kate put on her shoes and jacket. "I'll go see what I can find open, and get you some flannel bottoms to wear home while they get the paperwork ready."

He yawned. "I might take a nap."

"If you do, I'll put a voodoo on you. You're not about to go to sleep until I can," she threw at him as she left.

She was the first customer in the Dollar Store that morning. The only pajama bottoms they had were leftovers from Christmas, printed with Rudolph's antlers tangled up in lights. She didn't care if they had Care Bears or the Disney Princesses on them. She wanted the night to be over so she could go home, take a long hot shower, brush her teeth, and fall into bed for twelve hours. She picked up a package of plain white T-shirts. She thought about socks, but if the pair he wore the day before wouldn't do, he could just shove his bare feet down in his boots.

She went through the Dairy Queen drive-through window and picked up half a dozen sausage biscuits. She was working on the second one when she arrived back in his room. Hart was looking forlornly at the breakfast tray before him.

"I hate oatmeal," he whispered.

She held up the sack. "Want a sausage biscuit?"

He reached for the bag. "You just fell from heaven."

"So are you ready to go?"

"They haven't brought in the paperwork yet. I asked the breakfast lady and she said it'll take an hour or so."

He was on the second biscuit when she held up his new Rudolph britches.

"What the . . . ?" he sputtered.

"It's what they had. You have a choice: Rudolph or wearing a gown, or else staying here until I can go to your place and get some jeans," she said.

"Then Rudolph it is," he said.

She was running on raw nerves when the nurse finally came in with the papers to release Hart. She waited outside the room until he was dressed, then the nurse wheeled him out to the door, and, like a limo driver, Kate picked him up.

"Don't get used to this," she said, as she drove a couple of blocks to Highway 180 and turned east. In half an hour she'd have him unloaded and be on her way back into town to her own pillow, which looked better by the minute.

"I just want to sleep and sleep and sleep. Except that I missed feeding the cattle last night and I'll have to do chores when I get home. That'll take a couple of hours, and then I can fall in a heap," he said.

No, I do not feel guilty. I will not stay and help do chores. I'm sleepy too. He can call his dad or a neighbor. She fought with herself over what she wanted and what she should do, the two ideas diabolically opposed and neither willing to give an inch.

She looked in the mirror. Dark clouds were rolling off to the southwest. A storm was brewing and coming on fast. She turned on the radio to hear the DJ warning residents of Shackelford and Stephens counties to be aware that a thunderstorm, with possible hail and severe lightning, was approaching from the southwest. Abilene was being hit at that very moment with hail the size of golf balls and a fifty-mile wind. As of yet, no tornadoes had been sighted, but it was the beginning of the season. The DJ went on to remind everyone to keep batteries for a radio so that if the electricity went out, they could keep up-to-date on the weather news.

She couldn't leave him to do it all alone. Not with a bad hailstorm on the way.

"I'll help you get the chores done. You'll have to tell me what to do, since I'm not a cowgirl," she said.

"Thanks a lot. You've already done so much I hate to take advantage, but I won't turn down a bit of help right now, *chere*."

She bristled. "I'm not your *chere*, Hart."

"Today you are. It takes someone more than a friend to sit up all night entertaining me, and to offer to help with chores when I know you are dead tired. Tomorrow I might trade your halo in for a set of horns, but right now you are *chere*, darlin'."

"I'm too sleepy to argue with you," she said.

She barely glanced at the Ridge Motel when they passed it, but she did gaze longingly at the restaurant across the street from the courthouse. It would be opening in a couple of hours. Maybe she'd be back in town in time to run through and grab a plate of tamales to keep her hungry stomach from waking her up after an hour of sleep.

"Okay, tell me where to go," she said.

"Turn south on 183, go five miles."

"That sounds like directions to Theron and Fancy's place. Only you turn south on 283."

"It is about the same. If you could go as the crow flies, we are only twenty miles, give or take a couple, from each other," he said.

She looked at the odometer and drove four and a half miles. "Which way do I turn when the five miles is up?"

"Left at the big sign that says 'Rockin' D Ranch.' Can't miss it. Take the lane back to the house and we'll change trucks. I usually used Grandpa's old work truck for chores and general running around. I hate losing that truck."

She saw the sign and turned left. Half a mile down an oak-tree-lined lane, the house sprawled out in the center of a split-rail-fenced yard with mint-green grass promising that spring wasn't far away. She stopped and he bailed out of the truck, Rudolph pajama legs flapping in the wind, and opened the gate. He left it open and motioned for her to drive on inside. He did a half jog to the garage and pushed a button that raised the double doors. He pointed toward the empty space beside his truck. She drove it inside, happy that it would be out of the weather if the hail really was that big.

He opened the door for her and then crawled into the passenger's seat of his vehicle. She looked at him quizzically, and he shrugged. "Never have let a woman get behind the wheel of my vehicle, but if you'll drive, it'll make things faster. We might even get it done by the time those clouds catch up to us."

The big white truck rumbled to life, and she backed out through the gate without taking a smidgen of paint off the side. She really thought he should give her a standing ovation or at least a *chere* for her accomplishments, but he just pointed toward a big barn in the distance.

On his orders, she stopped a few feet back from the barn doors, and he went to open the doors and yelled at her to drive inside. She was out of the truck the moment the engine died. "What can I do now?"

"I've got to load about ten bags of this feed," he said.

She grabbed one end and he got the other. "Why don't the cows eat grass? It's green, isn't it?"

"We're in between right now. In another week, I can turn them out into the green pasture. Right now I'm feeding them enough to get them by until then."

By the ninth bag she was huffing. "What kind of cattle do you raise?"

"Angus mainly, but like Theron I'm interested in Longhorns too. Someday I'd like to get into rodeo stock just for the fun of it," he said.

They pitched in the last bag, and she leaned against the truck. That was every bit as good a workout as going to the gym for an hour. "Now what?"

"Now we go feed," he said.

With her help the two-hour job was over in just less than an hour. Thunder had begun to herald the oncoming storm by the time they were back at the house. The first raindrops fell about the time he flipped two switches in the garage; one rolled the big garage doors down, the other turned on lights.

"You might as well come on in and sit it out. Surely it will pass in a few minutes. Right now, the windshield wipers couldn't keep up anyway," he said.

Of all the dumb luck, she thought.

But he was right. With the wind, lightning, and rain, she'd be better off waiting a few minutes. She'd been up more than twenty-four hours already; another hour wouldn't make that much difference.

She retrieved her purse before they went inside, just in time to hear the ringtone that told her Mary was calling. She tried to sound cheery when she answered, but her hello came out flatter than her energy level.

"Where are you? Are you at the house?" Mary asked.

"I'm at Hart's ranch. I brought him home since he had no transportation, and helped him do the chores. We just got back to the house."

"Then stay there. Don't leave. Promise me," Mary said.

"What's the urgency?" Kate asked.

"There's a tornado on the ground between Breckenridge and Hart's ranch, about three miles south. If you start home you'll go right through it, and it's tearing up the area pretty good. We're watching it on the television set here at the restaurant. Besides, the hail and wind is horrible."

"How fast is it moving?" She put her hand over the phone's mouthpiece. "Turn on the television. There's a tornado between here and Breckenridge."

"Slow," Mary said. "It's going northwest like normal, so I don't think you'll get hit there except for the squall line. Just stay put."

"I can't believe you are telling me to do that," Kate said.

"Hart Ducaine don't scare me like a Texas tornado," she said. "Take care and call me before you start home."

"I will." Kate flipped the phone shut.

"Want the grand tour before I take a shower and shave?" he asked.

"Of course, and do it fast in case the lights go out. I want to know what I'm running into," she said.

"We're in the kitchen, as you can see. Grandma remodeled the year before she died, so it's fairly modern. Everything is only about twenty years old, anyway."

Kate took stock of the oversize country kitchen with a small wood table and four chairs in the center. A window above the sink overlooked the backyard, but all she could see at that point was driving gray rain. Cabinets circled three areas, with a bar separating the kitchen from the formal dining room. A bigger table, covered with a hand-crocheted cloth and surrounded by ten chairs, took center stage in that room. A corner buffet filled with good China and special dishes sat beside an enormous window that went from ceiling to floor.

"When it wasn't raining, Grandpa could sit there and watch his cattle grazing out beyond the yard fence. Grandma said that was the reason they had a rail fence instead of something more solid. He liked to look at his cows. Through this arch is the living room/foyer/den/office/library." Hart pointed as he talked.

A stone fireplace covered most of the west wall. The six-inch-thick oak mantel held family pictures that went back a hundred years or more. Kate wanted to take time to hear all the ancestor stories, but Hart steered her down a hallway door to the north of the fireplace.

"This is the wing I use. It's got two bedrooms and a bathroom. The one that breaks off on the other side of the fireplace goes into a hallway with four bedrooms and two bathrooms. That's the guest quarters. They were going to have a whole bunch of kids, but Daddy was their only chicken. So they used that guest wing for buyers at the cattle sale once a year. Since you've got to stay until the storm is over, you want to get a shower and borrow a pair of my pajama bottoms and a T-shirt? It would be a lot more comfortable. Maybe you'd even have time for a little nap before we see the sun again."

It sounded tempting, and she couldn't think of a single reason why she shouldn't sleep through the wind and rain. "I'd love to. Just show me the way."

"You can have one of the other bathrooms in the guest wing. This is the bedroom I claimed when I came home. Can't bring myself to sleep in Grandma and Grandpa's room. I'll have to clean it out someday, but I haven't been in any hurry." He opened the door into a room with an antique four-poster bed, deep plushy rugs covering areas of the shiny hardwood floor, a dresser with an array of his belt buckles and personal items arranged on the top, and a chest of drawers with a picture of him on the last bull he'd ridden.

He removed a pair of plaid pajamas and a T-shirt from a dresser drawer and handed them to Kate. "Follow me, and I'll show you the bathroom. I think there's a toothbrush in the drawer in there. Grandma was a wonderful hostess and kept extras of everything in case a buyer forgot something."

She followed Hart down a hallway with open doors on each side, showing off bedrooms that looked inviting to a sleep-deprived woman.

He stopped at a door and stood aside. "This one has a shower over a tub, so you can have a choice. Don't fall asleep and drown. Want me to wash your back?" He grinned.

"Jethro Hart," she said.

"Just checkin' to see if you would remember to double-name me. Man, you don't even let down your guard when you're tired, do you?"

She shut the door firmly in his face and locked it as loudly as she could. She turned on the water to fill the tub. If she fell asleep, so be it. Thunder hammered down on the house and the lights flickered. She hoped the hot-water tank was gas powered and not electric. Lightning zigzagged so close to the house that it lit up the room through the lace-covered tiny bathroom window facing the west.

Maw Maw Miller would have a pure Cajun hissy fit if she knew lightning was jumping around like ants on a hot griddle and Kate was getting into a bathtub of water. According to her, water drew lightning as bad as trees and cats. A sane person didn't stand under a tree; they didn't allow the cat in the house; and above all, they did not take a bath in a storm.

She crossed herself as a precaution before she sank into the tub with a moan. The hot water was wonderful and the soap on the edge of the tub smelled like roses. There was a bottle of shampoo with the same fragrance, so she dunked her head under the water and lathered her hair. She could have leaned back and stayed an hour or until the water got cold but she decided not to tempt fate. The storm still raged, and there was a possibility Maw

Maw was right, so she stepped out onto a rug and wrapped a fluffy white towel around her hair and one around her body.

A glance in the mirror revealed dark circles under her brown eyes and a face so tired it looked every minute of its thirty-one years. She picked up a bottle of rose-scented lotion and rubbed it on her arms and legs. Sure enough, there was a brand-new toothbrush still in the bubble wrap in the drawer and two kinds of toothpaste. She brushed her teeth, finished drying her hair, and dressed in Hart's pajama bottoms, which she had to roll twice at the waist and two turns on the legs. The T-shirt he gave her advertised a bull ride in Denver, Colorado, and hung to her knees, but it was comfortable.

She picked up her purse at the same time the cell phone rang. The noise startled her so that she dropped it on the floor, spilling the contents everywhere. She sat down on the tub and retrieved the phone first.

"Hello?"

"Are you still at the ranch?" Mary asked.

"Just got out of the tub and brushed my teeth. I'm going to take a nap before I leave. I don't even know if I could make it home. My energy is gone and I'd be dangerous on the road." She talked too fast.

"Were you in that tub alone?" Mary asked.

"Yes, Momma. I don't have energy to drive, much less let Hart wash my back, but he did offer," she said bluntly.

"The tornado has gone on but the wind and rain is to keep on for a while. Take your nap. Business is slow. I'll see you when I get home tonight," Mary laughed.

"I'll call when I leave," she said.

"You sound exhausted. Maw Maw used to say that what goes around comes around."

"Good night, Momma. I'm hanging up now," Kate said.

Hart was coming down the hallway when she opened the door.

"I heard a noise and you talking. I thought maybe you'd slipped and fallen." His mouth went suddenly dry at the sight of her standing there in pajamas that hung on her and her hair in a towel. She looked tired, but she was even more stunning than she'd been in the red satin dress at Theron's wedding.

"No, just a phone call," she managed to get out, without stumbling all over her words.

Water beads clung to his wet curls. A small tuft of light brown hair showed at the V-neck of his T-shirt, and he smelled like the Bayou Teche in the springtime. Clean and musky all rolled into one.

"How did you manage to keep that bandage dry and wash your hair?" She tried steering her mind away from what she'd like to do to such a delectable hunk of male flesh, even in her worn-out state.

"Wasn't easy. Took some acrobatics in the shower. I was glad there wasn't a window in the bathroom. Grandma would have my hide for getting into a shower with a lightning storm going on," he said.

She laughed. "Maw Maw Miller's fear of the same thing came to mind as I ran a tub of water. But I took a chance and won."

A crack as loud as dynamite at the front of the house made them both jump. Hart headed up the hallway in a hurry with her right behind him.

"Guess you're not going anywhere for a while," he said.

She looked out the window to see the rain working hard to put out the fire at the base of a smoking oak tree that one bolt of lightning had sent falling in front of the yard gates. It had split right down the middle of the trunk, but with the help of the wind, both pieces fell to the same side, branches sticking through the rail fence that had been broken in several places.

She moaned.

"You can get a good sleep rather than a nap. Tomorrow, when the rain stops, I'll get the chain saw out and clear the gate. Or you can have your Mom come get you when the weather clears up."

She headed for the sofa. "I'll think about that tomorrow. Right now I'm going to sleep."

He took her elbow and steered her toward the hallway. "I don't think so, *chere*. You can have the bedroom across the hallway from me. No arguments. And if you need a reason, it's because if I wake up disoriented with a bleed in my brain and need you, you can hear me when I call."

"I'm now a nurse?"

He opened the door to his grandparents' room and left her there. "You are my sleepy *chere*. Good night or good day, whatever it is. There's food in the fridge if you wake before I do. Make yourself at home."

She barely took time to think about where she was and the fact that his grandparents had slept in that room for their whole married life. She did notice the picture of Hart and his mother, Elisa, on the bedside table. Hart must have been about six and was a pretty boy even then. She wondered if a son that she and Hart shared would look like that.

"Probably not," she mumbled, as she tossed the towel from her hair on the floor, slid in between the sheets, and pulled the white chenille bedspread up around her chin. Tomorrow her hair would be all bumpy and lumpy since she hadn't taken time to brush it out straight, but right then, she simply did not care.

She slept fitfully. She dreamed of the bayou and dancing at a party at Maw Maw's place at a cousin's wedding. Zac was there, and they danced several times together in the sweltering-hot-summer Louisiana night. The stars twinkled and the moon was a big round ball of white in the black sky. The swamp smelled of ages past, and the trees swayed in the gentle breeze that didn't have a chance of cooling the temperatures.

Zac drew her into his arms and whispered soft Cajun words in her ear in a deep, sexy voice. She awoke with a start and sat straight up in bed. Thunder rolled in the far distance. Rain fell softly on the roof and against the window, but the wind was barely more than a Texas breeze.

She stretched the kinks out of her neck and looked at the big digital clock that looked so out of place in the antique bedroom. It was six o'clock, but she had no idea if that was in the evening or the next morning until she looked closely and saw the red dot beside the tiny P.M. at the bottom of the clock face.

She peeked out the door and heard soft snores still coming from the room across the hall. She tiptoed into the living room and flipped the light switch. A big, overstuffed, brown velvet sofa faced the fireplace. Brass lamps stood on tables at the end of the sofa, with a matching coffee table completing the grouping. On the other end of the room, a large-screen television hung on the wall in front of two oversize recliners with tables and lamps. It was evident where Hart sat all the time, because a James Lee Burke mystery lay on the table beside his chair, along with an empty tea glass.

She picked up the glass and carried it through the dining room to the kitchen. Her stomach growled, and she opened the refrigerator. She pulled out an apple and munched on it while she took stock of what was available. Maybe later she'd make a Cajun omelet and pan-fried toast.

A ringtone sent her scurrying to the bathroom, where she'd left her purse. She grabbed the phone on the fourth ring, just before it went to voice mail, not even looking at who was calling but expecting to hear her mother's voice.

"Hello. There's a tree down in front of the gate. It will be tomorrow before I can get there," she said hurriedly.

"Hello to you too, Kate. So there's a tree down. You must have had some bad weather over in your neck of the swamp," her former boss said.

"I thought you were Momma," she said.

"*Chere*, it's been a while since I've seen you, but there's no way I could be your momma," he said.

She laughed. "I'm sorry. I was up all night and slept all day. I'm disoriented."

"Want your old job back?" he asked abruptly.

She was stunned. "What did you say?"

"I've had two replacements in the past few months. Rudy can't work with either of them. He wants you to come home and so do I," he said.

Home? Was that where her heart was? In Louisiana?

"I'm shocked," she said.

He chuckled. "What? That Rudy can't work with the two replacements, or that I'm asking you to come back?"

"Just plain old shocked. How long have I got to think about it?"

"One month. The last replacement has given me a one-month notice."

"Can I call you back in a couple of days?"

"I'll be looking forward to it. And good luck with the tree."

"Thanks. I'll be in touch," she said, and looked at the phone for a full minute before she snapped it shut.

Hart stumbled into the living room, rubbing at his eyes. "Is it morning?"

"No, it's late evening. Hungry?"

"As a bear."

"Cajun omelet? I found eggs and frozen shrimp. Or Mexican. There's also onions, tomatoes, and jalapeños. You stock a pretty good refrigerator for a bachelor. Or has some woman been around that you didn't tell me about? Have you got a girlfriend and you let me sit with you all night? I may make your head look worse than it does now if the answer is yes, so you'd better lie to me really good."

"You make it, and I will eat. No girlfriend. I have a housekeeper. She comes in two days a week, does the laundry, runs the vacuum, and shops for me. I make a list and leave it on the bar. She's sixty years old, wide as she is tall, and cusses worse than you do. She has a family in Breckenridge and I don't think I would have called her to sit with me," he explained.

Kate smiled. "You lie really good. I'm proud of you."

"It's the truth. Swear it on Grandma's chocolate-chip cookie recipe," he said.

"Not the Bible."

"Lightning is over. Don't want to bring it back on."

She headed for the kitchen. "Truth then."

"Moselle is about forty. She's tall and skinny as a rail. Has a husband who is worthless and won't hold a job. Three kids that keep her drained for cash. I overpay her and invent things for her to do so she can make more money," he said.

"Truth on the Bible?"

"Swear it right on that part about 'Thou shalt not lie to the woman about to make you an omelet.'"

She decided on a Mexican omelet on the way to the kitchen. Peppers hot enough to make Hart's nose run. Lots of chopped tomatoes and sausage. By the time she got started, hash browns sounded good too. And then there was that can of biscuits; all she had to do was pop them open and put them in the oven. She found a can of cinnamon rolls and lined them up in the same pan with the biscuits, leaving a little space so they wouldn't touch and blend the flavors.

By the time they were ready to fill their plates right off the stove, she'd made a small bowl of sausage gravy. There was, after all, all that good-flavored grease going to waste if she didn't brown some flour in it and add milk.

Hart moaned when he saw the stove top. "God, woman, you've been holding out on me. I'm finding out you can cook too? Marry me and be my love, my sweet *chere*, forever and ever."

"Do you propose to every woman who makes you food?"

"No, just the ones who buy me Christmas pajamas." He cut a chunk of omelet and put it on one side of his plate, added two heaping spoons of hash browns, and covered two split biscuits with gravy.

"You really have turned into a bad boy," she said.

"If that means starved plumb-awful to death, then I'll take the title," he teased. He carried his plate to the table and forked a bite of omelet into his mouth. "Hot! God, this is good," he said.

"It's Mexican. Jalapeños," she said.

"I don't care if it's Korean or Chinese. It's dang good."

"Thank you." She sat down to his right at the small kitchen table.

It felt oh so right and yet oh so wrong. One part of her wanted to snuggle right into the big farmhouse, flirt with Hart, and make a home there. The other part said she didn't belong there and should run as fast as she could back to Louisiana. Back to the safety of a time-consuming job that left little time for romance.

She ate without tasting much, as she tried desperately to decide what to do. Coming on the wings of a lightning storm, the phone call was an omen—as if it had used the storm to bring the message. Telling her that what was ahead for Kate Miller in Texas was one big storm after another.

Go home, go home, her mind kept saying over and over as she shoved food into her mouth.

Texas is home. Hart is home, her heart said.

She wished she'd never heard the phone. If she'd only slept a little longer. But she hadn't, and the choice was there.

How was she supposed to know which road to take?

Chapter Nine

Kate awoke to sunshine pouring in the window and warming her face, and to the high-pitched whine of chain saws and men's deep voices. She bailed out of bed and looked out the window. Hart leaned against a fence post, and several young men were busy cleaning up the oak tree. He was dressed in faded Wranglers, a T-shirt with a plain gray hooded sweatshirt over it, and boots. His stained cowboy hat sat a little farther back on his head than usual. When the saws stopped, he pitched in and helped clear the brush from the usable timber.

The men used the blade of the saw to measure off eighteen-inch lengths and sawed through the various-sized branches, ranging anywhere from the size of Kate's arm to the size of Hart's waist. After a while they stopped again, and the whole bunch of them loaded the wood into wheelbarrows and disappeared around the end of the garage.

"Must be where the fireplace wood is stacked," she muttered.

It was time to go home, and Kate wasn't ready. She liked the ranch, enjoyed cooking and eating with Hart, loved the banter between them, the excitement of flirting. But—and there always seemed to be a *but*—she knew nothing about ranching, not one thing about a cow except that the udders were underneath and the horns on the head. Hart deserved someone who shared his love of the lifestyle.

Kate had known since she was sixteen that she wanted to be a detective. It was ingrained in her soul, and she felt alive when she was on a case. She lived and breathed putting the puzzles together, talking to witnesses, figuring out why something happened. That was her lifestyle, and few people outside of Rudy and other detectives would ever understand that it took as much dedication as what her brother Paul gave when he went into the priesthood.

She stripped the bed and folded the bedspread across the end of the mattress, took the sheets to the laundry room, put them in the washer, and started it. She went back to the bedroom and dressed in the clothing she'd worn to the ranch the day before, leaving the pajamas and T-shirt lying on the bed, and put her shoes on.

She pressed the garage-door button and, while it opened, got into her truck and started the engine. Hart was waiting beside the doors when she backed out. She applied pressure to the brake and rolled down the window.

"Thought you might stay and help do chores this morning," he said.

"Looks like you've got lots of help. Thanks for the bedroom and everything," she said.

"Thank you. I believe you did a little more this time than I did. Dinner Saturday night? You name the place and time."

"Call me. I'll think about it," she said.

"That's more than you usually say, so I'll take that as a good sign."

She managed a weak smile as she rolled up the window and headed toward home. Ten minutes later she was in her own bedroom and redressing in clean jeans and a bright orange T-shirt. She had caught up on her sleep and was ready to do a shift at the café. She heard Mary's footsteps going to the kitchen, and in a few minutes the aroma of strong coffee floated down the hallway to her bedroom. She hadn't realized how hungry she was until she smelled bacon.

She followed her nose to the kitchen, poured a cup of coffee, and sat down at the table. "You making enough for two?"

"I heard you roll in a few minutes ago. I'm making enough for four. Two wouldn't come close to feeding you," Mary said.

Kate sipped the coffee. "We didn't sleep together."

"I didn't ask."

"Captain Laysard called last night."

Mary cracked half a dozen eggs into a bowl and whipped them. "That why you didn't sleep with Hart?"

"No. It's . . . well, Laysard offered me my old job back," she blurted.

"And?" Mary asked.

"Maw Maw might say it was an omen. There was the storm, and I was with Hart out there at his place. And Laysard called."

"Maw Maw used to say, 'Don't let the green grass fool you.' You lookin' over the fence and thinking it's better in that pasture. Life is what you make it, Kate. Your daddy taught me that. I thought I couldn't leave Texas, but as long as I was with him, it turned out it didn't matter where I lived."

"I'm a detective. It's what I was trained for. It's what I like. I can never do that job in Breckenridge, not now," she said.

Mary dished up a plate full of scrambled eggs and sausage, added two pieces of pan-fried toast, and set it before her daughter. "You running to something, or away from something?"

Kate looked up at her. "Both maybe."

"Running away won't fix the problem. Running *to* leaves unfinished business behind. Go to Louisiana. It's time you paid your Maw Maw a visit. Sit on the old chair out in the backyard by the bayou and listen to the nutria and the tree frogs. She'll help you figure out everything. She's a wise old girl."

"How long will it take?" Kate whispered.

"Who knows? But when the answer comes to you, you'll know it's the right one and you won't be looking back at the other pasture all the time," Mary said.

Kate hugged Mary tightly. "I'll miss you."

"And I will miss you. That's only normal. Put your soul at peace and then come on back to Texas where you belong." Mary grinned.

"What if Louisiana is where I belong?"

"Then I will pitch a fit and you will change your mind," she teased.

"Momma, this thing with Hart . . ." Kate began but couldn't find the words.

"Which one—Hart, the man, or heart, the one in your chest?"

"I'm so confused right now."

"Pack your bags and get on out of here. If you don't go soon, I'll start crying just thinking about you not being here. Call me when you get there. And don't tell Maw Maw you are on the way. She loves surprises."

Kate's smile was halfhearted. "You can't surprise that woman. She's half voodoo witch. She'll be on the porch when I get there with one hand shading her eyes, declaring that a voice in the wind told her to get ready for company."

Mary finished her breakfast and carried both of their plates to the sink. "It's already warm in that part of the world, but you'll need a jacket at night. Tell everyone hello for me."

Kate hugged her mother again and went to the bedroom, where she opened a suitcase and began to pack. The advice was good. She needed to clear her mind, and there was no better place to do that than on the back side of a sugar plantation on the Bayou Teche.

A couple more long hugs an hour later at the café, where her mother had her hands knee-deep in tamales, almost convinced her to stay in Texas. But, as Mary said, she could come back any time she wanted. They could always use her at the café, and there was a possibility the police force would call her again if she put a little pressure on the chief.

Traffic was light, and she made good time. She stopped in Longview at a McDonald's for lunch and called Fancy while she ate in the truck. The sun was directly overhead, and the day was warm. McDonald's was doing a brisk business.

"Hello," Fancy said, out of breath.

"Hello. You sitting down?"

"Is it Aunt Maud?" Fancy's tone turned serious.

"No, I'm in Longview, Texas, on my way to Louisiana." She went on to tell Fancy the whole story.

"Running away won't solve a thing. I tried it, remember?"

"I'm not so sure I'm running. I just need to get my head on straight, decide what I want to do. Jesus, Fancy, I'm thirty-one years old and I'm trained to be a detective, not a waitress. Besides, I don't know jack squat about ranching," she said.

"That what's bothering you? It's Hart, isn't it?"

"I don't know. I do know I've got to get out away from him and make some decisions about me before I can get serious about him."

"Does he want serious?" Fancy asked.

"I think he does. All these years I would have given my soul for a chance at that man, and now I'm not real sure it's the right thing for me."

"Well, go to your grandmother's place and figure it out. Remember, the baby is due this fall, and I don't know anything about birthin' a baby, so you'd better be here by then to help Sophie with the cheerleading."

Kate giggled. "Surely it won't take me that long to get my head on straight."

"I'll call Sophie and fill her in. You get on back on the road so you won't be traveling so much after dark. Give her a ring when you get there, and she'll let me know you are safe. Deal?" Fancy asked.

"You got it. You going to call Hart for me too?"

"No, ma'am. That can of worms is all yours."

On that note, Kate's phone went silent; Fancy had hung up.

She caught Highway 49 south out of Shreveport, and by the time she reached Grand Bayou, she was ready to turn around and go back to Texas. She'd made a rash decision and feared it was totally the wrong one. She dialed the café's phone number and was glad to hear her mother's voice.

"If you are already in Jeanerette, you had to have flown. Please tell me you aren't on the side of a road waiting on paramedics," Mary said.

"I'm on the side of the road all right, but I'm fine. I had this panic attack and pulled off to make the decision whether to go on or turn around," Kate said.

"I'd like to say, turn around and be back in time for a late supper. But I'm not going to. You need to get some perspective, Kate, and you can't do it here with that good-looking Hart Ducaine showing up at any time of night or day. Kiss him or kill him, but make a decision."

Kate attempted a laugh; it came out a high-pitched giggle.

"Go on south. Where are you now?" Mary said.

"Just passed the exit to Grand Bayou."

"You *are* driving too fast. Slow down. Talk to you later," Mary said, and she was gone.

Kate pulled back out on the road and drove south. Two hours and four CDs later, she stopped in Alexandria for gas and a bathroom break. She picked up a burrito at the convenience store mini-deli and a Dr Pepper from the cold box.

Midafternoon found her in Opelousas. She'd be at Maw Maw's on the bayou by suppertime. It was supposed to be a ten-hour trip, but she'd made it in less than nine. Everything was familiar after she went through New Iberia, and when she turned off the main road onto a back street to her grandmother's place, for the first time she felt as if she really was going home.

Maw Maw Miller was a tiny, wizened woman who would have been the last in a million candidates to be the poster lady for a wrinkle-preventing night cream. Her face had weathered like soft leather into dozens of creases, but at the age of ninety her smile was still genuine and she was proud to have a mouth full of her own teeth. She might have weighed a hundred pounds if someone filled her pockets with rocks. Her short gray hair frizzed all over her head in natural curls. When she wore shoes they were size five, but that was only on Sunday morning. Any other time she favored rubber flip-flops from Wal-Mart.

She was standing on the porch with one hand shading her eyes when Kate drove up into the driveway. The phone rang in the seat beside her at the same time she turned off the engine. She picked it up, saw that it was Hart, and let it go to voice mail. He'd call back later, and Maw Maw would pitch a fit if she sat in the truck and tried to explain to him what she was doing in Louisiana. That, according to Maw Maw, would be rude.

"I knowed you'd be here tonight. *Etouffé* on the stove, and the milk warming for café au lait. Did you have a good trip? *Mais*, come on in and tell me about that man problems," Maw Maw said.

Kate bent to hug her. "How did you know?"

"Little whisper on the wind told me."

"What if I said there were no problems and I'd just come to

see you for a few days?" The aromas of Cajun stew and strong coffee blended, and Kate's stomach growled.

"I'd say you are lyin', *chere*. Only thing that puts that look on your face is a man. I'm old; I'm not crazy. And if you only came for a few days, then get in the truck and go on back to that foreign country they call Texas. Two women can't catch up on nothing in a couple of days. We need longer than that."

"You're right."

"Of course I am. Didn't live to be ninety to start making mistakes now. Come on in and draw up a chair. I didn't eat until you got here."

"Did Momma call?"

"No." Maw Maw shook her head.

What she didn't tell Kate was that she'd gotten up that morning missing her daughter-in-law and she'd called Mary. It was a little whisper in the wind—a soft voice on the telephone was the same thing, wasn't it?—that had told her to expect Kate for supper.

"Shrimp fresh?" Kate asked, as she lifted the pot from the pan and sniffed the steam.

"Any fresher, they'd still be wiggling. Old man Louviere just took them out of the trap this afternoon and brought them by. Make a cup of coffee and sit down. Got to heat up the bread."

"Hot French from LeJeune's?"

"Ain't nothing else to go with *étouffé*. Now tell me what about the man trouble?"

Kate started at the beginning, blushing only slightly when she had to tell Maw Maw that she'd spent a night in a motel with a man, and ended the story at the same time she took the last bite of good Cajun food.

"You love that man?" Maw Maw asked.

"I don't know. I'm attracted to him. Have been most of my life. But love is more than lust. It's something that has to go on forever, Maw Maw."

"Did he tell you he loves you?"

"If he did, it wasn't at a time I would believe him."

"Well, then you got a powerful lot of thinking to be doing.

Starting right now. Go on with you. There's a fishing pole by the back door. Take a lawn chair and get on to the bayou. It's not in this house you'll find the answers. It's out there. I'll wash up these dishes. Don't come in until you've got a fish for dinner tomorrow."

"I should make a couple of calls first," Kate said.

"Then get it done; but you can't take the phone with you. Can't figure out life with a phone stuck in your ear."

Folks didn't argue with Maw Maw, never had; and Kate wasn't about to start right then, not after eating her fill of *étouffé* and good French bread. She went out to the truck to bring in her things and made a quick call to Mary to let her know she had landed safely and already had supper. She asked her mother to phone Sophie.

Hart Ducaine would just have to wait. Maw Maw had said she should fish and think, and that's exactly what she would do. Maybe by tomorrow she could at least discuss her decision rationally with Hart.

"Just put it in the other bedroom," Maw Maw said.

Kate carried her things through the small living room furnished with an orange floral sofa bought the same year Kate was born. Maw Maw said a person didn't throw away good stuff because it was outdated or had gotten old. If so, they'd have done put her in the trash heap long ago. There wasn't a bit of dust on any of the shiny wooden tables or the hardwood floor. Maw Maw said a body never knew when they'd drop right down dead on the spot, and if the neighbors came to help the family, they weren't going to be talking about how she didn't keep a clean house. Even in the damp, swampy area of southern Louisiana, bugs simply did not take a chance on showing up in Maw Maw's house. According to her, roaches were the devil's spawn, and no self-respecting home would abide such varmints. If one had ever crossed her doorstep, it had to have been back before Kate's time.

The house was square, with a living room and kitchen/dining room on one side, two bedrooms on the other. Maw Maw's bedroom was always the same. White chenille bedspread covering a full-sized bed with mosquito netting around the sides because she liked the windows open and, unlike roaches, the mosquitoes weren't convinced of how mean she could be. A mirror so old that the silver on the back side had as many wrinkles as her face, hung on the wall above a dresser. Pictures of her late husband and eight sons hung on the walls.

She'd raised all eight sons in the second bedroom. The room had looked huge when Kate was a little girl and they'd come to Louisiana a couple of times a year to visit Maw Maw, but now that she was grown, she wondered how the single room had endured the testosterone levels of eight boys.

Four double beds lined the back wall, with just walking space between them. The white paint on the iron bedsteads had chipped in places. She chose the bed against the wall next to the window. Multicolored piecework quilts covered the tops of the beds, and not even one little dust bunny cowered in the corners under the beds.

Four mismatched dressers sat against the north wall. Doilies now graced the tops, but Kate couldn't imagine them being there when the Miller boys were all at home. A Bible and pictures of the grandchildren covered the dressers.

Kate unpacked her suitcase quickly into the empty drawers of the dresser nearest her bed, hung her clothing in the empty closet, and left her cell phone lying on the bed along with her purse.

Maw Maw had finished the cleanup in the kitchen and was sitting on the back porch with her crocheting when Kate joined her in the second weathered rocking chair.

"What are you making?" Kate asked.

"Dat Minnette, your cousin. Already she knows it's a girl she'll be having. Fall baby will need a blanket, yes?"

Kate remembered as a child listening carefully the first day she was in Louisiana. The dialect was strange to her Texan ears, but after twenty-four hours her brain adjusted, and she could understand the old Cajun way of saying things.

Maw Maw eyed her. "*Mais*, you?"

"I'm just thirty-one. There's still time for men and babies."

Maw Maw grunted and spieled off something under her breath in French that Kate definitely could not understand. The tone said that Kate had already wasted too much time.

"Me, I had eight boys when I was thirty-one," Maw Maw finally spoke in words Kate could understand.

Kate picked up a bamboo fishing pole and the rusted coffee can filled with worms from the edge of the porch. "Maybe I'll have eight boys when I am forty-one."

"Better get busy, yes?" Maw Maw didn't look up or miss a stitch.

Kate let her have the last word. She carried the bait and pole in one hand and an aluminum folding chair in the other. It was only the length of a football field to the bayou, where she set up shop under a cypress tree older than God and drooping with moss that swayed gently in the humid night breeze.

Somewhere to the south, she heard the plaintive cry of a nutria. Closer by a tree frog set up a soliloquy. A squirrel added his chattering to the mix, and one lonely old duck put in his two cents' worth. Whoever said a bayou night was as quiet as a tomb must have been deaf. But whoever said it was as peaceful as Heaven itself was a prophet.

She baited her hook and tossed the line out into the bayou, sat down in the chair, and watched the red and white bobbin by the light of the full moon. The breeze ruffled the water slightly, and the bobbin danced. She didn't know how long she'd been sitting there or when Maw Maw had brought a chair and pole and joined her, until the familiar ring of the phone jerked her from that pleasant plane where worries weren't allowed.

She jerked her head around to see Maw Maw handing the phone in her direction across three feet of space. "*Mais*, dat thing has howled worse than a loup-garou every five minutes. Thought it might be important."

"Hello," she answered on the fourth ring, just before it went to voice mail.

"Kate, where are you? I've been calling all day and I was worried. Why haven't you picked up the phone or returned my messages?" Hart asked.

"I'm in Louisiana at my grandmother Miller's house. I'm on the bayou fishing," she said.

"You are where? Good God, what are you doing in Louisiana? Did she die?"

"Sitting right here beside me with a fishing pole in her hands. Made me supper, so I guess the answer is no. My old boss at the force in New Iberia offered me my job back. I'm here to think about it."

Heavy silence filled her ears.

"Are you going to say anything?" she asked.

"The world isn't big enough to run from me." His tone dripped ice.

"Who says you are so important that I'd run from you?"

"You saying you're not?" he asked.

"You started it."

"And I'll finish it. How long did your boss give you to think about it?"

"I wouldn't think that would be a bit of your business," Kate snapped.

"Do you love me, Kate?"

"*Mais*, are you crazy as the loup-garou?" She reverted back to Cajun.

"This is what Fancy did when she figured out she was in love. She took off for her old stomping grounds. Theron told me all about it when I called their place to see if Fancy knew where you were."

"No," she lied.

"I was hoping you were and then you'd marry me."

"Is that a proposal? Because if it is, it was about as romantic as a cow chip in the punch bowl at a church social," she snapped.

"No, it wasn't a proposal. When I propose to you it will be with enough fanfare you won't have to guess," he said.

"Going to come riding up on a big white horse in all your shining . . ." The word escaped her again. Why couldn't she remember the old cliché?

"Shining armor?" He finished the sentence for her.

"Whatever. Are you?"

"If I make up my mind to propose, you won't be able to see who it is for the glare off my shining armor," he said.

"Are we fighting?"

"Could be. Want me to come down there so we can make up?"

"I want you to stay away so I can think," she said.

"Can't think with me in the same town?"

"I didn't say that, and I wouldn't admit it if it were the truth," she said.

"I'm not going to leave you alone," he said.

"Yes, you are."

"Good night, Kate. I'll be in touch tomorrow morning," he said, and hung up before she could say a word.

She looked at the phone as if it were the spawn of a gator and the devil.

"Dat the man, yes?" Maw Maw asked.

Kate nodded.

"The one when you were a girl?"

Kate nodded again.

"*Mais*, should've married him then. You'd have big strapping boys by now."

"You are right," Kate sighed.

"'Course I am." Maw Maw nodded slowly, and went back to fishing.

Chapter Ten

The night air was still warm enough to produce a sheen of sweat after a good fast dance. Kate wore a bright yellow sundress with spaghetti straps. Part of the handkerchief hemline touched the tops of her brown eel cowboy boots. She'd twisted her long dark hair up and gathered it with a wide yellow clip to keep it off her neck. A small silver cross hung barely above the swell of her breasts and matched big, loopy silver earrings that stopped an inch above her bare shoulders.

Maw Maw sat at a long table with other grandmothers, who kept a watchful eye on their kinfolk. The party that night was for a family whose home had burned the week before. Two big galvanized buckets were set on the edges of the stage, where the band kept lively music going. The whole building was an open-air pavilion, with the stage on one end, the crowd flowing out against the cars and trucks parked along the perimeter of the park grounds. Children danced with other children and adults when they could talk them into it. Teenagers flirted and disappeared into the shadows for a bit of hanky-panky. It didn't get out of hand, because if a mother or grandmother heard the faintest whisper of a kiss, they weren't above embarrassing a girl or boy. Twenty- and thirtysomething men and women danced and flirted but without the restriction of overprotective parents.

Kate was surprised to realize that there were fewer and fewer her age that weren't sitting on the sidelines with babies or with children almost old enough to be looking at those shadows where they could steal their first kisses.

Zac Verret kept his fiddle whining and the dancers hopping, and winked at her every time he caught her eye. During a break when someone put on an old country music CD, he beat a pathway to her side to ask for a dance.

He held out his hand. "The pretty Kate has come back to the swamp where she belongs. Come and dance with me, yes?" His voice was deep and mesmerizing. His black eyes sparkled with mischief.

She put her hand in his and let him lead her to the dance floor, where he wrapped his arms around her. His body melted against hers like a magnet attracts metal. She could hear his heartbeats as she laid her head on his shoulder and let him lead her around the floor in a two-step.

"Where have you been, *chere*? Why did you leave?"

"Momma wanted to go home to Texas. I was burned out at my job, so I went with her. Now I don't think I was as burned out as I thought."

"Ah, so Texas doesn't hold your heart like the bayou. *Mais*, what are you going to do?"

"Think about things."

"About me?" He tilted her chin back to see her eyes better. Such a lovely shade of light brown, almost the same color as her lightly toasted skin.

"Among other things. What have you been doing while I was gone?"

"Making many women happy," he laughed.

"You will never grow up, Zac."

"Don't get old, *chere*, and regret that you didn't do what you could while you were still young enough to do it."

He was talking in riddles, but she didn't care if he'd been spitting out the gospel according to Zac Verret in plain Cajun. He'd held her too tightly. His sexy warm breath had brushed her ear. And she'd felt absolutely nothing. Hart brushing her hand made the air around her crackle. Zac was handsome and talked such sweet Cajun, but his touch did nothing.

She sat down beside Maw Maw while Zac danced with another woman. His moves were the same. He drew her up to his body in a fluid movement. He looked into her eyes. He whispered in her ear. Not one surge of jealousy turned Kate a faint shade of mint green.

Then a woman tapped the lady on the shoulder and took her place with Zac. He held the new lady differently. A few inches separated him from her, and he wasn't nearly as flirty. He smiled at something she said and leaned forward to brush a kiss across her lips when the dance ended. When he picked up a beer and went back to the drums, she sat at a table close to the bandstand.

"That would be Zac Verret's fiancée," Maw Maw said.

Kate jerked her head around to stare at her grandmother. Surely the lady was teasing or joking. "But . . ." she stammered.

"Holds her like a lady, and you he holds too tight and whispers in your ear. I don't like it, *chere*," Maw Maw whispered behind her hand.

"I didn't know he was engaged," Kate said.

"Now you do."

"Who is she? She looks older than him."

"*Mais*, so do you. That's because you are older than him. He's Minnette's age. Barely twenty-five."

"He told me he was thirty-two last year," Kate said.

"And you believed a drummer. You need to go home to Texas if you are that gullible. She is Charlene Broussard from down in New Orleans. She's going to take his band to the big time with her money."

"Rich, is she?" Kate asked.

"Got more gold than Midas."

"Hmmm," Kate said.

"Find someone else, Kate. Find a good Cajun man who will love you and not hold another woman in his arms like Zac Verret just did you. Charlene will get a ring on her finger, but she'll never get his heart. It's too fickle to give to one woman."

Before Kate could make another comment, her cousin, Minnette, pulled up a chair and sat down beside her.

"So tell me, what man is it in Texas that sent you skittering back to Louisiana?" Minnette asked.

"Hello to you too. I hear you got married and are already expecting a baby," Kate said.

"Don't change the subject. I have the sight, like Maw Maw. I can see it in your face."

"And besides, you have a cell phone and the gossip is already producing a vine," Kate said.

Minnette giggled. "Just answer the question. What's his name and why are you here?"

"His name is Hart Ducaine, and I need time to think."

"I remember that name. I was only ten years old when you moved here, but I thought you were the most beautiful cousin I had. Hart Ducaine. He's the one who broke your heart when you were a kid, right?"

"How did you know that, and how did you remember it?" Kate frowned.

"Because I heard you telling my older sister Charlotte about him, and I remembered it because I couldn't imagine why a mother would name a kid such a thing."

"So what are you naming your baby?" Kate changed the subject again.

"It's a girl, so her name will be Janette."

"Sounds Cajun."

"Good. I want it to sound that way. That's my husband over there with my brother, Vincent. What do you think?" Minnette asked.

Kate expected someone who looked like a movie star. What she saw was a dark-haired man with brown eyes, who was already overweight and was barely an inch taller than Minnette. He glanced over toward them and blew his wife a kiss.

"After all the hunks, he's not what you thought I'd wind up with, is he?" Minnette whispered.

Kate put up the palms of her hands. "I'm not saying a word."

"That's a good move, *chere*. I'd hate to have to mop up the dance floor with you. His name is Claud Thibodeaux. He's twenty-eight years old, and he's a teacher at the middle school in New Iberia. I fell in love with him when I realized that he thinks I'm beautiful just the way I am, and he's lucky to have me, and that I don't need to lose weight."

"You are beautiful, and he is very lucky, and you are the only one who ever worried about your weight," Kate said.

"I know it, and every day I give thanks for him. He married me and doesn't want to change a thing about me. He likes my cooking, doesn't care if I want to go visiting and not clean the house some days, wants a house full of kids with me, and never looks at another woman the way he looks at me."

"Then you are the lucky one," Kate said.

"So does Hart Ducaine look at another woman the way he looks at you?"

"I wouldn't know. I haven't been in a place to test that out."

"Bring him down here, *chere*. I'll test him and then I'll call Mary Margaret, Alvera, and then Vanessa. If he can't see any of them because his eyes are only on you, then we might give him a good grade on the test."

"Did you bring in the troops with Claud?" Kate smiled.

"Oh, yes. I even tested him with Corrine."

"You didn't," Kate gasped. Corrine was the most beautiful cousin in the family. Twenty-one last summer just before Kate moved back to Texas, and could run Angelina Jolie a race for oozing beauty out every pore of her slim body.

Minnette nodded.

"She did just that," Maw Maw said. "Poor old Claud didn't know what he'd been hit with when Corrine flirted with him at the engagement dance. But he passed the test just fine."

Kate wasn't sure Hart could endure that kind of harsh testing. It might be worth a try when she was absolutely sure he was what she wanted. The clock ticked loudly inside her head and heart. Three weeks and she had to give Laysard an answer concerning the job. If she came back, would she ever find anyone who made her feel the way that Hart did?

"So Claud proved that he loves you. What makes you love him?" Kate asked.

"It's the way my heart feels when I'm with him. I can't tell it in words. It's just there, and I couldn't outrun it or make it go away."

"Did you try to escape it?"

"You bet I did. After the first couple of dates—and he sent me roses the next day after both of them, by the way—I broke it off and went out with a couple of other guys. They were barbarians compared to Claud. No respect. No roses. And all I could think about the whole time I was with them was that I'd rather be with Claud."

"Why did you break it off if he was so good to you?"

"Because it scared me. I was afraid."

"Why?"

Minnette shrugged. "Who knows? Settling down is scary. One man for the rest of my life. To promise to love him until death, that in the church before God and Maw Maw. Tell me that's not scary and I'll call you a liar. But you already know how scary a commitment that is, or you wouldn't be in Louisiana fishing the bayou every night and trying to think things out that are impossible. I'm going to dance with Claud now. Before long the belly will get in the way."

Kate watched Claud as Minnette approached. He saw an angel floating on a puffy cloud instead of a slightly pregnant lady in a red satin top.

"She's settling down. When the baby comes she'll dress like a mother," Maw Maw said.

"I wouldn't count on it." Kate laughed.

"See that man coming this way? That is Bubba Boudreaux. His granddaddy and my brother were friends. He's a good man. You dance with him and be nice," Maw Maw said.

Bubba held out his hand to Kate. "Like to dance?"

"I'd love to," Kate said.

It was a slow dance, and Bubba was light on his feet. He was well over six feet tall and had arms of steel and not a spare ounce of fat on his large frame. His eyes were green and full of life. He wore his hair short and had a cap line across his tanned forehead. He held her like Zac did Charlene, with respect.

"So what do you do for a living?" she asked.

"I'm a fisherman. Got three boats now and a crew that brings in the best shrimp in the south," he said. "What about you?"

"I was a detective over at New Iberia. Nowadays I'm a waitress."

"What made the change?"

"Thought I was burned out. Now I'm not so sure."

"What're you up to while you're figuring it out?"

"Staying over at Maw Maw's place and fishing."

"Good way to figure it all out. Want to go get some breakfast with me after this is over? I make a mean breakfast gumbo."

"Just breakfast?"

"That's up to you. It can be anything you want it to be. You are a lovely lady. I wouldn't treat you bad."

"Pretty straightforward, though, aren't you?"

"That's me. Old Bubba don't know no way else to be with the ladies. He's not got a way with words like Zac has."

"You know Zac?" Kate asked.

"He's my cousin."

"And what has he said about me?"

"He just smiled when I asked him about the pretty lady he was hugged up to when I got here. He's engaged, you know. I wondered why he was dancing so close to you. You don't look like his kind."

"What's his kind?" she asked.

"Yaw," he answered.

She smiled. She hadn't heard that term used in months. *Yaw* meant half stupid, not even worthy of a whole stupid.

"Well, thank you for not thinking I'm yaw," she said.

"Breakfast, then?" Bubba asked when the dance ended.

"I'll think about it while we dance again," she said.

Maybe a fisherman by the name of Bubba was just what she needed to get Hart out of her heart and mind. He'd be right at home on the bayou and would like sitting with a cup of café au lait in the evenings beside the bayou, just watching the water flowing eternally down the state and to the gulf. They would share the same likes and dislikes; gumbo for late-night breakfast being one of them. Perhaps Kate Miller had just met her Claud.

Hart dressed with care, even if his heart wasn't in a party. It was a regular occurrence in Albany. On the weekend before or after St. Patrick's Day, there was a barn dance at his folks' place. He put on fresh-from-the-laundry starched jeans, a plaid shirt, and his ostrich boots. His stitches had been removed a few days before, but the scar was still pink. He could, however, set his hat where it belonged without too much pain, and it covered the ugly.

He picked up his cell phone and called Kate; after four rings it went to voice mail again, as it had for the past three days. "Call me when you have time. We've got things to talk about. If

I don't hear from you by the end of this next week, I'm getting in the truck and heading that way. So if you don't want to see me, you'd best be calling me," he said.

He locked the door behind him and pushed the button to open the garage door. Somewhere deep inside his heart, he hoped that one day he'd push it and there she'd be, waiting in her truck right outside the gate. It didn't happen that evening any more than it had in previous days. The last time he saw her, she was headed home after spending the night with him when the tornado went through.

"What happened?" he wondered aloud.

Nothing fell from the cloudy skies above him in the form of an answer. God seemed to be silent that night. Not even the devil came up with an answer for him, so when he pulled his big truck into the driveway and headed back to the barn, he was still wondering what he should have done differently.

"Hey, look what just walked in the door. I believe it's T-R-O-U-B-L-E," the band singer announced through the microphone. "Let's have a little Travis Tritt by that name, even if the song is about a woman walking in the door. Old Hart has been his share of trouble in his day, so this one is for him."

Hart waved and an old friend appeared at his elbow.

"Hello, Darlene," he said.

"Hi, darlin'. Come on out here and give me the first dance. I'll be the envy of all the women in the place," she whispered.

He removed his hat and hung it on a hook just inside the barn doors. The dance was fast enough that she didn't glue herself to his chest, and for that he was thankful. Darlene had chased him for years and swore someday he'd get tired and let her run him to ground. So far, he was still on the move.

"Thank you," she whispered, as she kissed him on the cheek when the dance was finished. "I've got a room reserved at America's just in case you are feeling lonely. Number 101. Knock three times."

He smiled as she walked away.

Theron grabbed his arm and led him to the table he and Fancy had claimed, along with Sophie and the preacher. Feeling like a fifth wheel, Hart slid into a chair with his back to the wall so he could see everyone who came through the doors. He hoped that maybe Kate would have a change of heart and show up. He'd told her about the party in a voice message and invited her to go with him.

"Darlene trying to put the make on you again?" Theron asked.

"Never stops."

"Kate know about her?" Fancy asked.

"Don't think she'd care," Hart said forlornly.

"I talked to her a while ago. She asked about you," Sophie said.

Hart grabbed a Coke from a tray carried by a passing waiter and gulped down a fourth of it before coming up for air. "Then why doesn't she return my calls?"

"You sure you are even interested in her," Sophie said, "or are you just intrigued because she's run away from you? She's opinionated, brassy as the devil, bossy, and is making you miserable."

"Hart, she'll come back home. Give her time," said Fancy. "She's got to figure it all out for herself. She loved being a detective."

"Then why did she ever leave it in the first place?" he asked.

"Told me she was burned out," Fancy replied. "I think a case went wrong. She never would talk about it, but when her mother wanted to move back to Texas, she quit her job. It had to be something like that for her to walk away from the job. Maybe someday she'll talk to you about it."

"She won't even talk to me about the weather," Hart said. "But enough. You are here to enjoy a party. Don't let me drag you down. Theron, have you even asked this pretty lady to dance?"

"I guess I'd better, or you'll be getting ahead of me." Theron stood up and held his hand out to Fancy. "Mrs. Warren, would you care to dance with your husband?"

"Yes, sir, I do believe I would like that very much."

"Sophie?" Hart asked.

"Don't look at me," Marcus said. "I can't dance worth a flip. I came for the music and the good food. Y'all go on out there and enjoy yourselves."

"Care to dance with me?" Hart asked.

"I'd love to," Sophie said.

It was a slow dance and he held her close, but there were no sparks or electricity between them. Sophie was a fine-looking woman in her designer jeans, boots, and Western-cut lace blouse with ruffles at the sleeves and neck, but she didn't do a bit more for Hart than Darlene did.

"Why don't you just go down there and make her talk?" Sophie asked.

"You think that's what I need to do?"

"Either that or get over her. She's playing with fire, giving you time to think with Darlene chomping at the bit."

"I'm not interested in Darlene."

"How do you know, if you don't give her a chance?"

"I thought you were Kate's friend."

"Fancy and I have been her best friends since we started school."

"Then why are you trying to get me to forget her?"

The dance ended and they stood on the floor facing each other, oblivious to the people around them. "I'm not. I'm saying you need to talk to her or call her and tell her to get on with her life. This limbo isn't doing either of you a bit of good."

"You know something I don't?" Hart frowned.

Sophie started toward the table and he followed.

"You didn't answer me." A vise clamped down on his heart and squeezed the life's blood from it.

"No, I didn't. I don't know a blessed thing that you don't know. I'm just telling you what I think. You can't solve a thing over a cell phone or by waiting. Get right in her face and tell her how you feel. Don't beat around the bush. Say it, and loud enough the whole county or parish or whatever the hell they have in Louisiana can hear it. Stand on the rooftop. Kate doesn't understand anything but straightforward, and you hurt her bad way back when, so you have to scream really loud."

"She's talking about the shining thing," Fancy said from the end of the table, where she'd sat down after the dance finished.

Theron had gone to get her a glass of tea and another plate of barbecue.

"What?" Hart's brow wrinkled, making the scar ache.

"When we first got back to Texas from the four corners of the US of A, or so it seemed, we talked about our three magic words," Fancy explained.

"I love you?" Marcus asked.

Sophie poked him on the arm. "Don't let Theron hear you saying that."

"You know what I mean. 'I love you' is every woman's three magic words. They want to hear it," Marcus said.

"Who died and made you so danged smart?" Sophie asked.

Marcus stuck his nose in the air. "Hard to believe you were ever a preacher's wife."

"Hard to believe a preacher would act like a two-bit womanizer, but he did."

"So if it's not 'I love you,' then what were the magic words?" Marcus asked.

Hart kept the laughter inside. Sophie would lead that man a dog's life for sure, and Theron kept throwing them together. "I'd be interested in knowing what they are too," he said.

"Well, mine was 'a forever thing,'" said Fancy. "That's what I wanted. Not three words that can change with the wind. I wanted Theron to promise me a forever thing that would last beyond 'I love you' and right on through eternity. At first he didn't want to offer such a thing, but he finally came around."

"Took me a while to figure it all out." Theron rejoined them and put a plate of food in front of Fancy, along with a glass of sweet tea. "But when I did, I didn't stutter. I took care of it, didn't I, honey?"

She reached up and patted his cheek. "Yes, you did. I got my forever thing and a daughter to boot."

Hart pretended he'd never heard the story before.

"So what's your three magic words, Sophie?" he asked.

"It's 'life after wife.' I won't ever marry again unless a man can offer me a life after the marriage. Seems they're all willing to promise a woman the moon and stars and half the sun before the marriage, but afterward they aren't so interested, so I want a life after I become the wife."

"And Kate's?" he asked, his heart almost stopping as he waited.

Both Sophie and Fancy laughed.

"Well?" he asked.

"She wants a knight in shining . . ." Fancy paused.

"Armor?" Hart asked.

"No. Whatever." Sophie burst into giggles.

"What?" Marcus asked.

"A knight in shining whatever. She never can remember the word *armor*," Fancy said.

"For real? But that's more than three magic words," Hart said.

"In shining whatever. Those are her three words. Until someone can give her that, she's not interested."

"What is it? 'I love you' is words. 'In shining whatever' doesn't make a bit of sense," Hart said.

"You figure it out and take it to her, and maybe she'll listen to you," Sophie said.

Darlene tapped Hart on the shoulder and wiggled her rear end. "This is a fast one, darlin'. Dance with me?"

Hart stood up. "Excuse me, folks."

He danced two with Darlene, one with his mother, and a couple with other women at the party. The whole time, he thought about that "whatever" thing. Understanding Kate was more complex than he'd bargained for. Maybe he'd better try to forget her. How could he produce an "in shining whatever" when he had no idea what it was or where to buy it?

Forgetting Kate would be impossible. She'd been in his subconscious ever since that summer when they were teenagers. He'd measured every woman after that by her yardstick, and they'd all come up short. Now she was within his grasp, and he had no idea how to close the distance between them.

He pondered it all evening. The dance ended at midnight, and then he helped his father and mother take down decorations until two in the morning. By the time he drove home, he'd forgotten all about Darlene in the motel until he saw the sign. It might be a lot easier to forget Kate if he knocked three times.

He pulled into the parking lot and turned off the engine.

Chapter Eleven

Kate stretched the kinks from her back and adjusted the big, wide-brimmed straw hat, then walked on her knees to the next spot in the garden she was weeding. She reached across the tender little green onion plants and pulled up the dandelions and other green shoots that did not belong in Maw Maw's vegetable patch. The potato plants were a couple of inches tall, and the beans were beginning to sprout.

"Good morning, Kate," Hart said.

She almost said good morning back to him, but she kept working without looking up. She'd heard his voice more than a dozen times a day in the past weeks and turned, way too often, to find that he wasn't standing in the doorway, sitting beside her on the bayou, or even right behind the shower curtain.

"You not even speaking to me?" he asked.

She did look up then. Her eyes widened and all the air left her lungs.

"I thought . . ." she stammered.

"You thought what? That I was in Texas?"

She was on her feet instantly. "Don't put words in my mouth. What are you doing here?"

Of all the scenarios he'd envisioned, her tone and the look on her face weren't among them. He had hoped she would rush into his arms.

Of all the scenarios Kate had envisioned, him finding her on her knees in a vegetable garden wasn't among them.

"I told you I was coming down here if you didn't answer my messages," he said.

"Oh," she said flatly.

"*Mais*, y'all goin' to stand out there in the hot sun all afternoon?" Maw Maw yelled from the back porch. "Come on in the house and have some café au lait and beignets. They're hot out of the grease and I just shook powdered sugar on them."

"We've been summoned," Kate said.

Hart followed her into the house, wondering the whole time what he was doing there. It had seemed like such a good idea the night before. He'd called the foreman of his ranch and told him he was taking a trip. He had given him his cell phone number in case of emergencies, packed a bag, and booked a flight from Dallas to New Orleans. When he arrived at noon, he rented a car and drove to Jeanerette, asked the proprietor of LeJeune's bakery for directions to the Miller place, and there he was, wishing he'd never come to Louisiana.

Maw Maw issued orders when they opened the back door. "Wash your hands and set up the table. I've already met your young man, so you don't have to be introducing us, Kate. I reckon the weeding will wait until tomorrow morning. You'll be needing a shower after you have some beignets."

"Obey," Kate said, with a glance over her shoulder at Hart.

He joined her at the kitchen sink and soaped up his hands. Their fingers got entangled as they rinsed them under the faucet, and the jolt they both got rendered them speechless.

Hart watched Kate pick up one of the square-looking donuts covered with white powder and bite into it. He followed her lead and almost swooned. Krispy Kremes would have taken a backseat to them in any connoisseur's taste buds. The coffee was strong, hot, and sweet—not necessarily his normal choice, but delicious with the beignets.

"So tell me what brings you off to the bayou and sugar plantation world?" Maw Maw joined them.

Hart was glad he had a mouth full of food so that he could collect his thoughts.

"Other than my granddaughter," Maw Maw added.

"That's about it," Hart said, once he'd swallowed.

"Then I'll hang up the sheet," she said.

Hart looked at her so funny that Kate started giggling. It

turned into a full-fledged roar that brought tears to her eyes. When she wiped at them, she smeared powdered sugar across her face. She reminded Hart of a reverse-painted Indian from the old Saturday morning Western reruns.

"You know the rules," Maw Maw said seriously, but a grin tickled the corners of her mouth.

"Yes, I do." Kate nodded, still chuckling under her breath. "And I'll help you hang up the sheets. Bring in your bags, Hart. I guess you've passed the test enough to be invited to stay right here."

"I can stay in a hotel," he offered.

"You want to know my Kate?" Maw Maw cut her eyes around at him.

"Yes, ma'am, I sure do."

"You can't do that in a hotel. I'll get the sheets. You can help Kate hang them," she said. "But eat your beignets first. Man shouldn't be rushed through his afternoon lagniappe."

Hart looked at Kate.

"It means something extra. This is something extra over and above regular food."

"I like it. When you come back to Texas, can you start making these?"

"Who says she's going back to Texas, young man?"

Kate laughed again. "We'll hang the sheets and then I'm doing some fishing this afternoon. You can help me with both. How long can you stay?"

Maw Maw clucked her tongue. "That's rude, Kate Miller. You don't ask him how long he can stay. That's up to him. Our home is open for him to stay here as long as he likes. While you two fish in the bayou, I'll call up Minnette. We'll have a party in the backyard tomorrow night. Vincent can bring the hog in the morning."

"Don't go to any trouble, ma'am. I can take you both out to dinner," Hart said.

"*Mais*, later, maybe yes. But not until you've had a taste of our hospitality. I've got shopping to do in town. LeJeune's for bread to go with gumbo for supper. You catch anything, we'll have that for dinner tomorrow. Vincent loves fish chowder." Maw

Maw made plans as she removed her apron and slipped her bare feet into rubber flip-flops.

"Want me to drive you?" Kate asked.

"I might be old but I can still drive. Me and the old truck have an agreement. It don't stop on me, and I won't shove it off into the bayou," she said.

She picked up her purse from the rocking chair in the living room and looked back in the kitchen. She shook her finger at Kate. "You take care of the sheets before you go fishing. *Mon dieu*, I won't have you sleeping in the same room with Hart Ducaine."

"We will, Maw Maw. When you return, the sheets will be up," Kate said.

The screen door slammed, and the old rusted truck engine purred to life. Kate looked across the table at Hart, still unable to believe that he was there.

"I was going to call, but I didn't have it together enough to talk to you," she said.

"You got it together now?"

She shook her head.

"When you do, let me know. Now, what's this about sheets? Honest, I can stay in a hotel. I didn't come down here to impose," Hart said.

"You'll offend her if you do, and no one in their right mind would offend Maw Maw. She'll put a gris-gris bag somewhere you won't ever find it, full of things that will bring you bad luck. She's full-blood Cajun. You ever heard that song about being country when country wasn't cool?"

Hart nodded.

"Well, that's Maw Maw with the Cajun. When it wasn't socially acceptable to be considered Cajun, she was one, and she didn't give a rat's hiney if it was never acceptable. She was who she was, and what anyone thought of her couldn't change it a bit."

"What's that got to do with a gr . . . gr . . . whatever you said . . . bag?"

"She believes in the old ways. Voodoo. Bad luck. Good luck. And she'll help it along if she sees fit. So don't offend her."

"The sheets?"

He wanted to reach across the table and touch Kate's hand, run the edge of his palm down her cheekbone or kiss her long and passionately. But something was drastically different. What if he'd waited too long, and someone else had already claimed her heart?

"House is big for a bayou home, but it's only got two bedrooms, and one of those belongs to Maw Maw. The other one has four full-sized beds in it. When more than one family is here at the same time, or when members of the opposite sex stay in the room, sheets are hung from the ceiling to create walls."

"That's supposed to keep me away from you?"

"You want to suffer the wrath of Maw Maw Miller? If not, you'll stay on your side of the sheets, darlin'."

"Was that an endearment or a sarcastic remark?"

"You decide. You're big and tall. Grab a kitchen chair. I'll get the sheets and then we'll go fishing. You'll be amazed what you can learn with a bamboo pole in your hands," she told him.

He pushed the chair back and washed the sugar from his fingers at the kitchen sink.

"This is awkward," he said.

When he said that, her breath caught in her chest. She was sure he was going to tell her that it was over.

"Maybe we'd better talk before we put up the sheets," she said.

"You don't want me here?" he asked.

"Do you want to be here?"

"I am sick of worrying about what to say or not say. I'm scared to death that you are going to tell me there's already someone new in your life and you're just being nice to a friend from Texas. That's what is awkward."

She smiled. "I was worried that you'd come to Louisiana to tell me to stay here and not bother coming back, that there was someone new in your life. Is there?"

"There could have been. There was a party a couple of days ago."

"The big St. Patrick's barn dance. I had dreams about you inviting me to go to that dance, but it was always Stephanie who was looking for a pretty green dress to wear to it," she said.

"That's in the past. You could have gone this year if you'd come home," he said.

"I had a party to attend here," she said.

"Darlene—you remember her from high school? Had the worst reputation of any girl in school. She's been chasing me for years. She's between husbands number three and four."

Kate's heart turned bullfrog green. She'd snatch that hussy baldheaded and then slap her for having no hair as soon as she got back to Texas.

"What happened?" she asked between clenched teeth.

"She rented a room at the America's Best and invited me to come spend a little time with her. I actually pulled into the parking lot and sat there staring at the room for ten minutes. I thought about knocking on the door, but I figured it would take more than Darlene to erase you from my mind."

Kate let out a lungful of pent-up air. She didn't even realize she'd been holding her breath until it gushed out. "And?"

"I went on home. Made arrangements to come down here and have it out with you. One way or the other, I've got to find some peace. You are driving me crazy."

A smile tickled the edges of Kate's full mouth. At least she wasn't alone in her misery, but she wasn't ready to lay all her cards on the table just yet. She was still weighing the pros and cons of taking her old job back and hadn't made up her mind yet.

"What if when you find your peace, you figure out I'm not in it?" she asked.

"Then at least I'll know I've been dreaming about a ghost for all these years," he said.

"Fair enough. Let's get our job done so we can go to the bayou. Tomorrow will be very busy, since Maw Maw has called for a hog. That means everyone is invited to come and look at you, cowboy. You'd better watch your step. I've got a whole beaucoup of gorgeous cousins that won't care if you've got a scar on your head."

He grinned. "Now that's an interesting idea."

Kate led the way back to the bedroom and opened a bottom dresser drawer. She brought out a sheet with big pink daisies scattered all over it, then a blue and green plaid one, and one with Rudolph pulling Santa's sleigh. "See those hooks up there?" She pointed to the ceiling.

He looked up.

"We are going to string these sheets on the twine and fasten it to the hooks. You will have a cubbyhole with a bed and dresser in it when we are done."

"What if I get up at night to go sit on the porch or go to the bathroom or have a cold beignet?"

"I'll be safe in my cubbyhole. We are going to make your walls and then mine."

"Why two?"

Kate shrugged. "Because that's the way. You want to question Maw Maw, go right ahead."

He didn't ask any more questions. They made his walls and then she removed three sheets for her end of the room. This time she chose three solid pink ones.

"Why did I get the psychedelic walls and you get girly pink?"

"When you wake up, you need to realize where you are and not think they are real walls. Next time you come to Louisiana you might get plain ones," she added.

He wondered briefly if that comment meant she had chosen to stay, but decided that he had a week to change her mind if she had. This time he wasn't letting go as easily as he had in the past.

She was standing on the bed holding the sheet up when she lost her footing and fell backward. He reached out and caught her before she hit the floor, and in her fear, she wrapped her arms around his neck tightly and buried her face in his chest.

"Little clumsy there," he said hoarsely. Her body against his felt so right and so good that he didn't want to put her down.

"The bed threw me. I'm not clumsy," she protested, but she didn't wiggle out of his embrace.

She licked her lips when he tipped her chin up with his fist and lowered his mouth to hers. Fireworks on the Fourth of July didn't compare to the sparks that lit up the bedroom. She leaned in so close that she could feel his heart thumping.

"Where are y'all?" Maw Maw yelled, as she opened the screen door.

Kate bounded out of Hart's arms as if they were prepubescent teenagers. "Back here. We're just finishing putting up the sheets."

They heard her opening cabinet doors and putting away groceries, then the flapping sound of flip-flops hitting the soles of her feet as she made her way to the bedroom door. "I'm going to talk to Minnette up at the courthouse about the *cochon de lait* tomorrow night. Finish this job and get out of the bedroom. Ain't no place for a couple who ain't married to be lingerin'. Puts idees in your mind."

"Maw Maw!" Kate blushed.

"I was young once upon a time and I ain't yaw now," she said with a huff, leaving them standing there speechless.

Hart raised an eyebrow at Kate.

"Remember? *Cochon de lait* is a get-together. I told you while you were in the hospital about the words they use down here," she said.

"*Yaw?*" He said it with a Texas twang, and it sounded odd.

"You're not saying it right, but it means half stupid, not worthy of a whole stupid," she explained. "You'll get on to it and in a couple of days you won't even hear the Cajun anymore."

"I doubt that, but we'd best get out of the bedroom before I start getting *idees*," he said, giving the last word several syllables.

She slapped at the air close to his arm but was careful to not touch him again, or the *idees* wouldn't be his but hers, even if Maw Maw brewed up her worst gris-gris bag.

At that rebellious thought, Kate's blush was so crimson that it actually itched. But not as much as that place so deep inside her heart.

"Fishing?" Hart asked.

"You might want to change clothes. It's hot and sultry on the bayou this time of day. You bring anything other than starched Wranglers and button-down shirts?"

"Got a pair of jean shorts and a few T-shirts," he answered.

"Put 'em on while I get the jug of iced tea ready. We'll take some of the cold beignets with us to nibble on if we get hungry before suppertime."

In a few minutes he joined her in the kitchen. His shorts were wrinkled and worn and the orange T-shirt had a white silhouette of the Texas Longhorns symbol. He'd hung his hat on the bedpost and opted for a cap with the Rockin' D logo across the brim.

Kate still wore her faded denim capris and an oversize red-and-white-striped knit shirt that fell to below her hips. Her dark hair was pulled up with a big plastic clip that kept it off her neck but let the ends poke out every which way. She'd long since sweated off any traces of makeup and had eaten off her lipstick with the beignets.

Hart thought she was absolutely adorable.

He carried the cooler with the tea and snacks and the can of worms. She carried two lawn chairs, stuck two bamboo poles under her arm, and led the way down a path through the cypress and live oaks.

A soft breeze blew the dry drooping moss, and twice it hit Hart in the face. He pushed it aside without losing any of his cargo. It was years and years since he'd been fishing, and never with a bamboo pole. The last time had been off the coast of Galveston when he was down there on the rodeo rounds; he and several other bull riders booked a fishing boat and went out into the gulf on a deep-sea excursion.

Kate finally stopped near a twisted live oak tree in front of a body of water he would have called a creek, and popped open the lightweight aluminum lawn chairs. She reached out and took the can of worms from him and carefully baited her own hook, making sure the long earthworm was threaded on the hook well enough to keep the fish from cleaning it off without taking the hook. She tossed the line out into the bayou and got comfortable in her chair.

Hart followed her example and waited for her to start the conversation.

Five minutes later she hadn't said a word.

He leaned over to see if she'd fallen asleep.

Ten minutes. Nothing.

Fifteen, and he cleared his throat.

Twenty. He gave up and watched the bobble dancing in the gently rolling stream.

Thirty, and he was deep in his own thoughts. He'd given up bull riding because he was ready to come home and settle down on the ranch. His grandfather's passing seemed to be the sign that the time had arrived. Then there was Kate, the love of his life, at the wedding. From there it had been an emotional roller coaster that had him doing everything but cussing most days. He thought about Kate. He dreamed about her. He couldn't get her out of his mind.

But was it love?

Like Fancy and Sophie said at the party, what were those three words all men feared and women wanted to hear? They were important, yes, but were they the be-all and end-all of an existence? He did love Kate. He'd loved her when they were too young to even know what love was, and he still did; but could he live with her? She'd come to Louisiana to think about the job offer. Would she ever be happy as a rancher's wife? Was he kidding himself that he could make her happy?

Kate could feel his tension when they first sat down. She wanted to talk; she really did. But she didn't know where to start. Did she tell him she'd loved him her whole life, and that all other men were measured by him? Or that she was terrified to let him know how much she cared about him, because she couldn't bear another heartache? She waited for him to talk, but he didn't say a word. Finally, she felt the tension ease as he watched the bobble.

The breeze picked up slightly, and the sun dipped a little lower in the east, sending rays of pink and yellow across the bayou. Minty-green leaves said spring had arrived and winter was over. One mother duck led the way to the edge of the bayou, and six little yellow babies followed her. Ignoring them, she hit the water with a splash, and, fearlessly, they went in right behind her, bobbing up and down like the red and white plastic balls on the fishing line.

"You ready to talk?" Kate asked.

"You?"

She shook her head.

"Then I guess we'll fish some more," he said.

The sun eased its way across the sky a while longer, and twilight set in, the trees becoming silhouettes in the dusky evening. They'd been on the bayou for hours and had eaten every last crumb of the leftover beignets and drunk a gallon of sweet tea. Still they fished.

"Y'all ever going to come in the house?" Maw Maw yelled from the tree line.

"In a minute. We didn't even get a bite yet," Kate answered.

"I bought some clams for chowder tomorrow, so don't worry about it. Come on in when you give up on it," Maw Maw said, and disappeared.

"Hungry?" Kate asked when it was full dark.

"Little bit."

"Figured anything out?"

"Haven't even scratched the surface," Hart said.

"Now you know why I didn't call you."

"Do we have to figure it all out before we talk?" he asked.

"Not all of it."

"I have trouble keeping my hands off you," he said.

"That's physical attraction. We're attracted to each other. Always have been, but that doesn't mean we could make it in a forever setting like Fancy and Theron, does it?"

"Never know until you try," he offered.

"And that I'm not willing to do until I figure out if I can make it last. Marriage is a one-time thing for me. Divorce is out of the question. If I make a mistake, I'll have to live with it forever. I'm not going to make a mistake. I won't do it if I can't at least think I'm going to get one of those cakes with the golden bells on top."

"What's it going to take to convince you?"

"I'll tell you when I figure it out. Are you proposing?"

"No, not right now."

"Why?"

"I need to fish some more. Maybe for a long time."

"Let's go eat supper. Maw Maw has made gumbo and bought good bread. Besides, she's going to put you through the wringer now that you're staying here. How do you like dominoes?"

Hart frowned. "What's dominoes got to do with anything?"

"You think you're staying here for free? Maw Maw loves dominoes. She saw a sucker when you knocked on the door. We will be playing, and she's not above cheating if she gets behind. You have to watch her like a hawk, because she likes to win."

His eyes came near to popping right out of his head. "You're lying."

"Keep thinking like that and you'll lose your shirt. Ever play poker?"

He blinked several times. "Of course."

"She's got that kind of face, and she takes it serious. How much money you got in your pocket?"

He stuttered and stammered.

"I don't mean dollars but change. You are about to lose every dime of it."

"I don't think so."

She gathered up the gear and shared the load with him. "Don't forget the worms. She'll burn your breakfast if you lose the worms."

He picked up the coffee can and walked beside Kate back to the house. She warmed the gumbo and sliced the bread. He ate until he couldn't hold another bite, and then he helped with the cleanup.

Maw Maw brought out the dominoes. At midnight, when she declared it was bedtime, he didn't have a single penny in his pocket and was very grateful that they hadn't played for folding money.

He took a quick shower and went to bed. Kate rustled against the curtains that made his walls on her way to her end of the room. He laced his fingers under his head and watched the moon sitting high in the sky outside the window. Kate was just a few feet away. He could hear her soft breath and the squeak of the bedsprings when she turned over in bed. He wanted to go to her, gather her into his arms, and just hold her until she slept. He shut his eyes and slept more peacefully than he had in weeks.

Kate would have been willing to strangle him with a length of twine leftover from hanging the sheets if she'd known how good he felt. Every raw nerve in her body kept her from sleeping. She wanted to cuddle up in his arms and listen to his heartbeat on her cheek. But she didn't succumb to her desires, even if it did take all the willpower she had left.

Maw Maw put her winnings in a quart jar on her dresser. That Hart Ducaine would make a fine grandson-in-law. If it took meddling, she was just the one to do it.

Chapter Twelve

Not a single white puffy cloud floated in the clear blue sky that spring morning. Kate sat on the back porch in her cut-off sweat bottoms and an oversize T-shirt with a picture of Betty Boop on the front. She held a mug of café au lait in her hand and still had a bit of powdered sugar around her mouth. Maw Maw had been up long enough to make fresh beignets for breakfast. That meant she was quite taken with Hart Ducaine.

It took a lot to charm Maw Maw Miller. She could see right through deception. But Kate still didn't know where *she* stood with Hart. She was drawn to him physically. That she loved him wasn't a big revelation, but did she like him enough to live with him forever, if he should ask? Therein lay one big, black question mark. Was Kate just a passing fancy like before? Could she trust him?

Maw Maw pulled her rocker out of the sun and sat down with a cup of coffee.

"I like the man," she said.

"I love him. I don't know if I like him and I don't know if I can hold on to him even if things did work out. I couldn't before, and I was a lot younger," Kate said.

"Don't be so serious. He's here and it's a pretty day. Go show him around the parish. Have a good time. You're thinking too hard with your head and not enough with your heart. Got a party tonight. Vincent has a hog and he's on his way over to put it in the pit. Either you lighten up, or Corrine is going to sashay in here and Hart Ducaine is going to slip right through your fingers."

"Did I hear my name?" Hart came out onto the porch. He

was already dressed in jeans and a three-button polo shirt the same color as his eyes. He carried a cup of coffee in one hand and a saucer piled high with beignets in the other. "A man could get used to finding these on the table."

"You did hear your name, and a man ought to find beignets on the table at least once a week," Maw Maw said. "Kate knows how to make them. She's been holding out on you, *cher.*"

"I can be a *cher*? I thought that was only for girls." Hart sat down and braced his back against the porch post.

"Is *darlin'* only for boys?" Kate asked.

"No, ma'am. You can call me that anytime you want," he said.

"Okay then, darlin'"—she smiled—"finish your breakfast, put on your best walkin' shoes, and get ready for the grand tour."

Maw Maw winked at her.

"Of what?" Hart asked.

"Why, the whole parish, that's what. We'll take in the whole thing and be back in time to clean up for the *cochon de lait* tonight. Vincent is on his way with the hog," Kate said.

Hart raised an eyebrow.

"There's a pit about halfway from here to the bayou. He's the best at cooking a whole pig for a party. Who's playing, Maw Maw?"

Hart raised the other eyebrow.

"*Cochon de lait* ain't worth nothin' without a band," Maw Maw said. "Zac and the Gators is comin' round tonight. That boy can make a fiddle tell a story, can't he? I told Minnette to tell him they could eat all they wanted, so they're playin' for free. Said they needed to practice anyway. Whole family is coming. Minnette got the beans started last night. They'll be good and thick by suppertime."

"Maw Maw loves a party," Kate said. "Minnette makes the best baked beans in the parish. Everyone is always after her to bring them. I hope she's got two pots going. I can eat one all by myself."

"She knows to make two pots when you are home," Maw Maw said. "Want to know her secret?" she whispered toward Hart.

He nodded.

"She starts out with pork-n-beans right out of the can, adds some kidney beans, a pound of bacon, and a pint of chopped-up ham, peppers, onions, and spicy barbecue sauce, but that's not her secret. It's a double shot of Jack Daniels and a tablespoon of red pepper flakes. That's her secret—and it makes the beans right tasty with barbecued pork," Maw Maw said, as if she were sharing secrets from the top chef at the White House.

"I'll be looking forward to a plateful," Hart said seriously.

"Who's making gumbo?" Kate asked.

"Wouldn't let nobody else do that, not while I'm alive," Maw Maw said. "But that's enough talk about food and the *cochon de lait.* You two get on out of here and let an old woman fix up the gumbo. I'll see you by five o'clock this evening. Everyone is coming round after six."

Kate finished the last sip of her coffee and stood up. "How long will it take you to be ready?"

Hart polished off the last bite of his donut. "Five minutes to put on my shoes."

They met in the living room in less than that. Kate had changed into jeans and a light brown knit shirt that hugged every curve of her body. Beignets and gumbo hadn't put a pound on her in the weeks she'd been in Louisiana.

"You got any preferences today?" she asked.

"I'd be happy sitting on the bayou watching you fish," he said.

She shook her finger under his nose. "Flattery will get you zilch."

"That was fact, *chere,* not flattery," he teased.

"I'll be the tour guide. We'll drive to New Iberia and start with the courthouse and maybe do the Dave Robicheaux walk," she said.

"I'd like that. Old Dave is a man after my own heart."

She drove her truck and he sat in the passenger's seat. She pulled over on the side of the street in one spot and pointed to an enormous live oak. "See that tree with the moss drooping?"

He looked. It was big, he'd give it that much, but he felt like saying, *So what? It's not nearly as impressive as you are in that tight-fitting shirt.*

"That is the Gebert Oak. It was planted in 1834, before Texas was even a state. There was a lady who lived to be a hundred and five who told stories about sitting in the branches of that oak tree and watching the Yankees march into town."

"You do know your history," he said.

"Don't get sassy with me. One part of me is hot-blooded and brassy. The other is hotter-blooded and laid-back. They do battle with each other. Maw Maw taught me Cajun ways that summer we moved down here. She taught me to think about things," she said.

He had no idea what she was trying to say, but he didn't ask. Just listening to words coming out of her mouth in that soft Southern accent was enough. She could tell him how each leaf was formed on that live oak and how the twisted limbs meant something profound, and he'd be more than glad to listen.

Next she took him to the courthouse, parked the truck, and marched inside as if she owned the whole building. Her former boss, Captain Laysard, left his desk and gave her a hug. She made introductions and Laysard sized him up. Hart figured he'd passed the test when the man stuck out his hand.

"You going to be the one that keeps my best detective from coming back to work for me?" Laysard asked.

"I wouldn't know, sir," Hart said.

"If you are, it's possible that some gators might go against their natural distaste for Texans and do me a favor and chew on your carcass," Laysard said, without a hint of a smile.

"She's pretty good, is she?" Hart asked.

"Don't know why you'd be asking me such a nonsense question. I heard it took her one day to figure out what happened over there in Texas to that woman the police thought you killed," he said.

"Could have been a fluke," Hart said.

"I'm going to see Minnette about the party. You two old tomcats can circle each other while I'm gone or sit down and talk sensible," Kate said.

"Want to circle or have a cup of coffee?" Laysard asked.

"Coffee sounds better to me, but if you're going to throw me in the bayou with the gators, would you please make sure I'm real dead?" Hart asked.

"Just testing you, son," Laysard said. "Kate's daddy and me

grew up together. I gave her a place on the force more as a favor to him than because I wanted a female officer. She proved me wrong time and time again. She's good at what she does. I'd be glad to take her back, but only if she wants to be here." Laysard poured two cups of coffee and handed one to Hart.

"Trust you take it black like a man and not sissified up with milk and sugar?"

"This will do just fine," Hart said.

"Now, tell me about your career in the bull riding business. I always had a hankering to do some of that, but my bones is way too old now for any such thing. Heard tell you were ranching over in central Texas since you give it up."

So Hart had been researched . . . or else Kate talked about him as much as he did about her.

"That's right. Last ride was too close. Thought I'd just retire on top," Hart said.

"She watched every ride, you know. Whole time she was here, she bet on you every time," Laysard said.

Hart was stunned into silence.

"She dated some, but nothing serious. Not that the fellows around here didn't want to lasso her. Just, she wouldn't have none of it. I knew the first time I heard her mention your name why that was."

Hart wondered if all the people in Louisiana were so personal. He'd only just met the man.

"Guess I'm meddling," Laysard said, "but I thought maybe you'd want to know that before you go on back to Texas without her."

Kate poked her head in the door without knocking. "I see y'all decided to talk rather than throw Hart in the swamp."

"You be careful, *chere*," Laysard said gruffly.

"Only stating the truth. Maw Maw is having a little *cochon de lait* tonight. You and Rosetta come on down there and have some barbecue with us. Six o'clock or anytime after. Pig might run out since Vincent is doing the cooking, so I wouldn't be too late," she said.

Laysard looked at Hart seriously. "She must like you. Never

knew Jeannie Miller to give a party for someone she didn't like. Mostly they wind up floatin' down the bayou."

"Guess I'm lucky," Hart said.

Laysard turned his eyes toward Kate. "Who's making the gumbo?"

"Maw Maw. And Minnette is doing the beans."

"I'll call Rosetta and tell her to put the pork chops back in the freezer. I wouldn't miss a chance at a meal like that for nothin'. Save me a dance, *chere*."

"You got it." Kate tugged on Hart's arm.

He set the empty coffee cup on the counter and let her lead him out of the office. "That was the worst coffee I've ever had in my life. Jesus, take me somewhere so I can buy a Dr Pepper and get the taste out of my mouth," he whispered.

Kate giggled. "Tastes like a combination of road tar and cow crap, doesn't it?"

"Worse," he said.

"Probably been brewing a week. He keeps that pot special as a joke. The good stuff is in the break room. Anybody who drinks that is either crazy as an outhouse rat or else meaner than a junkyard dog," she said.

"Well, I hope he thinks I'm meaner than a junkyard dog. I bet that stuff is radioactive. A teaspoon of it would cure liver cancer."

"It might," Kate said.

They were on the steps leaving the big white courthouse when she got tickled and stumbled. He caught her before she fell. Carrying her like a new bride, he caught a movement in his peripheral vision and looked up. Laysard was standing in the window and giving him a thumbs-up. Hart nodded slightly and carried her all the way to the bottom of the steps and to her truck before putting her down.

He brushed a sweet kiss on her lips after he helped her inside the truck.

"Whew!" she said.

"Yep," he agreed.

He took in the sights of downtown New Iberia as she drove.

"James Lee Burke was right. Main Street is beautiful. What's that thing on the corner with all the wrought iron?"

"That would be the Gouguenheim. It's a hotel, but it started out more than a hundred years ago as a clothing store on the ground floor with the Elks Lodge on the top. Because of its stucco walls and metal roof, it stopped the fire back at the end of the eighteen hundreds. It stood empty for a long time, but the Jordans have restored it. Want to spend a night there?"

"Why should I? I've got beignets and coffee waiting for me in the place I'm staying," he said.

"And a sassy old bird who likes you because you let her cheat at dominoes."

"Was it that obvious?"

"Not to her. She thinks she got away with it."

"So I lost two dollars and ninety-one cents. I couldn't buy one beignet with that much money, and it made her feel good."

"Makes me wonder what other kind of cheating you'd let go on right under your nose?"

"If you're talking about what I think you are, the answer is, not a single penny's worth. Dominoes is one thing. Marriage is another."

"You got that right," she agreed.

They did the tourist's tour of Avery Island, where Tabasco sauce is made, and then it was lunchtime. She drove them back into town and parked down the block from Victor's Cafeteria.

"It's smaller than I thought. When I read about it in his books, I figured it was a lot bigger," Hart said, as they waited in line behind a dozen other people.

He had the jambalaya, fried okra, and black-eyed peas cooked with a generous amount of bacon. The pecan praline cheesecake took his eye, so he added a piece of it to his tray. Kate had the same and put two pieces of cheesecake on her tray.

"Don't say a word. I don't get this stuff very often and I always want more than one piece. We'll share the third one because you're going to want more too. I guarantee it."

"Maybe we better put on a fourth one, if it's that good," he said.

"I would, but that's the last one," she told him.

They sat at a table near the back. People came and went, stopping to talk to friends and family, much like the Eagle's Nest in Albany or the Amigos in Breckenridge. Accents changed. Decorations changed. But human nature stayed the same, no matter the climate or the nationality.

"So what do you think of Victor's?" she asked.

"Good food. Nice folks. No wonder Dave likes it here. You eat in this place often when you were on the force?"

"Yes, I did. My partner and I talked our way through a lot of crimes over a chunk of cheesecake."

He held up a bite on the end of the fork. "So this stuff is magic. If I eat it, I'll know what happened in the past and what will happen in the future."

She poked at his arm with a forefinger. "You are in magic country. You never know what revelation you might get with that. Who knows? Maw Maw might have called down here and had some kind of voodoo put in the praline syrup. You sure you're ready to face the truth?"

He put the cheesecake in his mouth and shut his eyes, appreciating the flavor. When he finished chewing, he blinked and, sure enough, the magic was there. He'd made a big mistake in the past when he broke up with her. She would have stood by him no matter what he wanted to do. Bull riding. Ranching. Teaching. He would have had her support because she loved him. The future? What he saw didn't scare him one bit, not anymore. It looked absolutely delightful.

"So?"

"What?" he asked.

"You ready to face the truth?"

"I already did, and I'm getting my half of your second chunk of this stuff."

She didn't ask anything more, because she wasn't so sure she was ready to face a blessed thing. Maw Maw said everything happened for a reason. She'd left Texas for a reason. She came to Louisiana for a reason. Now Hart was there for a reason. But what was it—other than to send her into more turmoil? Just when she thought she had the business of moving back to New Iberia and working at the force all figured out, she'd looked up from the vegetable garden to see Hart Ducaine. Now she didn't know what she wanted, and she was right back to where she'd been in Texas.

She and Hart had a battle of the forks for the last bite and ended up splitting it into two measly pieces, because neither of them would give it up. While she was sipping the last of her sweet tea, something Maw Maw said when she was determined to go into law enforcement came back to her mind.

"When you make the right decision," Maw Maw had said to Kate, "there will be no doubt, and your soul will rest easy. When it's not resting easy, that means you haven't made the right decision. It's not for your momma or your daddy or even me to decide, *chere*. Your big life decisions are for you to decide. If you let someone else do it for you, it might not be right, and you'll get to be an old woman with regrets. Me, I have no regrets. I made my decisions, and my soul has rested easy."

Mais, Maw Maw, there is no bigger one than the one facing me. I love him, but I also love my job, and I can't have both. So what do I do?

As surely as if Jeannie Miller had been sitting on her shoulder, she heard the soft Cajun whisper, *Make it so there are no regrets when you are ninety.*

"What are you thinking about, Kate? You look like you just saw a ghost," Hart asked.

"Nothing," she snapped.

He put his palms up and frowned. "Hey, don't get mad at me. I was just asking."

She stood up. "You ready to go?"

He picked up the tab lying on the table and went to the front of the cafeteria to pay. Something had sure changed her mood in a matter of seconds. Maybe he should have conceded and let her have that last bite of cheesecake. Had he just failed some kind of Cajun test?

He paid the bill, surprised that it was under twenty dollars, and they stepped out into a humid, hot afternoon. Diagonally across the street was Bojangles, a seafood place that he made a mental note to bring Kate to later in the week. The name sounded familiar, but he supposed it was something he'd read in one of Burke's books.

Once inside the truck again, she turned on the air conditioning, and he sighed with relief. Texas might be hot in July, but it was never this humid.

"Little hot for you, is it?" she asked.

"Little bit. What was that all about back there?"

"I was thinking," she said.

"Well, don't do it anymore. It makes you mean."

"If you don't like it, go home."

"Are you spoiling for a fight?"

She thought about her reaction when she'd first realized he wasn't a dream. She didn't want to fight with him then, far from it. She pulled over to the side of the road right up next to the sugarcane, which had been planted out as far as possible. She turned around to face him and drank in the sight of his face, the scar that the bull left and the one the car wreck had given him. She reached up and touched his sharp jawline, moved forward enough that she could kiss him, and wrapped her arms around his neck.

The sparks dancing around in the cab of the hot truck made the outside humidity seem as dry as the Sahara Desert. He kissed back, tasting the remnants of sweet tea and praline cheesecake.

When she finally leaned back and looked him right in the eyes, she said, "That's what I've been spoiling for ever since you arrived. Why did you drive this far and not even kiss me like you meant it when you first got here?"

"I was afraid you'd slap me or your grandmother would kill me," he said.

She kissed him again. "Does that feel like a slap?"

"Rejection is the same if you're eighteen or thirty-three. I almost turned around in Dallas and went home. It took a lot of persuasion to make me keep going." He hugged her tightly.

She shivered. "From whom?"

"Fancy and Sophie. And I even called Theron."

She brushed a sweet kiss across his eyelids. "Why'd you call them and not me?"

"You wouldn't answer my calls, remember? For all I knew, you'd already found someone else."

"And if I had?"

"I was going to war with them," he said.

"Oh, really?" She settled back into the driver's seat and put the truck in gear.

"Is there something you need to tell me before this party thing tonight?" he asked, suddenly afraid of the answer.

"His name is Bubba Boudreaux. Common name down here. He danced with me and asked me to his place for breakfast. He makes a mean gumbo breakfast."

"And?" Hart asked.

He had no right to feel jealous or angry. He hadn't actually stepped up and asked Kate to marry him, had he? He'd only asked her to dinner; so if she wanted to go to Bubba's place and have breakfast, he had no right to be angry with her.

"And we talked a couple of hours. Then I went home. I told him I was straightening out some things in my life, and he said when I got them straight to come on back and we'd see what we could cook up."

"He going to be at the party tonight?"

"Of course. He's a good friend of Minnette's husband, Claud. Bubba is a fisherman and loves the bayou," she offered.

"In other words, you two have more in common than we do," Hart said through clenched teeth.

"Probably. What are you going to do about that?" she asked, as she started driving.

"Fish some more at the bayou."

She jerked her head around to stare at him. That was absolutely the last answer she would have expected.

"That's what you've been doing all these weeks, and you don't know yet what you're going to do about all that. So I guess I'd better fish some more and try to figure out what I'm going to do about Bubba the fisherman and Kate the detective."

She finally smiled. "You sure are keeping your cards close to your chest. I bet you are a heck of a poker player."

He grinned back at her. "Yes, I am. I could whip you solid, lady."

"You are on. One night before you leave we'll have a game. I learned to play poker at my dad's knee and won a fortune from my partner when we were on stakeouts."

He chuckled. "I learned to play at my grandpa's knee, and, honey, it's a long way in a travel trailer from one bull ride to the next."

"What does that mean?"

He laughed aloud.

"Hart Ducaine, were there women in that trailer?"

"Like you said, darlin', I keep my cards pretty close to my heart. You want to tell me anything about the men you kept company with?"

"No," she said, loud enough that the words echoed off the truck's windshield.

"What's good for the goose is good for the gander," he said, intoning his grandmother's favorite adage.

"Well, gander Ducaine, you can get ready to lose when we play poker, because I won't let you win and I won't let you cheat."

"I won't need to cheat," he said.

"We'll see about that. I'm changing the subject before we fight. This is LeJeune's bakery, and we're going in here to get some bread and ginger cakes for tonight. Party in these parts isn't a real one without good bread to sop up the juices."

"So you don't want to fight?"

"I do not. I'm thinking about having a couple of ginger cakes and a Coke down by the bayou before we do any more sightseeing," she answered.

"But we just had lunch."

"And I worked up an appetite kissing you."

Hart reached across the console and ran a thumb down her jawline to the tender part of her neck. "I'd like to help you work up another appetite. I'd like to send you a class-five emotional tornado."

"You already did. That's why I'm in Louisiana."

Chapter Thirteen

The people began to gather at six o'clock. Women toted covered dishes and desserts. Men carried lawn chairs, and kids brought fishing poles and bait. The party tables were set up halfway between the house and the bayou in a clearing among the cypress and oak trees. Vinyl cloths covered two eight-foot folding tables, which had seen so many *cochons de lait* that if they could talk, the stories they would tell would be scandalous. Desserts went on one table. Food on the other. A smaller table was set up at the end of the food table to hold paper plates, napkins, plastic cutlery, and cups for tea or coffee. A child's swimming pool had been inflated and filled with ice early in the day, and canned soda pop and beer were chilled in it.

Maw Maw had already set her Crock-Pot full of gumbo on the table and claimed a chair half an hour before Kate and Hart made it home. She and Vincent nursed a cold soda pop and visited while he took care of mopping his own recipe for barbecue sauce on the hog turning slowly in the pit.

Kate and Hart hurriedly changed clothes and joined the party. The tables were full, chairs were everywhere with people in them talking, the band was setting up in a corner under the shade of an ancient live oak, and kids were running back and forth to the bayou. Kate had introduced Hart to a dozen cousins when Zac drug the bow across his fiddle for the first time and picked up the microphone.

"I understand we're celebrating something or other tonight. Could it be that Kate has found a fellow?"

Everyone laughed and looked at Hart, who did his best not to blush. Settling down on the biggest, meanest bull in the rodeo wasn't as intimidating as meeting all these people. Could Kate truly be related to all of them?

"So, since this is a party because she's come home where she belongs and should have never left, we'll let her and that cowboy who's come to visit have the first dance. This one is for you, *chere*," Zac said.

The band went straight into a Cajun song, and Kate led Hart to the floor. It was a fast song that didn't call for the two of them to melt together, and he did his best to follow her every footstep. Zac's fiddle whined, and the singer sang in what Hart supposed was French.

"What are they saying?" he asked Kate, when they got close enough to each other to talk.

"It's called 'La femme que j'ai jamais ublié.'"

"And that is?"

"It translates to 'The Woman I Never Forgot.'"

"It's nice of him to play something like that, because I didn't ever forget you," Hart said.

Kate laughed. "He's not playing it for you, believe me."

Hart cocked his head to one side and looked around. There were a dozen or more couples on the floor, including Claud and Minnette. He wondered who Zac was playing the song for; then the band went into another fast song, and Kate grabbed his hand and pulled him away from the dancing to meet more people.

"What's that?" he asked.

"It's a party," she said.

"No, the music. No one is singing, but it's a toe-stomping tune."

"Oh, that's just the 'Bayou Teche.'"

"No, I don't mean the sound of the bayou. The music. What's the name of it?"

She laughed and repeated what she'd just said. "That's the name of the piece they are playing. The kids love it and it's a good dance number. Not as lyrical as when they sing, but it's a good warm-up song."

She led him over to the table where Maw Maw sat with other women her age. Maw Maw made introductions and asked Hart if he was hungry yet.

"Just smelling that barbecue makes my mouth water," he said.

"*Mais*, good man, yes?" Maw Maw looked at her friends, who all nodded.

Zac and the band started a waltz and Maw Maw shooed them both off to the dance area, promising that the food would be served within thirty minutes. "Can't eat before full dark. It's too hot, *chere*," she explained.

Hart didn't have a bit of trouble dancing to the waltz. The accordion and fiddle blended together, and even without words he could almost hear a singer talking about the hot Louisiana night in a copse of live oaks, where he danced with the woman he could never forget.

"So you like the waltz better than the fast dancing?" Kate whispered.

The warmth of her breath in his ear shot desire though his body that he had difficulty controlling. "I like holding you."

"Remember that line, because Corrine is here," she said.

"What's that got to do with anything?"

"You'll see."

A minute later, a tall, dark-haired woman with the blackest eyes Hart had ever seen tapped Kate on the shoulder and took her place in Hart's arms. She melted her body next to his and wrapped both arms around his neck. She was tall enough that she laid her head on his shoulder as if it were made to fit in the crook.

"I'm Corrine, Kate's cousin. And you are one handsome cowboy," she said, in a thick Southern accent that had most men melting at her feet. "So tell me all about yourself while we dance the Cajun waltz."

"Not much to tell," he said.

"You are a bull rider, no? And you fill out those jeans really well, yes? And *cher*, I bet you are a man who would not mind Corrine kissing you, right?"

Hart wasn't sure he'd heard the woman right. Surely she wasn't coming on to him that quickly, and she was Kate's kinfolk. What kind of family had he gotten tangled up with?

"So is the big, pretty cowboy tongue-tied? Maybe I could kiss away the fear of speaking. Want to take a walk with me to the bayou?"

He pushed her back a step. "What is this?"

"It's flirting," she laughed. "You think about my offer and later, after we eat, give me a wink and I'll slip away to the bayou."

When the waltz ended, he searched frantically for Kate. He'd been propositioned before, but never so blatantly. Maybe all Corrine's attributes went to making a lovely body and face, and nothing was left over to make a brain.

He felt a touch on his shoulder and spun around.

"Lookin' for me?" Kate asked.

"What is that?" He grabbed her hand and led her away from the noise toward the bayou.

"A waltz," she said.

"No, that woman. Corrine."

"She's my cousin. Your tone says you didn't like her. Be careful, Hart, she's kinfolk, and we don't abide people talking about our kin," she warned him.

"I don't care if she's the queen of Cajun and talking about her will get me strung up for treason. Keep her away from me."

Kate put back her head and laughed so loud that it echoed in the trees, and the children at the edge of the bayou looked back to see what was happening.

"Did I hear my name, *cher*?" Corrine appeared like a creeping panther from the shadows.

Hart squeezed Kate's hand so hard that she feared he'd break her fingers.

"Corrine, this is my friend, Hart Ducaine," Kate said. "I think you met him on the dance floor."

"Did he pass?" Corrine asked.

"He did. You can go on and have a good time now."

"He's a good man, Kate. Don't be lettin' him get away from you now." Corrine disappeared into the same shadows she'd come out of.

Hart's grip relaxed. "Explain."

"You asking or demanding?"

"I don't care which one. What was that all about on the dance floor?"

Kate didn't like his tone one bit. "We don't have a dance floor. This is just a simple family get-together."

He dropped her hand. "You know what I mean."

"It's a family joke. When a new man comes on the scene, we turn Corrine loose on him first thing. If she can turn his head, then it's plain that he's not interested in the girl who brought him to the party."

"It's not funny," Hart said.

"Loosen up. Have a beer. Don't be an old grouch because she came on to you. You passed the test."

"I don't like it that I was even given a test," Hart said.

"I'm going back to the party. When you get through pouting you can join me," she said tersely, as she turned around and left him standing there.

"I'm not pouting," he said, but she was already gone.

Music drifted through the trees on one side of him and, on the other, the laughter of children rang out into the dusk. Hart sat down on the ground and braced his back against a tree, listening to both. They'd had such a good day and had even talked a little about the history between them. He'd thought they were making progress until she let her cousin make a complete fool of him.

Women!

Too bad it was against the law to shoot them. Had it been legal, Corrine would have been on the top of the list, with Kate not far behind her.

Another bit of music started, this time with Zac's fiddle taking center stage. Suddenly it became very clear what Zac had been singing about. He was literally singing to Kate and telling her she was the woman he'd never forgotten.

"*Mais*, you scared me, no?" a little girl about ten years old said when she stumbled over his foot.

"Sorry about that," Hart said.

"I'm going to hide behind the tree. Don't you tell Vinnie where I am, no?" She eyed Hart.

"I won't tell."

She darted behind the tree and sat down, but he could still hear her breathing. "What's your name?" he asked.

"I'm Julietta. You'd be the sorry Texan who came to snatch our Kate back over there, no?"

Hart smiled. "I suppose I am."

The only noise that filtered through the trees was the fiddle. The tune Zac was teasing from the strings almost sounded Irish. Hart could imagine Kate swishing her skirt tails around and the sweat beading on her upper lip.

"You'd best go on back to your Texas, because my Uncle Bubba, he says he's goin' to marry Kate. He says he's goin' to turn your head around with Corrine."

The smile faded. "Oh really, is that what your Uncle Bubba says?"

"That's right, yes, it is. Uncle Bubba says now that Zac is goin' to marry the rich lady, that he's got a chance with Kate. They both like to fish," Julietta said.

Jealousy crept up from the green grass beneath Hart and down from the gray moss hanging in the trees. Who was this Bubba, anyway?

A tall, gangly kid with a blond mop of hair and clear blue eyes came running out from the bayou. "Hey, y'all seen a little red-haired girl?"

Hart shook his head, and the kid ran on toward the house. Julietta giggled and took off back toward the bayou.

Zac's Southern voice came through the microphone as Hart watched Julietta disappear into the night. "Hey, y'all, Bubba asked me to play this here song for Kate Miller."

The fiddle began to send its whining notes out through the air, and the singer talked about his Louisiana woman being down in the bayou country and before the sun went down that evening, he was going to marry that Cajun baby. He said he wouldn't change his Cajun baby for all the gold in the land.

Hart seriously thought about sneaking around the end of the house, collecting his things, and leaving right then. But Maw Maw had not created the fiasco, and it wouldn't be fair to her to leave when she'd gone to so much trouble making a party for him. He stood up, dusted the butt of his jeans with the back of his hand, and went back to the crowd.

Candles had been lit and were blazing everywhere. From the smell, he knew they were Citronella to chase off the mosquitoes.

One got through the aroma and bit him soundly on the neck. He slapped at it, and Maw Maw motioned for him to come to her table.

"We're ready to eat now that you're back from the bayou. Were you fishin' with the kids?" she asked.

He spotted Kate out in the dancing area, swishing around a big, tall fellow that looked at her like she was made of pure gold. No doubt he was the Bubba who'd had the song sung for her. The singer was doing something about dancing with the boogie queen. Kate was surely filling that place, and Bubba was watching every movement with raw desire in his eyes.

"*Mais?*" Maw Maw asked.

He had to think for a minute to remember that that word was the same as "Well?" in Texas language.

"I'm sorry. I was helping the kids play hide-and-seek. Julietta was hiding behind me, and I had to tell some little kid I hadn't seen her. Is that cheating?" he asked.

"All's fair in hide-and-seek and love." Maw Maw smiled.

She clapped her hands at the end of the song. "Time to eat. Vincent says the pig is ready, so line up and get y'all a plate."

No one needed a second invitation. Zac and the band members put down their instruments and headed off to the tables. Zac stopped at Kate's side long enough to run a forefinger up her bare arm from elbow to shoulder and whisper something in her ear. She laughed and swatted at him.

Corrine was suddenly beside Hart, arm looped in his. "Come and lead me to the table, yes?"

He carefully removed her arm. "Sorry, ma'am, but Maw Maw Miller is my date tonight. I'm escorting her to the table."

Maw Maw smiled and took his arm. When she had her plate filled, he helped carry it to the table before going back for his own food. Kate waited for him to return like a dutiful guest who'd just realized she'd brought the wrong fellow to the shindig.

"Still mad at me?" she whispered.

"Never was mad at you," he said stoically.

"You don't lie none so hot, Hart Ducaine," she hissed.

"Darlin', I hold the record for being stupid. You are doing the same thing to me that I did to you back when we were kids.

I thought we were both adults now and had gotten past my teenage mistake. Evidently I was wrong," he whispered back to her.

Julietta grabbed Hart's hand and looked up at him. "Since Uncle Bubba is going to marry Kate, I guess you can sit with me for supper."

Hart smiled down at the impish red-haired girl. "*Chere*, I would love to do just that, but I've done promised Maw Maw Miller I'd sit with her. You want to tell her that you've stolen me away from her?"

Julietta shuddered. "*Mais*, not me, no? Maw Maw might put a spell on me and turn me into a swamp frog. You go on and sit with her. I'm glad you're goin' to be my aunt, Miss Kate. Are you goin' to wear a white dress to the weddin'? Y'all goin' to live on Uncle Bubba's boat?"

Kate was speechless.

Julietta ran off to find a little friend to sit with.

Hart picked up a disposable plate and filled it to the brim. He tucked plastic cutlery into his shirt pocket and grabbed a can of Coke with the other hand. Kate loaded her plate and followed him to Maw Maw's table.

"I heard tell you'd done give your hand over to Bubba Boudreaux. Why's that, Kate Miller?" Maw Maw shook her red fork at Kate.

"I did no such thing," Kate protested.

"Bring a feller down here from Texas. Make him drive all this way just to see you when you was goin' to marry up with Bubba, yes? That's not Cajun manners, no? You and me will talk later, after this *cochon de lait* is over."

"Maw Maw, I didn't say yes to Bubba. He didn't even ask me yet. And I didn't bring this Texan all the way down here. He flew, for one thing, and only drove from New Orleans. And I didn't ask him. He came uninvited."

"No sense in you being rude," Maw Maw said.

"She's just giving me a taste of my own medicine, ma'am," Hart said. "Only, when I broke her heart, we were just kids. She's showing me that in her world she's the princess and I'm the outsider. I'll be leaving as soon as I eat."

"Where you goin' this time of night?" Maw Maw shot him a mean look.

"Nearest hotel until morning, and then I'm going home where I belong. Kate has found her world. I need to find mine. I do thank you for a lovely party," Hart said.

Maw Maw threw up her hands. "Eat your food, boy. I'll talk to you too. Kids!"

Kate's heart dropped six feet below ground level and died right then and there. They'd gotten along so well all day long, and now he'd taken offense at a silly family joke. Maybe that was proof positive that she didn't need to be with him. What was it he'd just said? He was the outsider in her world. Well, she'd been the outsider in his, back when he was the glory child of Shackelford County.

Tears dammed up behind her lashes, but she blinked them back. She wasn't going to have black mascara streaks down her face, especially at a gathering where Corrine was. But, by the same token, she couldn't force a bite of food down her throat. She sipped at the sweet tea, and even it was tasteless.

"You not hungry?" Vesta, one of Maw Maw's closest friends, had been watching Kate.

"Just hot from all that dancin'," Kate said quickly, an orange-sized lump in her throat. "I'll eat a bunch later when I cool off."

He was going home, and she was staying behind. It wasn't supposed to work like that. He was supposed to stay a week and play poker with her before he left. He was supposed to convince her that her place was in Texas, learning how to be a rancher's wife.

She excused herself by pointing at the house like she had to use the restroom and went straight to her part of the bedroom. When she passed the sheets dividing his share of the room, she caught a whiff of his aftershave but didn't slow down. She retrieved her cell phone from her purse and punched in the familiar numbers.

"Hello." Fancy answered on the second ring.

"It didn't work. He came yesterday, and he's already going

home. When Theron came to Florida to see you, you went home with him," Kate said.

"What did you fight about?" Fancy asked.

Kate told her the Corrine story.

Fancy laughed until she got the hiccups. "Too many people. Get the weatherman to send you an ice storm where you have to spend a few days in a cabin together."

"Not possible in Louisiana, darlin'," Kate said sarcastically.

"I guess not in the middle of March, either. You shouldn't have pulled that trick on him. You two are at the fragile stage anyway, and that wasn't very nice."

"You're taking his side. Some friend you are," Kate said.

"I'm calling it like I see it. Think about your history," Fancy told her.

"What's that got to do with anything?"

"You don't trust him."

Kate chewed on that for a few seconds.

"Well?" Fancy said.

"I guess I don't. But he didn't succumb to Corrine and her tricks," Kate said defensively.

"You still don't trust him, and he doesn't trust you, either. If you're going to build anything, it has to be on a trust foundation. Go on back out to your party and start making a foundation."

"But he's going to a hotel," Kate whispered.

"You didn't have a bit of trouble finding the Ridge, did you? Why do you have qualms now? Can you not talk in a hotel room again?"

"I want it to be right between us," Kate said.

"Well, it'll never get to that point with you in the house talkin' to me and Corrine out there in the yard, right?" Fancy said.

"Okay, I'll do what I can. I'll call you tomorrow," Kate said.

"You better. I'm already biting my nails," Fancy said.

Kate flipped the phone shut and went back out in the yard. "Bye and thanks for listening to me."

Hart wasn't at the table with Maw Maw, so she figured he'd gone back to the bayou to pout some more. Not willing and not ready to talk yet, she danced a couple of times with Zac to music from a CD player. Then the band went back to the corner and the real music started. She looked around for Bubba. If she was going to have the name, she'd have the game. She'd show Hart Ducaine that he wasn't the only man in the world and she didn't have to put up with his pouting.

Minnette grabbed her arm and startled her. "Where you been, *chere*? Where's that good-lookin' Texan? Y'all had a fight, yes?"

"I was in the house and I don't know where Hart is, and yes we had a fight."

"He hug up too close to Corrine?"

"No, he passed that test as well as Claud did, I'm sure. We just had an argument because he got mad over the test. I think he's really upset because he thinks I'm rubbing my family in his face. It's complicated," Kate said.

"Sounds like it. We're just family, and we like him."

"Like I said, complicated in the biggest way."

Claud wrapped both arms around Minnette from behind. "Come and dance with me, *chere*."

Minnette turned around and put her arms around his neck. and they began to sway to the waltz Zac was coaxing out of his fiddle.

Kate went to the table where Maw Maw was having Corrine's famous cheesecake for dessert and asked if she'd seen Hart or Bubba.

"They left together," Maw Maw said.

"Did he know who Bubba was?" Kate asked, wide-eyed.

"Don't reckon he did. I introduced them myself, but I reckon I called Bubba by his given name. Never did like nicknames. Call a kid by what you named him. And that boy is Jedidiah Boudreaux in my books," Maw Maw said.

"Dear Jesus, what have you done?" Kate asked.

"Me? Didn't do nothin' I wouldn't do again, so I ain't done no sin. You was mean to your man, so Jedidiah done took him out on his boat to show him about shrimpin'," Maw Maw said.

"Why would he do a fool thing like that?" Kate said.

"Guess because Hart wants to learn about it 'fore he goes home tomorrow mornin'. Shame he couldn't stay the whole week. He promised to take us to dinner, and I had my heart set on something from down at Victor's. Y'all had any of that cheese-cake down there? Why, it's almost, but not quite, as good as Cor-rine's. That woman is going to catch her a man one of these days and fatten him plumb up on cheesecake." Maw Maw turned to her friends and ignored Kate.

Kate had no idea which way Bubba would be taking his boats out, so all she could do was wait—the one thing she didn't do well. If patience was indeed a virtue necessary for admittance into heaven, Kate was going to have to give her ticket to Min-nette or her mother.

She walked to the bayou, but even the children had been called back to the yard after dark settled in. She sat down at the edge of the water and wondered how things could get so messed up in twenty-four hours. They'd fished there in the peaceful surroundings just the night before, and now Hart was out on some stupid boat with Bubba, no doubt getting sloppy drunk.

"Hey *chere*, what are you doin' down here?" Zac asked, so close to her that she jumped.

"Party over?" she asked.

"Breaking up. Kids are cranky. Mommas are tired. Daddies have to work tomorrow. Good party, though. Good food. Your Maw Maw, she does know how to make a good *cochon de lait*. Come and let me hold you. You look sad."

"You are engaged."

"What does that have to do with us?"

"Everything," Kate said.

He reached over and touched her bare arm, but nothing hap-pened. Not even a tingle like she got when Hart just acciden-tally brushed against her skin.

"Come home with me, *chere*. I'll chase away the blues," he whispered.

She shook her head. "I won't be the cheating hussy in your life. You want to cheat, you go find someone else."

"Remember that I offered. Here's a Coke. Corrine said you were down here pouting and asked me to bring it to you. She said she can tell when a man has a wandering eye, and your Texan, *mais*, he did have one."

Kate took the Coke. "Corrine just thinks she knows Hart. If she wants to see a wandering eye, she needs to look into yours."

"You know how to stab a man in the heart." Zac pretended to plunge an imaginary knife into his own chest. "This Hart man is a fool to let you out of his sight. I'm leaving. You drink your Coke and pout all night if you want to, yes?"

She set her jaw and didn't say another word to him.

Rotten men!

All of them. She tilted the can back and guzzled half the soda before she came up for air and let go with a loud, unlady-like burp.

She listened to the toads and the crickets and a nutria some-where in the distance. Hart had spoken the gospel truth when he said she was home in Louisiana. And since she was ready to accept that, then she'd just make up her mind right then and there to go back to work for Laysard. She'd tell him tomorrow and call her mother, Fancy, and Sophie as soon as she did. They'd all pitch a hissy fit, but it's what she was going to do.

Her mind was made up.

To celebrate finally making the decision, she tilted the can back and finished it off. She was thinking about how the deci-sion didn't feel right, when Minnette sat down beside her.

"Zac said you were down here by the bayou. Me and Claud we're fixin' to go home. Want to come on over and have a cup of coffee with me and talk awhile?"

"Why not?" Kate said. When she stood up, she noticed that the trees were weaving, but then she'd jumped up really fast.

"Whoa!" she reached out.

Minnette grabbed her arm and flipped it over her shoulder. "Careful, *chere*. Before I married Claud there was days when I thought I'd like to put a dagger through his sorry heart. You feel like that tonight?"

Kate giggled and nodded. "I just jumped up too fast."

"Come on. We'll talk all night. I'll just call up Maw Maw and tell her you'll be stayin' over with me tonight. How's that?"

"Don't care where I stay tonight. Hart's mad at me and gone off fishin'."

"Oh, honey, he'll be over it come mornin'. I guarantee it,"

Minnette giggled with her and, arm in arm, they headed for Minnette's car.

"You don't know Hart Ducaine. He won't be over it by mornin'." Kate melted into the passenger's seat and leaned her head back. She shut her eyes just for a minute, and heard Minnette getting into the driver's side and the engine starting up, and felt the car begin to move.

"You are a good cousin to take care of me. You really think he'll be over it in the mornin'?"

" 'Course I do, *chere*. He won't go home tomorrow. I bet he stays the rest of the week."

"I want to believe you, but everything is so . . ." She didn't finish the sentence, but she heard Minnette laughing in the background as everything went black.

Chapter Fourteen

Hart followed Bubba out to the boat. Kate could just worry, or maybe she wouldn't worry at all.

"Maw Maw calls me Jedidiah, but everyone else calls me Bubba. I reckon you can call me Bubba too."

"So you're goin' to marry Kate?" Hart asked, when he'd settled into the pirogue. There seemed to be a lot of baggage on one end, but he figured that was fishing gear. Who knew what all they'd need for fishing in the backwaters of a Louisiana swamp. In the distance he heard a woman crying out for help and his eyes began to search the murky night for her.

"Sounds spooky if you ain't used to it," Bubba said in his thick accent.

"Who is it?" Hart whispered, his words only slightly slurred.

"Not who. What. It's a nutria."

"And that is?" Hart asked.

Bubba shoved off with a pole of some kind and began to maneuver through the cypress knees and the algae scum on top of the water. "It's this animal that was brought to these parts and accidentally let loose. Least that's what we're told. Old folks say it was on purpose to wipe out the swamp lands. Don't know how in the hell nutria is goin' to wipe out the swamps, but that's what they think."

"What does it look like?" Hart looked around. All he saw was a couple of snakes the size of an Angus bull slithering down trees and into the water.

"Those'd be cotton moccasins. Don't want to be pesterin' 'em none. They can be right mean and their bite'll put you in the hospital if you're lucky," Bubba said.

"And if you're not lucky?"

"Why, then you go to the morgue."

"So when do we start fishin'?" Hart asked.

"Little bit yet. Got to get on down to the good spot. You just be comfortable," Bubba said.

The strange haunting sounds of the swamp let him know he didn't want to be truly alone in this place. "So tell me about this nutria thing. Is it like a bird?"

"More like a beaver without a flat tail. Kind of like a big old twenty-five-pound rat. They breed like rats too. The momma can give birth, and a couple of days later the females are ready to breed again."

"Good Lord," Hart said.

Bubba pointed with his rowing pole. "Yep, and they have three or four litters a year, so you do the math. Hey, look at that gator."

Hart looked in time to see the critter yawn. All those teeth looked mighty vicious, or maybe it was the reflection of the moon. Nothing could be that big. Not even a swamp rat.

He realized Bubba was pulling his chain about the nutria thing. Why wouldn't he? Hart was a greenhorn in the swamp, and Bubba was in love with Kate. He'd go home tomorrow and tell everyone about the crazy stories he'd told and they'd all have a laugh at Hart's expense. Hart didn't care how big the beaver thing was—twenty pounds or just a plain old Texas-sized rat of about one pound—because he was going home in the morning.

Angry, *yes.*

In love with Kate, *yes.*

Facing reality, *yes.*

There, the yeses had the vote. There were no nays, so it was really over.

"*Mais*, we're about there," Bubba said, after an hour of sliding down the water.

"Hey, man, if you're in love with Kate, why'd you invite me to go fishin' with you? Tell me that before we break out the fishin' equipment."

"Kate Miller?" Bubba asked.

"You brought me out here to feed me to the gators so you can have her, didn't you? I'm not stupid."

It was Bubba's turn to laugh. "I'd like to have a turn at Kate. That's a fact, but I'm not in love with her. Where'd you get that?"

"Little girl told me."

"Julietta? Little imp. Last week I was talkin' about Kate Miller. This week I was talking about Kate Faucheaux. Now that's the woman Julietta heard me sayin' I'd like to marry up with. She's the daughter of a fisherman and has a whole fleet of boats. She's almost as good a shrimper as I am and pretty as a picture."

Hart felt a little better, but not much. "Okay, then, let's fish."

"We will, my friend. But we got to get the nets out of the old shack."

"What old shack?" Hart asked.

"Folks used to live out in the swamps more than they do these days. There's an old place back in here where a man raised up a family. He was a shrimper, Cajun man. Had a bunch of kids who lived on this island in the swamp. Pretty place, really. Ain't been too much touched by the modern world. Anyway, that's where we'll dock up and get our nets," Bubba said.

"And then what?"

"Then we go on down the swamp to the fishin' hole. I bet you catch a bunch of fish," Bubba said.

Five minutes later, a house sitting up on stilts appeared among the trees. Moonlight showed it to be sitting on a small island. Hart recognized an outhouse down a grown-over path several hundred feet from the main house. A set of steps that didn't look too sturdy led up to the screened porch around the outside of the place.

Bubba pointed at the outhouse, once he'd tied the pirogue to a stump and was standing on grassy land. "You got to go, go ahead. I'll get the nets."

Hart shook his head. "I'll help you."

"Okay, go on up in the house. Nets is up there over in the corner. I'm goin' to the outhouse. Be out in a minute," Bubba said.

Hart climbed the steps one at a time and carefully. They felt like they could break under him at any time. He'd barely made it to the top when he heard Bubba yell his name.

"What?" he turned and yelled back.

"I'll be seein' you in a few days," Bubba hollered. "Left you some supplies on the bank there. You can take them on up to the house."

"You miserable Cajun," Hart screamed.

"Don't come gunnin' for me. It was Maw Maw's idea, and I ain't goin' agin her for nothin'," Bubba yelled back, and then there was nothing but silence.

Hart leaned against a tree and shook his head. He pinched his arm and it hurt, so he wasn't dreaming. He'd been suckered into a fishing trip by an old woman and a redneck Cajun to teach him—what? Manners? Had he been that rude at the dinner party, the *cochon* whatever? Or were they just getting rid of him so Bubba could have a few days to talk Kate into staying?

Hart was going home. He'd told them that. He wasn't staying in Louisiana but one more night, and then he would be out of Kate's presence and back in his own sweet Texas. So why'd they have to pull a stunt like this?

Bubba said he'd left supplies on the bank. So that's what was in the boat instead of fishing stuff. Hart jogged in that direction to find two burlap bags full of food stuff. No bottled water. Just cans of beans and boxes of macaroni and cheese. At least that's what he could see by the light of the moon. He dragged them over to the steps and looked up. He had to get it inside in case of rain.

He figured the best way was to unload the sacks at the bottom of the stairs and carry items up a few at a time. So he loaded his arms with groceries and carefully put a boot on the first step. It didn't even creak. The wood must be petrified to be that sturdy. Six trips later, he decided the wood would hold up the Statue of Liberty, and he slung the rest of the food over his shoulder and toted the remainder all at once.

He'd worked up a sweat getting the supplies to the screened porch and then realized he didn't have a key to get inside the place. He stomped the floor without any thought of bringing down the house with his big boots, and was surprised when he found both the screen door and the wooden one open. Couldn't be much of a house if they didn't even lock it up.

Once he had all the supplies moved inside the door, he slid

down to the floor and put his head in his hands. Bubba said he'd come back and get him in a few days. Did that mean the other five he had planned to be out of Texas or did it mean a month? He stood up and looked around. Moonlight flowed through the windows enough that he could see a kitchen of sorts over at the back of the room. The cabinets looked like crates turned up on their sides and nailed to the wall. A table with a small galvanized tub was pushed up under a window. Surely that wasn't the sink.

He squinted and decided that it was. He got to his feet and inspected the thing. There was a pipe running down the wall with an elbow at the end and a faucet attached to it. He turned it, and cold water shot out into the tub. He quickly turned it off and looked up, hoping to find a cord to turn on a light.

"Well, stupid," he chastised himself after a few seconds.

There was a red lantern sitting on the kitchen table surrounded by three mismatched wooden chairs and a rusty metal chair that folded. Matches were in an old coffee can that had been painted yellow with the word MATCHES in big black letters on the side. He struck one against the bottom of his boot and lit the lantern.

He carried it around the rest of the house. It wasn't something he'd want to live in for a lifetime or even for a month, but it would keep the wind and rain off until Bubba came back. As soon as that big bruiser of a Cajun got him back to roads and highways, Hart intended to bust him right in the nose for this stunt. He didn't care if it was Maw Maw's idea. Bubba was big enough and mean enough to say no to that withered-up little granny.

The living room was small and sported a few old wooden chairs with the paint long since peeled off in layers. A deck of playing cards lay in the middle of a small folding table pushed up in one corner. Two chairs matching the oddball one in the kitchen were pushed up under it.

In the second room he found a bed with sheets, two pillows, and a quilt folded neatly on the end. The thought that he didn't have to sleep on the rough wood floors made him sigh. The second thought, that he had only the clothing on his back, made him mad all over again.

He dropped all his sweaty things on the floor and went back to the kitchen, where he found a washcloth in one of the cabinets and washed his face and arms. Feeling a bit less grimy, he went back to the bedroom, opened the windows to let the night breezes in, and made the bed. Then he stretched out on the bed and pulled the sheet up to his waist.

His grandfather always said things looked much better in the morning. Hart hoped he was right. He shut his eyes and fell into a deep sleep born of physical and mental exhaustion.

Kate roused up slightly when they reached Minnette's house. She remembered hearing Claud's laughter at her feeble attempts to get into the house, and thinking that surely she was coming down with the flu and it was making her light-headed.

"Your refrigerator is making a loud noise," she mumbled when Minnette laid her on the bed and covered her with a blanket.

Claud just laughed louder.

"Where's Minnette?" Kate asked.

"Don't worry, *chere*," said Claud. "She's tired and gone to bed. You just sleep. Tomorrow will look much better."

"I'm sick," she muttered.

"Not as bad as you might think. Shut your eyes and rest. It's been a long night."

She tried to open her eyes. She heard a nutria in the distance and could smell the swamp. Minnette lived in New Iberia, in town. Kate wondered why she could hear the sounds of the swamp at night.

Sometime later, she felt strong arms picking her up and carrying her to another room. For a minute she thought it was Hart, but he had probably already caught a red-eye flight back to Dallas and was home in his bed.

That story Maw Maw told about him going fishing with Bubba Boudreaux was a "save face" tale. She didn't want everyone at the party to think that Kate couldn't keep a man around for twenty-four hours without running him off with her sharp tongue.

She had fitful dreams after someone laid her down on a bed. She and Hart were fishing on the bayou, and she could hear the night sounds of the swamp. A cool breeze blew over her face, bringing with it the faint odor of his shaving lotion. Sometime later she felt the warmth of the sun as it streamed into Minnette's spare bedroom through the window.

Expecting to be aching with the flu, she opened one eye barely a slit and got ready for the pain when the sunlight hit. When it didn't do anything, she ventured the other one, only to see a rough wooden wall in front of her. Minnette's spare room looked like a creation out of a Martha Stewart home, with silk wisteria garland draped over the four-poster bed and around the mirror on the antique vanity. The walls had been papered in a trailing-ivy pattern; there was no way she was at Minnette's place, not with weathered wood boards covering the wall across the room from the bed.

She blinked several times. Maybe she was still dreaming. The only time in her life she'd awakened to a wall like that was back when she was about seventeen and her father insisted they go fishing way out in the swamp. It was where Maw Maw grew up with all her brothers and sisters, out on a little island. She remembered waking up and wondering where she was that day too.

Shutting her eyes tightly and trying desperately to remember how she would have gotten in a swamp shack, she slowly touched her forehead. She wasn't dreaming. It was real. But she could not remember how she got to the fishing shack. Had she and Bubba Boudreax gone fishing?

She was trying to figure it out, when someone on the other side of the bed flopped over, threw a bare arm over her, and snored loudly in her ear. She screamed and jumped up so fast she got a head rush, slipped on the rag rug, and landed square on her fanny on the bare floor.

The first thing she did was check to see how many clothes she was wearing. She sighed in relief when she saw that she still wore the sundress she'd had on the night before. Her shoes were sitting by the door beside two duffel bags. She recognized one as hers, the other as Hart Ducaine's.

She crawled across the floor and peeked over the edge of the bed to find Hart staring at her through wide eyes.

"What are you doing here?" she asked.

He blinked a dozen times. "I got left here by Bubba last

night. He said Maw Maw made him do it. He said he'd come back and get me in a few days. Why are you here?"

She bristled. "I don't know why I'm here or how I got here. I went home with Minnette," she said.

"I don't want to talk to you." Hart turned his back to her and shut his eyes. "Wake me when Bubba comes back."

She bounced on the bed and slapped him on the shoulder. "Well, I don't want to talk to you either, so I'm going home. I know where the old pirogue is hiding back behind the outhouse. You want to go with me, I might be nice and let you. You want to stick around till Bubba comes back for you, that's fine by me. What were those people thinking when they put us out here together?"

He rolled over to face her. "Did I hear you say there's a boat that will get us off here?"

"Emergency boat, and I remember the way back out of here. We can catch a ride into town. I've got credit cards in my purse," she said.

"Well, halle-dang-lujah!" He was out of the bed so fast, he looked like a blur.

Kate slipped her feet into her sandals and rifled through the duffel bag for her purse, but it wasn't there. It posed a setback, but nothing she couldn't overcome. Surely Hart had a couple of credit cards or a few dollars in cash in his jeans.

"Those fools didn't bring my purse. What have you got?" she asked.

He stuck his hand in his hip pocket and came back with nothing. No wallet. No comb. He found the exact same thing in his front pockets. Not even a bit of change. Bubba must have picked his pocket.

"I'm orderin' one of Maw Maw's gris-gris bags!" She kicked the wall.

"We'll hitch," he said.

"In different directions, I'm here to tell you."

When he was fully dressed, he picked up his duffel bag and followed her out onto the screened-in porch, where she stopped dead in her tracks. He ran into her backside and, if he hadn't grabbed her, she would have gone sprawling.

"I'm sorry," he said.

She pointed to a piece of paper tacked to the doorjamb. Written in lovely handwriting was a note:

Don't come hunting me down when you get back. Bubba will come and get you both in a few days. It was all Maw Maw's idea. She said if you two were on an island together without any interference, you'd come to your senses. We just did what she told us to do. Bubba left supplies with Hart, but I was afraid she'd forget the essentials, so I made Claud bring a garbage-bagful too. It'll be setting on the dock, because I'm pretty sure he'll be in a hurry to get out of there before Hart wakes up. Oh, and one other thing. There's a storm brewing off the coast and the old emergency boat ain't there, chere. Bubba hooked onto it as he left and brought it back with him. Looks like a big tropical but not a hurricane. Hang on to that cowboy and maybe you won't blow away. He'll keep you safe. Love, Minnette

"They drugged me, Hart. Some relatives they are," Kate fumed.

Hart read the note and sat down on the porch floor with a thud. Hope that sprang eternal had just been killed with a bullet called a note. If he hadn't been a grown man, he would have cried.

"We are stuck," she whispered.

"Guess so."

"I'm not going to come to my senses, whatever that means. I'm going to live through this, get back home, and take my old job back. Then I'm never speaking to my relatives again."

"I plan on a brawl out in a barroom parking lot. Bubba Boudreaux is going down for this, and I'm never speaking to your relatives again, either."

"What did you bring in with you?" Kate asked.

"It's all inside the door. Mostly beans and rice and macaroni and cheese," he said.

"Whatever Maw Maw had in the cabinet, probably. Well, go on down there and bring back whatever Minnette sent," she said.

"Why should I bring anything back? I toted up the batch left with me. You go get whatever they sent with you," he said.

It was mean, but he didn't care. Look what being a gentleman and resisting Corrine's joke got him. Kidnapped. Thrown out in the swamp with Kate, who hated him.

"Can you cook?"

"Not very much, but I reckon I can heat up a can of beans if it comes to that or starving," he said.

"I can make something out of nothing. So I'll cook; but you have to go get that bag out there," she said.

"I'll live on beans straight out of a can. Right now I don't think I'll need food for a week." He picked up his duffel and went back into the house with it. It was a silly fight, but Kate was not going to dominate the whole week, and if he didn't stop it right there, she certainly would.

She jumped up, stomped the wood floor of the porch, and went back inside to look at what was sitting inside the door. Cans of beans. Two bags of rice. A dozen boxes of Kraft macaroni and cheese. A couple of cans of black-eyed peas. A jar of jalapeño peppers and two onions. Two large cans of ham shaped in an oval.

"Hart Ducaine, if you don't go get that bag, then you can't have a bit of my coffee. Maw Maw didn't pack any for you, and I know Minnette wouldn't leave me out here without any, so there'll be some in my bag down by the dock."

That stopped him in his tracks. He dropped the duffel in the middle of the floor and turned around. "You aren't playing fair."

"All's fair in swamp living. It's the he-man's job to bring in the bag and the she-woman's job to make the coffee."

He stormed out the door, slamming both the screen door into the house and the one off the screened porch as loudly as possible. The big black garbage bag waited on the grassy place where Bubba and Claud had tied up their boats. He untied the top and, sure enough, there were two cans of coffee. He removed one can and hid it in a cooler on the porch before he went inside.

A man needed a little bit of leverage when dealing with an alligator.

"Thank you. Now that wasn't so hard, was it? Doesn't even

Carolyn Brown

look heavy," she said when he carried it back inside, slung over his shoulder like a bag of chicken feed.

"Where do you want it?"

"Right there is fine. I'll unpack it and put the other things away, then we'll go fishin' for some meat to go with the beans and rice."

He dropped it where he stood and went back out to sit on the porch. He chose the old metal folding chair, mostly because it looked sturdier than the wooden one. He'd done his day's work, so she could cook.

Kidnapped man bring in coffee.

Sassy woman cook breakfast.

A smile tickled the corners of his mouth. He tried to keep it at bay, but it spread until he was chuckling. Maw Maw had sure played a trick on them, and he wasn't so sure, now that he was awake and there was a promise of coffee, that he minded so much. A week should give him and Kate plenty of time to make a lot of decisions.

He didn't smell anything coming from the house when she opened the door. She tossed him a package containing two of those pastries that require a toaster to heat. He felt like he'd been cheated and very justified in hiding his own coffee.

"It ain't bacon and eggs," he said.

"Go find me a hen house and slaughter a hog, and we'll have bacon and eggs," she said.

"I don't remember you being this mean in the morning," he said.

"Well, remember me just like this when you go back to Texas, because this is the real me. Come on. If we're going to have meat, we'll have to fish."

"What are we using for bait, or am I eating it?" he asked.

"We'll dig worms. There's no shortage of them in the swamp. If we don't catch fish, then we'll put the worms in the macaroni and cheese. It's good protein," she said.

He grinned. "Yum, yum."

She shook her finger at him. "Don't be sarcastic with me. This is all your fault." She led the way down the steps and picked up a small shovel stored up under the house beside a rusty old coffee can.

"And, pray tell me, just how is this my fault? It wasn't my crazy relatives who put us out here on something so small we couldn't cuss a cat without getting a hair in our mouth," he said.

"If you hadn't got all heated up over Corrine testing you, then we wouldn't have fought; and if we hadn't had a fight, then you wouldn't have told Maw Maw you were going home."

"I'd say you're lookin' at it all wrong. Give me that shovel. You can't get it deep enough to find worms," he said.

She threw it at him.

He jumped back to keep from being hit in the knees.

She popped a hand on each hip. "How am I looking at it all wrong?"

"If you hadn't let your cousin come on to me and acted like you were . . ." He stomped the shovel into the soft earth.

"Like I was what?"

He turned the dirt over, and, sure enough, a dozen earthworms wiggled toward the top. "All high and mighty, in with your relatives."

She produced a rusty soup can from behind her back and gathered worms into it. "That would be the pot calling the kettle black. You wouldn't even take me on a proper date, and you were broken up with Stephanie back then."

He rolled his eyes and sunk the shovel into another place.

She squatted and got ready to harvest the worms. "Don't you make that face at me. You know I'm right."

He stuck the shovel into the dirt and squatted so close to her, she could feel his warm breath on her face. "You want to know why I didn't ask you to the movies or to the Eagle's Nest for a hamburger? Do you really want to know?"

"Give it to me. I'm a big girl."

"Because I was scared your daddy would beat the devil out of me. You were fifteen, and he was a big man. He'd already told a couple of guys that if he caught them around you, they'd never see the light of day again," Hart said.

She tried to speak, but no words came out. Finally she inhaled deeply and whispered, "Why didn't you tell me that before now?"

"Kinda makes me look like even a worse wuss, don't it? Big old football star scared of your daddy. Really would put brownie points on my side, wouldn't it?"

"I figured it was because you were ashamed of me because I was part Hispanic," she said.

He leaned forward and brushed a kiss across her lips. "Never crossed my mind. Now are we going to fish or fight some more? I'm about hungry enough, I might start eating these worms if we don't catch our dinner pretty soon."

Chapter Fifteen

When they had a can full of worms, Kate picked up two bamboo poles leaning against the back of the house. Hart put the shovel back and followed her toward the place where the boats docked. It could hardly be called a dock since it was only a two-foot wooden porch out into the water, with a couple of tall posts at the end to tie up a canoe.

"Just how big is this place, anyway?"

Irritation had been replaced by curiosity and, besides, he couldn't stay angry at Kate for very long. She was so darned cute barefoot and in that little sundress. Even though it wasn't a tropical paradise, it was definitely a remote island, and they were alone.

"Big enough to support a family. They had a garden spot and a milk cow and some goats." She looked out across the bayou, shook her head, and followed the shoreline to the far side of the island. A live oak had stood proud and tall at one time, overlooking the swamp, but lightning struck it long before she was born; possibly all the way back when Maw Maw ran all over the island in her bare feet and black braids. It had fallen, and the weather and wild animals had eaten away at the limbs, until it was finally the perfect place to lean against or sit on while fishing.

"That's where we sit," she said.

He baited the hook on one of the poles, tossed it out into the swamp, and sat down to wait. He could get used to this fishing idea real quick. "Who lived here?"

"It's Maw Maw's land and house. It belonged to her family, and she's the last survivor of that generation. She'll leave it to one of her children," Kate said.

"I feel sorry for whoever gets it," he mumbled.

"What did you say?"

"Not a thing. Why didn't we fish where Bubba docked the boat?"

"Fish ain't bitin' there," she said.

"How do you know that? Are you just jerking me around like Bubba did about the twenty-pound rats?"

"What?" She looked over her shoulder at him, and her heart threw in a little extra beat.

"Some big animal out there in the swamp called a nutrition that looks like a rat or a small beaver without a flat tail and weighs more than twenty pounds. I heard a bird making a weird noise, and he told me a cock-and-bull story."

"That would be a nutria, and it's not a cock-and-bull story. They're nocturnal, so they're asleep right now, but when night comes, I'll try to show you one," she said.

His eyebrows almost touched the scar across the top of his forehead. "Are you serious? There's a twenty-pound rat out here?"

"More like an undersized beaver. Want to catch one and fry it? Some folks say they're really good."

"No, thank you. Worms look better than fried rat."

"You eat squirrel, and it's nothing but a rat with a fluffy tail," she said.

"That's different."

"Why? Because you've been raised on that idea. Well, folks around here are raised on the nutria idea. You will get tired of fish three times a day before we leave here, so you might change your mind."

"How long do you really think they'll leave us out here?"

"I reckon Maw Maw will consult her voodoo friends. That would be those four old ladies sitting at the table with her last night. They'll read the tea leaves or throw some dirt in the wind, and see how long it takes to filter back down to earth," she said.

"What does that have to do with us?"

"Nothing, but believe me, they'll know the minute we stop fighting and figure we've been here long enough," she said.

"Guess we are here forever." He smiled.

She giggled. "Kind of like Adam and Eve. Reckon this is the real spot for the old Garden of Eden?"

"Hummmph," he snorted. "More like the place where the devil was thrown when he got pitched out of the Pearly Gates."

Kate placed a finger over her full lips. "Shhhh, that kind of talk will go straight from your mouth to Maw Maw's ears on the wings of a dove, and we'll be here until St. Peter sets up a snow-cone stand in Hades."

"How did y'all get running water in this place? Is there a well?" he asked after fifteen minutes.

She answered with one word. "Cisterns."

After another ten minutes he ventured another question. "Would you tell me what you are talking about?"

"Cisterns. Used to be a big galvanized tub on top of the house; now it's a plastic one. Rainwater goes in and comes out the faucet in the kitchen."

"Then that water's been up there for years if it hasn't rained. It could be polluted with all kinds of ugly things."

"Rains right often here, and there's a top on the cistern. Water flows off the top of the metal roof into pipes that have a filter that prevents leaves and varmints like plain old house rats from getting into it. The one out in the side yard up in a tree doesn't have a top or a pipe. Water goes in and comes out the bottom when you turn on the shower."

His eyebrows went up. "You mean we get to take a bath?"

"A fast one. There's a system. You wet down. Turn it off. Soap up and then turn it back on and get the soap off in a hurry," she said.

"I could do that."

"I have no doubt. You'll want to take one in the middle of the day, after we catch our dinner and supper."

"Why's that?" he asked.

"Because that's the way we do things."

Something took her bobble to the bottom of the swamp, and she flipped a nice big bass up on the bank.

"There's dinner." She removed the hook and put the fish on a stringer, which she staked a couple of feet from the water. Then she eased it back down into the water.

He caught a catfish next, and she followed it with another bass. The sun was straight up when she caught a catfish and declared that was enough for dinner and supper.

"I might be hungrier than that. Those two dried-up toaster things you gave me didn't do much to keep body and soul together," he said.

"Then you can eat lots of beans and rice. You want to fish some more, you can do it after we have dinner," she told him. "Just remember that what you catch you eat that day, because there is no refrigerator and we don't waste."

"Bossy, ain't you?"

"It's been said by experts. You any good at cleaning fish?"

"I can do a fair job, I expect. You want steaks or fillets?"

"Fillets," she said.

"What do I do with the leftovers?"

"Toss them out into the swamp down by the boat dock. There's alligators that will appreciate a good meal."

He turned his head and studied her face. She wasn't teasing. Twenty-pound rats and alligators—how did anyone ever live there and raise kids?

"I'm going to start a fire in the cookstove and put on the rice. That'll take the better part of an hour. You think you can have these ready by then?" she asked.

He nodded. A fire in the cookstove meant they really were living primitive. No gas. No electricity. Showers from a cistern. Outdoor bathroom. Maw Maw must think she had a mansion in that little two-bedroom house on the bayou.

They stopped at the bottom of the steps up to the house, and she pointed to the right. "Over there, you'll find a shelf attached to two support pilings with a dishpan on it. That's the fish-cleaning table. Get some water from the shower. I'll bring you the fillet knife and a bowl to put the meat into."

He hauled the stringer with the flopping fish to the side of the house and laid them on the ground, picked up the white metal dishpan, and looked around for the shower. It was under a cypress tree, with the cistern located a few feet up in the branches. The pipe ran from the bottom of the oversize plastic tub to a fairly modern-looking shower head with a switch on the side to turn the stream loose. He held the pan up and turned. It filled so fast that it ran over before he could get it turned off. He quickly looked around to be sure Kate didn't see him wasting water, and then frowned.

He cared what she thought, or he wouldn't have checked the house over a quart of spilled water. That was not a comforting thought. Not when she'd already declared that she was going back to her old job as soon as they were rescued.

Kate pulled a small box made from a wooden crate more than eighty years before out from under the cabinet and set it on the table. It held mismatched spoons, forks, and an assortment of knives. She carefully moved pieces aside until she found the fillet knife with a long, slender, tapered blade with a sharp edge and a perfectly maintained point. She chose an enameled blue metal bowl from the cabinet and was on her way to take them to Hart, when she could have sworn she heard her father's voice.

Katy, don't slam the door in the face of opportunity. This is the time to listen to your heart and make decisions that will affect your whole life.

It was what he'd said when she got the scholarship to go to college. What on earth would that have to do with being stranded on an island with Hart Ducaine?

Hart was carefully toting an overfull basin of water from the shower to the table, when she rounded the corner of the house.

"You wastin' water?" she asked sternly.

"No, ma'am. What I spilled only went to water the grass," he answered.

She held up the things she'd brought. "Smarty-pants! Knife. Bowl."

"Water. Fish," he said right back at her.

"We've got days out here. Don't use up all your cuteness the first day," she said.

"*Chere*, I wouldn't use them all up if we were out here for a year."

"And don't call me *chere*. It's an endearment that you don't use if you don't mean it," she said.

"You are lyin' to me, Kate. Your grandmother called me that

the whole time she was planning to put me on this place with you. It's not an endearment. It's a curse. No one would put someone they loved out here on this island with you for a whole week."

"Just clean the fish and don't cut your finger off. I'd have to stitch you up, and I've never been real good with embroidery." She flounced back into the house.

Until that moment, Hart hadn't considered what they'd do if one of them got hurt or sick. What if Kate fell down the stairs and broke her arm? What if that woodstove blew up in her face and she was burned badly?

Kate lit a few handfuls of kindling in the stove and waited for it to catch before she threw in several sticks of wood. The house would be hotter 'n blue blazes in a few minutes, but to boil water for rice, the stove had to be hot. She'd cook enough for two meals and hope that the place cooled off by night. If not, they'd be taking the mattress off the bed and moving it to the screened-in porch.

She groaned, not at the idea of sleeping on the porch, but that there was only one mattress. That meant one of them had to sleep on the hard floor.

What she'd give for a cell phone to talk to Fancy or Sophie right then couldn't be measured in dollars and cents. During Thanksgiving a few months before, Fancy had gotten stranded in a cabin with Theron and his daughter, Tina. She hadn't taken her cell-phone charger with her, and she was only able to make one call. Kate had thought the whole thing was hilarious.

Fancy and Theron had been attracted to each other from the night he'd stopped her for what he supposed was drunk driving, and carted her off to jail. They'd fought it tooth, nail, hair, and eyeball and then found themselves trapped in a cabin during an ice storm. It didn't end happily-ever-after then, either. They continued to declare they were unsuited for each other, even after she moved back to Florida.

"Just like I am doing right now. If this were a romance novel, the plot would be pretty blasted similar," she mumbled, as she put three cups of rice and six cups of water into a pan and set it on the stove. "She didn't have a history with Theron and she sure didn't ruin her life by pining after him for years."

"Who are you talking to?" Hart asked from the doorway.

"Myself," she said. "Try it sometime. You'll be amazed at what good company it is."

He handed her a bowl brimming with fish fillets. "How you planning on cooking those?"

"Until they're done," she said.

"Good. I hate raw fish. Sushi is not my thing," he said.

"Go sit on the porch and get out of my hair," she said. Cooking in a hot house, looking at his sexy lips, and him standing there made too much heat in one room.

"With pleasure," he said.

A movement on the door caught his eye when he sat down in his old rusty chair. He looked down to see a cockroach the size of a small mouse, crawling through a gap in the screen. If something that big could get inside, then a mosquito would have no problems at all.

"Y'all got any tools in this place? Screen has come unfastened. Won't keep out a roach, much less a 'skeeter," he yelled.

She didn't answer but slid a wooden box out the door in a few seconds. Two one-pound coffee cans were filled with used nails and screws of every description and size. There was a hammer, two screwdrivers, several pieces of screen wire, pliers, and even a crank-operated drill. He set about killing the roach and fixing the screen. Then on the off chance there were other loose places, he made a careful study all around the porch, repairing as he went. The smell of frying fish wafted out the door as he worked, and his stomach growled loudly.

"How long until dinner?" he hollered.

"It'll be ready when it gets ready. You don't rush anything on a wood stove," she yelled back.

He remembered a creaky step leading up to the porch and carried his box of tools down to the culprit, repaired it, and checked each piece of wood the whole way up to the top. Maybe it would prevent Kate from falling and breaking her arm or leg.

By the time he reached the top, the aroma coming from the

cooking really had his stomach grumbling. If she didn't hurry up and get it ready, he might change his mind about sushi. Or they might have to fish again in the afternoon, because he ate dinner and supper all in one meal.

Nutria didn't sound too bad, either. Did a person grill it or dig a pit and turn it on a skewer? He had plenty of time to do either.

Kate knew the fish recipe from memory but had to do some major substitutions. There was no fresh garlic, so she used garlic powder. There was plenty of pepper sauce, red wine vinegar, and soy sauce, thanks to Minnette. And the family always kept flour and cornmeal in the house. She'd never tell Hart, but various family members were always bringing their sleeping bags and coming to the place to fish. Maw Maw came at least twice a year, but they'd made her promise not to come alone anymore since the time she took a tumble down the stairs.

Kate added salt and pepper to the hot pepper sauce and poured the sauce over the fillets. Usually she'd let it marinate all night, but she didn't think Hart would wait that long. She let it soak up the sauce only as long as it took the grease to get hot in the iron skillet. When that time came, she rolled the fish in a mixture of equal parts flour and cornmeal and started frying the fillets hot and fast.

Hart had done a good job when he cut the fish up. The pieces cooked fast and uniformly. While they fried, she stirred up a jar of strawberry jam, half a cup of red wine vinegar, a tablespoon of soy sauce, and two tablespoons of horseradish into a small sauce pan, and set it on top of the stove to boil.

The rice was dry by the time she took the last of the fish from the grease. The beans were hot, and the sauce had hit a boil. So dinner and supper were both ready. As soon as the firewood burned out, the house could begin to cool down. She set a dented aluminum kettle full of water on the stove and a saucepan filled with cornmeal, sugar, and a little water.

"Hey, you want to take the card table out to the far corner of the porch? It'll be a little cooler there than in here," she said from the screen door.

He was too hungry to argue. He carried the table out and went back to help her carry the food. He met her toting out a pan of beans, and their arms brushed. Neither the heat in the house nor the boiling-hot beans could match what ignited between them. But they kept going without saying a word.

He set up the chairs, the metal one for him and the wooden one he'd repaired for her, and went back inside to help carry an enormous platter of fried fish. She had a pan of rice in one hand and a smaller one of a scrumptious-smelling stuff that he thought might be dessert.

They set the food in the middle of the table, and she took the chair nearest to the screen, hoping for a breeze.

She bowed her head. "You say grace."

He was reaching for a piece of fish, but he laid the fork down and bowed his head to give a short prayer of thanksgiving for the food.

She didn't wait for him but filled half her plate with rice and topped that off with beans. "Oops, forgot the pepper sauce," she said, already pushing back her chair and heading for the kitchen.

Hart was no stranger to beans and rice. He'd traveled enough with the rodeo rounds to have eaten many different foods. Beans and rice was one of his favorites, but he didn't understand why she needed pepper sauce.

She returned and shook a bottle of peppered vinegar over her beans and handed it to him when she was finished.

"Don't need it," he said.

"Can't take the heat?"

"We talking about what's in that bottle or what's between us?"

She was speechless.

"Both," she finally said.

"Fair enough. I can take it, all of it." He doused the beans with the sauce and filled his mouth. It was really good. He chanced a look at the bottle, remembering the name so he could buy some when he got back to Texas.

She put three pieces of fish on her plate and added a table-spoon of the stuff he'd thought was dessert beside them. She cut a bite off with the edge of her fork and dipped it into the sauce before putting it in her mouth. She'd forgotten how good Cajun fish was until that moment. It was definitely a sign that she should stay in Louisiana.

"What is that?" he asked.

"Fish sauce. Try it."

"Hot?"

"Not too much. Kind of sweet and sour at the same time. Has strawberry jam in it."

He put half a tablespoon on his plate. If he didn't like it, he wasn't listening to her carry on about wasting good food. The burst of flavor sent him back for more immediately. He might ask the woman to marry him for her cooking alone.

Marry me! He choked just thinking the words. *Well, isn't that what you've been beating around the bush about? That's the ultimate thing you want, isn't it? Most people your age who admit they love a woman are thinking of the next step. Why does it come as a surprise to you?*

"Something down your windpipe, or are you a wuss and can't handle the hot after all?" she asked.

"Down the windpipe," he lied.

"I'll get us a glass of tea. Forgot to bring that out too. No ice, but it's sweet." She was up before he could catch a second wind, and back before he could process the argument with his conscience.

"Thank you," he said.

"Did that hurt very much?"

"What? The choking?"

"No, saying thank you to me?"

He grinned. "Much worse than choking. Good food. Catfish is wonderful but got a little hot taste to it."

"It's Maw Maw's recipe. They grew strawberries here when she was a young girl. She still loves them in everything. That's what makes the sauce sweet. The hot comes from marinating the catfish in hot sauce before it's fried. It's even better if it can marinate all night."

"You think maybe Minnette was wrong about the storm? Don't look like there's a cloud in the sky," he said.

"No, it's coming. I can smell it."

"Are you kidding me again?"

She slowly shook her head. "Take a deep breath. What do you smell?"

"Fish, beans and rice, and sweet sauce," he said.

"You're Texan. Inland Texan at that, so your nose hasn't been trained to smell a storm. It's coming, all right. We might be housebound all day tomorrow if it hits tonight."

His mind went into overdrive. What would they eat if it stormed? What if it blew the house down and they were killed?

She read his mind. "Don't worry. You won't starve. Minnette threw in a couple of those little canned hams. And the house withstood Katrina. I don't think we have to worry about a tropical squall. You about finished?"

"One more piece of fish," he said.

She waited for him to eat it, then began to gather up the dishes and food. Without being asked, he helped. He set everything on the kitchen table, and she set about covering what they'd have for supper with a clean dish towel, putting the dirty dishes into the dish tub, and running a little cold water on them.

"You think that will get them clean?" He leaned against the wall as far away from the hot stove as he could get.

"Not by itself, but this will." She added a squirt of dish soap, grabbed a potholder, and poured steaming water from the kettle into the dishwater, adding a bit more to an oversize bowl on the other side. "Want a cup of coffee before this gets cold?"

"I'd love one. How do you make it?"

"Like this." She pulled out a drip pot from inside the cabinets, put coffee grounds in the top, and poured the rest of the hot water through it.

"What's that stuff?" He stretched his neck and peered into the other pot bubbling on the stove.

"Cornmeal mush. Country pancakes for breakfast." She quickly greased the inside of a loaf pan and poured the boiling mixture into it.

He wrinkled his nose slightly.

"Trust me, darlin'," she drawled. "You'll like it much better than what you had this morning."

He picked up a tea towel, fished the dishes from the rinsing water, and dried them. "So what do we do the rest of the day? Supper is already cooked and breakfast is cooking."

She looked up to see him raise one eyebrow.

"What does that mean?"

"Torture couldn't make me say what I was thinking we could do with the rest of the day," he said.

She smiled. "I've got ways of torture you don't even know about."

"I don't doubt it, but I'm a strong man. I'd even ask you to go to the Eagle's Nest these days and take my chances with your dad." He grinned.

"Okay, I'll let you have that point. I'm not sure I want to know what you were thinking, anyway. We can either take a shower or I'll show you around the place. If the storm comes we might not get another chance."

"Why not? Is it going to last until God calls us away from Earth?" Hart chuckled.

She cocked her head to one side. Had he gone daft after less than twenty-four hours without the comforts of his Texas ranch?

"You said that they wouldn't come get us until we stopped fighting. I reckon the horns will blow announcing the end of the Earth before that happens," he said.

"Hush! Shower or tour?"

"Tour. I prefer my shower before bedtime."

"You might be sorry. I'm tough enough to take it. You might not be," she said.

"I'm tougher than you any day of the week," he said, wondering the whole time what she was talking about; but he'd be hung from a live oak before he asked her to explain.

She slipped her feet into rubber flip-flops at the door and motioned for him to do the same. "You don't want to ruin your good boots."

He looked at the black rubber shoes. "You think those will fit me?"

"They fit Daddy, and there's no way you are as big as he was."

There was an inch of room left behind his heel, and he tried to scoot his foot back so she wouldn't have the satisfaction of being right.

"Won't work," she laughed. "Actually those are Bubba's. Daddy had a small foot, but you still can't fill his boots. Come on, we'll go walk off lunch."

"Lunch? I thought it was dinner and supper out here on paradise island."

"Slip of the tongue; and you know exactly what I meant."

The whole place looked different now that his stomach was full. Water lilies floated on the water. Big white birds nested in the trees. The ever-present moss swayed in the wind.

He was looking up at an owl sitting on the branch of an enormous cypress when she poked him on the arm. That much physical contact caused him to jump.

"Look," she whispered, and pointed to the edge of the water, in among the leaves and twigs.

"Lizards?" he whispered back.

"No, baby gators. Three of them. Aren't they cute?"

"Where's the momma?"

"Somewhere pretty close. Just keep an eye out. They can be vicious and Daddy said they can come out of the water doing about thirty miles an hour, which is a lot faster than you can run."

The skin crawled on the back of his neck, and the scar on his forehead began to itch. "I vote that we leave them alone and get out of this spot."

"Ahhh, and I had notions of taking one home for a pet."

"If you're not kiddin', then you are crazy," he said.

"*Mon dieu*, you are full of nice things to say about me today. I've got a feeling when the voodoo queens meet tonight, the consensus will be to leave us out here a while longer."

"I wasn't joking when I said we may be here for a long time. We may have to populate the island all by ourselves, because it's the same as being the last man and woman on earth," he said.

"Guess the human race is about to die then," she said, giggling.

Chapter Sixteen

The night was even heavier with humidity than the day had been. The nutria weren't making as much noise. Tree frogs and crickets were still. The moss, dripping from the trees like stringy gray spiderwebs all tangled together, hung limp. Not a single ripple disturbed the water, giving it a glassy appearance, as if someone could actually walk out of the swamp right on top of it.

Supper was over, and Kate and Hart had ignored each other all evening. He'd sat on the porch, leaning back in that old chair, deep in thought. She'd opened all the windows to let in what little air could be enticed into flowing through the house, and stretched out on the bed and fought with herself.

In this corner was Kate, the detective who loved her job.

In that one was Kate, the woman who loved Hart Ducaine.

At dusk she gathered up a towel and a bar of soap and went outside. "I'm taking my shower. You want one when I'm done or not?"

"You want to sleep with me without one?" he asked right back.

Kate stopped so fast, she had to reach out to keep from tumbling forward. "I'm not sleeping with you."

"One bed, and I'm not sleeping on the floor. That roach I saw this morning could carry me out there to your bionic gators," he said.

She inhaled deeply, searching for a comeback. Nothing came to mind, so she let him have the last word and went on to the shower. Years ago, one of her relatives had hung a round rod from the trees. Using plastic rings, they'd attached a couple of cheap shower curtains to make a circle. Kate stepped inside, undressed, and tossed her clothing out on a chair sitting at the base of a tree.

That uneasy feeling that meant someone was watching swept over her about the time she turned on the water. She looked up, but there were no birds in the trees and the shower had been deliberately set where it was so that no one from the porch could peer over the top. She checked the ground; not a single spider, bug, or critter of any kind.

Hart was watching the shower from the corner of the porch. Though he couldn't see her, she could feel it. She braced herself for the first spray of cold water. Like diving into a cold creek or bayou, even on a hot humid night, the water would startle her. She'd bite her tongue plumb off at the root before she made a noise.

She finished the shower, wrapped the towel around her clean body, slipped a pair of flip-flops onto her feet, and headed up the stairs. The sight of her with her long black hair streaming down her back, water droplets on her lightly toasted skin, and those full lips sucked all the air out of Hart's lungs.

"Your turn," she said, and disappeared into the house. A couple of minutes later, she tossed out a towel. "Soap is on the chair beside the shower. Bring it in when you are done."

He plodded out to the shower in flip-flops, stepped inside the curtains, peeled out of every stitch of clothing, and put it on the chair as he'd seen her do. He was thinking about her when he turned on the water.

"Holy Mother of God," he yelled when the cold water hit his sweaty skin.

Her voice singsonged above the rush of the cold water. "I told you I was tougher than you."

"You are a devil woman," he yelled back, when he could breathe again.

Her laugh echoed through the still night.

He finished bathing and wrapped the towel around him like a loincloth, picked up his clothing in one hand and the soap in the other, slipped his feet into the flip-flops, and headed back to the house. Thunder rumbled somewhere in the distance, and dark clouds covered the moon.

So Minnette had been right. There was a storm coming. Hart didn't know which was more ferocious, the squall coming off the gulf or the one in his soul. He tossed his clothing on the floor and picked up his duffel bag.

Kate, in an oversize white T-shirt, was sitting on the bed with her knees drawn up to her chin, watching out the open window. He carried the bag to the screened-in porch and dressed in a gauze undershirt and a pair of black knit sleeping shorts that barely reached his knees.

"Looks like we got a choice," he said.

"About what?"

She was not sleeping on the same mattress with him. He could sneeze and get that idea right out of his head!

"It's about to rain. We can take that mattress off the bed and put it on the floor in the living room as far away from the windows as possible. Or we can shut all the windows and get stinkin' sweaty again," he said.

She looked up. Wet, plastered-down blond hair made the scar more visible. She wanted to kiss it but refrained. She was going to stay in Louisiana. Hart was going back to Texas. And never the twain would meet again, unless she ran across him when she went home to visit Fancy, Sophie, and her relatives.

Home? She frowned.

"It's not that tough of a decision, Kate. Heat or mattress on the floor," he said.

"Mattress on the floor. I'll put a pillow between us. We'll each get half of it, and you are not to get into my space," she said.

"Wouldn't dream of getting into your space. Now if you'll get off the bed, I'll move it. Thunder is getting closer all the time. Rain will be here before long, and it'll get wet next to the window. Feel the way the wind is already blowing in there." He held up his hand.

"Don't tell me what to do," she protested.

"Don't be controlling. We're here together, Kate Miller. You don't have to have the upper hand on every decision," he countered.

"Well, you're not God," she snapped.

"I don't want to be. He gets blamed for too many mistakes. I can barely stay ahead of my own."

"Floor, then." She picked up the bottom end of the mattress and helped him carry it to the living room. "There used to be two or three beds in here and two in the other room. Maw Maw said it was wall-to-wall people at night. When the weather was nice, they fought over who got to carry their beds to the screened porch."

He was amazed that she'd offered information with no barbs.

"So, you ready for bed?" she asked.

He nodded. "I'm even ready for sleep, so don't try any funny stuff like hopping over the pillow."

"In your dreams," she snapped, and found an extra pillow to divide the bed. She laced her fingers behind her neck when she was stretched out on her half. Her eyes were wide open, and she didn't think she could sleep with Hart on one side and a storm approaching outside. But in seconds her eyes fluttered, and she was asleep.

Propped up on an elbow, Hart drank in his fill of her lying there so peacefully. Long, lean legs. No excess fat anywhere in spite of a very healthy appetite. Silky dark hair that begged for a man's hands to touch. Lips that he wanted to kiss so badly.

Thunder rattled through the trees and she slept on, but when the first flash of lightning lit up the room, she jumped six inches over the pillow and grabbed Hart in a death grip.

She buried her face in his chest and shut her eyes tightly. "Hold me."

He wrapped her in his arms. "It's just lightning. The storm will pass."

"But it's here now."

He wished it would last until they were rescued, if it meant he could sink his face into her freshly washed hair and smell the sweetness until then.

She looked up into his face about the same time the next flash zigzagged its way through the window. She'd been dreaming they were in a boat trying to get back to civilization, when a hurricane hit. It overturned the boat, and she was hanging onto the bottom, searching for Hart in every lightning flash. She shut her eyes tightly and wrapped her arms around his neck.

"Were you here when Katrina hit?" he asked.

He felt her gulp before she nodded. "It was horrible. We were called to New Orleans to help with security. The smell. The destruction. It scared the bejesus out of me."

"I didn't think anything could scare you," he said. He made no effort to release her, and she made none to shake free of his embrace.

Losing you again. Loneliness. Hurricanes. She listed the three top things that could scare her right then. The first one terrified her as much as the storm. She was a complete idiot. There she was, in a place where no one could disturb her time with him, where she had his undivided attention; and she was fighting it tooth, nail, hair, and eyeball, as Maw Maw said.

She opened her eyes to see him looking down. Their gaze caught, and a million years danced in front of them. Suddenly, the past didn't matter, only the present. When he lowered his head to kiss her, she raised her chin slightly to meet him halfway.

When the kiss ended, she cuddled into his chest. "Hold me, Hart. Don't ever let me go."

"I won't," he whispered.

Later, when the thunder ended and the first round had ended on a note so high that it rivaled the squall, she eased out of his arms and went back to her side of the bed.

I'm still staying, she thought. The storm had passed, and her vision hadn't changed.

He pushed a strand of hair back behind her ear. "Your hair mesmerizes me. It always has. I used to watch it swing back and forth when you walked out across the playground that summer. What are we going to do about us?"

Kate snuggled closer to him. "I don't want to talk about it right now. No talking. Just sleeping until we have to get up."

"Why?"

"Because I hate good-byes and I hate decisions. I've got to think things through again. Give me some time."

The wind howled and thunder rolled as the squall line traveled on up the line. Even when it was no more than a distant rumble, Hart still couldn't sleep. He faced every single demon from the past fifteen years before he finally fell asleep.

He awoke to the warmth of sun on his face and the smell of ham frying in an iron skillet.

"We've got fried ham, biscuits, and gravy this morning," she said.

"Looks like a fine day for fishing," he said.

Kate had awakened at peace with the world. She didn't care that morning if she took Laysard's offer of a job or turned it down. She didn't give a damn if she and Hart spent the rest of their lives right there on that island. The air flowing through the house was crisp and clean and smelled fresh. She was in love. It might take Hart a while to catch up, but that was okay too. So long as he didn't drag his feet too badly.

"Storm washed up a cow, and you've already milked it this morning?" he asked as he rolled off the mattress, stood up, and stretched.

"No, an alligator. I had to sweet-talk it pretty good to get the thing to stand still, but the milk is really sweet and makes the best gravy," she said.

"I'm going out to check the damage," he said.

"You got about five minutes, so don't go far." Her voice had lost its edge, and she sounded sweet, like a wife making breakfast for her husband.

He nodded and made it to the bottom of the stairs before he saw the animal staring up at him. He stopped in his tracks and backed up two steps. "Kate, come here," he yelled.

She slammed the door and didn't make any attempt to be quiet. Still the thing didn't move. "What's wrong? Did a gator come looking for refuge?"

He pointed. "What is that thing?"

"That, *cher*, is a nutria. Remember the twenty-pound rat you thought we were lying about? Well, there it is."

"Will it attack me?"

"It can smell fear at a hundred yards. You might be in big trouble," she teased.

"I'm serious. It looks pretty mean."

She clapped her hands, and the animal lumbered out across the yard and into the trees. "There now. The big mean rat is gone and the little boy can go out and play after the rain. If that gravy burns, I'm holding you responsible," she said, as she made a beeline back into the house.

He walked around the house, and sure enough, it looked the same. One shower curtain had gotten tangled up in the tree, but when he pulled it down, there wasn't even a tear in the plastic. Later, he'd check the rest of the island and the boat dock. When he made it back inside, she looked up from the table with a smile.

"Just in time," she said.

He washed his hands and face at the kitchen sink, dried them on a towel hanging from a large nail driven into the end of the cabinet, and sat down at the table.

Kate removed biscuits from a cast-iron apparatus that sat on top of the woodstove, and piled them up in a crock bowl. She filled a smaller bowl with gravy and put several slabs of fried ham on a platter. On another platter, she stacked half a dozen pieces of fried mush.

"How did you really make this gravy?" he asked.

"Milk out of a can." She split two biscuits and covered them with gravy, adding a layer of black pepper when she was finished.

"Well, it's good. I love cooked breakfast," he said.

"As opposed to raw breakfast?"

"No, as opposed to cold cereal or those things out of boxes that you put in a toaster. I've always liked breakfast. Eggs. Pancakes. All of it."

"Me too," she said.

"Do you realize we just talked without fighting?"

"I did. Thank you for holding me in the storm. I've always been afraid of them," she said.

"Is that what it takes to make you play nice?" he drawled.

She smiled. "And what does it take for you to play nice?"

"For you not to cross me," he said.

"Then you aren't going to play nice very often. I'm not one of those mealy-mouthed women who walk three steps behind and one to the right. I speak my mind."

"That you do, and you are very opinionated."

"Point proven. I do speak my mind, and you want a sweet little ranchin' woman. We don't mix, and I'm not sure we can survive."

"Survive what?"

"Boredom. Living together without television, jobs, electricity, indoor plumbing, books, magazines. Nothing to escape with. Can we do it, Hart?"

"I guess we are about to find out," he said.

"I guess we are. I'm going out for an early-morning shower. The water will be wonderful, fresh rainwater. Besides, I'm all sticky from the heat in here."

"I'll do cleanup, and then let's go fish. I could eat some more like you made yesterday," he said.

"Thanks," she said, and headed out the door.

Her voice, singing something from the Zac Brown band about having to go where the boat leaves from, floated through the window. It didn't make a bit of sense to him why she'd be singing that song. He finished the cleanup, and following her example, threw a towel over the leftovers before he picked up his towel and headed toward the shower. By the time he got there, she was finished and going back toward the house.

A song played in her head as she got dressed.

Sugarland singing "Stay."

Why that song came to her mind was a complete mystery. It was about a woman begging her lover to stay with her instead of going home to his wife. Then it dawned on her that the song was about her situation. She was worried that one day another woman would call, and Hart would leave her again. She hadn't fully gotten over the past. The lines of the song said something about loving a man she had to share.

That's exactly what Kate was running from: fear of having her heart torn to pieces again. She'd never trusted another man after Hart and, now that he was back in her life, she found she was slow to trust him.

She was waiting on the screened porch when he returned from his shower. He dressed in the house and went back out to the porch in shorts, a clean T-shirt, and flip-flops.

"Ready to fish, or do you want to talk?" he asked.

"Fishing is fine," she said in a hollow voice.

"I can always eat more fried ham for dinner," he offered.

"No, I want to fish. Actually, I need to fish," she snapped.

"Don't bite at me, darlin', unless you want me to bite back."

"You wouldn't dare."

"I don't mean to hurt you, and you know it. I'd never hurt you, Kate. I care too much about you to hurt you."

She jumped up.

Cared about her.

She was in love with him. Considering refusing Laysard's offer and he *cared for her*? At least it was enough that he wouldn't hurt her. Was she supposed to be grateful for that and any other little crumbs he left for her to pick up?

"I'm going fishing now. You can come with me or stay up here and care about me."

He stifled a groan. *Women!*

Understanding nuclear chemistry was easy compared to understanding a woman. When he reached the place where he didn't want to strangle Kate, he went to the fishing spot.

She was sitting on the log when he got there. He sat as far away from her as possible and dropped his line in the water. What on earth had made her do a 180-degree turnaround?

He pondered the question for more than an hour before he caught the first fish of the day. A big, five-pound channel catfish that would make two meals all by itself. Finally the answer came to him in the peaceful quiet of the swamp that, strangely enough, was never really quiet.

She was terrified to let anyone into her life. Once upon a time she'd trusted him with her heart. He'd been young and stupid and didn't value the gift. To make her understand that he was a grown man and not a kid anymore, would take a lot.

Kate caught a bass half the size of Hart's catfish and put it on the stringer with his catch. They carried them back to the house without a word.

He set about filleting them at the side of the house.

She went upstairs to stoke up the fire in the stove again.

She swore, as she poked at the embers and added wood, that

she would never take an electric cook stove for granted again. She'd decided on baked beans and macaroni and cheese to go with grilled blackened fish. For blackened fish, Hart would have to start the charcoal, and she'd have to talk to him to explain where everything was kept. She changed her mind and decided to fry the catch.

"Hey, I found a cast-iron hibachi up under the house. We got any charcoal? You know how to make blackened fish? I ordered it when I was doing the circuit down in New Orleans, and it was really good," he said cheerfully.

She wanted to slap that happiness right out of him. "It's under the cabinet over there with the lighter. Set it right there, and I'll get it ready. You start the charcoal and get it red hot."

"Hoe cake?" he asked.

"Cornbread or biscuit?"

He found the charcoal and carried it back outside. "Either one is fine with me."

She added brown sugar, mustard, ketchup, and onion flakes to two cans of pork and beans, and put them on to simmer. When the water for the macaroni began to boil, she prepared it and set it on a cast-iron trivet to keep it warm. She mixed all the spices together and was very grateful for the pound of butter that Minnette had put in the bag. She melted one stick of butter and flopped each fillet into it.

She carried the bowl of fish out to the porch and handed it to Hart. His hand brushed hers, and she wasn't even surprised at the jolt that passed between them or the way his eyes went soft when he looked at her. That they were attracted to each other wasn't an issue. That much was a given. It was the idea of a forever thing like Fancy talked about.

"Take the grills off and put this right down on the coals when they get hot. You want real blackened fish, this is the way to do it."

He obeyed and watched in amazement as she deftly turned white fillets into blackened fish. That done, she put the grills back on the hibachi and set a small cast-iron skillet on top, added a pat of butter, and poured in cornbread mixture when the butter was hot.

He helped carry the food to the table. They sat down and he bowed his head, expecting her to ask him to say grace.

"Father, receive our thanks for this food and this day. Bless both. Amen," she said.

"You mean that?" he asked as he heaped his plate.

"What?"

"Thanking God for this day?"

"I think I do," she said.

"Why?"

"Could be worse. I could be in the morgue."

He shivered. "Don't say things like that."

"Why, Hart Ducaine, are you superstitious?" She laughed, and it was music to his ears.

"Yes, ma'am, I am that. I always did the exact same thing when I rode a bull. Chewed the same brand of gum. Carried the same things in my pockets. Called my mother five minutes before I went to the arena," he admitted.

"And if you didn't? Did it make a difference?"

"Never did give it a chance," he said. "How about you? Superstitious or not?"

"Think, man! Maw Maw and her voodoo cronies? I'm half Cajun."

"That mean yes?"

"No! I was just jerking you around. I'm not superstitious at all. I think we make our own fate and answer for our own choices."

"That, darlin', we agree on, for sure," he said.

Chapter Seventeen

Kate looked for Bubba or Claud all day. In the evening, mists rose from the swamp and covered the island in a thin blanket of fog. Even in that, she had no doubt either of them could find their way through the cypress knees to the boat dock. But bedtime came, and they didn't.

She took another shower to cool her sweaty skin and slipped into a clean white nightshirt. Two days, and now it would be three nights. Surely Maw Maw hadn't died and the rest of the family forgotten about her stranded on the island.

"Good night, Hart," she said, and rolled over to face the wall.

God was punishing Kate; she felt like a second-grader who had disappointed her teacher. Before she could dwell on that thought, Maw Maw's Cajun accent whispered in her ear as softly as if she'd truly slipped into the room.

God isn't punishing you, no. Only t'ing you done wrong was trustin' in a boy, but he's a man now, yes. You got unfinished business, child. Finish it, and you'll have the peace you crave.

I'm trying, Maw Maw. I really am. I want him to hold me so bad, but I want my three magic words. They might be silly, but I want them. Fancy got hers, and someday Sophie will find someone to give her life after wife. I want my knight in shining whatever, and Hart isn't a knight.

You be sure, yes. He might be one of those whatever t'ings, yes. Finish the business. Good night, Kate.

Kate stole glances all around the room, but Maw Maw hadn't slipped onto the island. At least, not in body. Unfinished business. Kate faced her soul in that moment and realized she would never know what was down the pathway with Hart at the end if she didn't take it.

She was going home to Texas for a month before giving Laysard an answer. If the position had to be filled before that, then so be it. But she wasn't ready to stay in Louisiana.

Of course, she had no intention of making life easy for Hart by telling him that when the morning dawned. It might not work out at all, but when she was Maw Maw's age, by golly, she wouldn't be looking back with regrets. Laysard's job was a paycheck, and she could get one of those anywhere.

She slept the sleep reserved for innocent children and old Southern women who only remembered the good things in their past. When she awoke it was to the aroma of coffee. She opened her eyes to find Hart sitting on the side of the bed with a cup of steaming coffee right under her nose.

She sat up and took it from him. "Thank you."

"Fire is started. Coffee is made. Didn't know what you wanted to do about food this morning. It's raining," he said.

"So you've never fished in the rain. It's just water. It won't melt you."

"They bite in the rain?"

"It's water. They live in it. They're hungry, they bite," she said.

"We've still got catfish left from last night, and beans. Want it for breakfast?" The day was totally gray, with the mists still hovering on the ground and soft rain falling from a sky the same color as the mist. Catfish and beans didn't sound so bad for breakfast. In her working days she had eaten cold pizza, jambalaya, gumbo, and a multitude of other things right from the refrigerator.

"Bring it out to the porch so we can watch the rain," she said.

He grinned. "So I'm cooking breakfast?"

The layer of cold surrounding her heart melted. "Guess you are."

He carried the food and a couple of bowls out to the table. She picked up a piece of catfish with her fingers and began to eat.

"No grace?" he asked.

"Already told God thank you for this twice. Reckon he knows I'm grateful." She spooned cold beans into a bowl.

"Think they'll come rescue us today?"

Fishing in the rain wasn't his idea of a wonderful morning.

She kept eating. "If we don't fight, they might."

"What is it with this arguing? Did Maw Maw expect us to get over our personalities? We're always going to argue. That doesn't mean we don't care about each other," he said.

Care. There was that word again. It had four letters, just like love, but it just didn't carry the weight that love did.

"You should have been around when Paw Paw was alive. Those two could bring down the house with their arguing." Kate grinned.

"You got a piece of bean right there on your front tooth," he said.

She shut her mouth, ran her tongue around her teeth, and removed it. "They're sticky when they sit all night."

"You were saying about your grandfather?"

"He was a tall, skinny man. Maw Maw was pure Cajun. Still goes back to French when she's really mad. He worked on a sugar plantation and fell in love with her when she was fifteen. Some of the men who worked for him wanted to go to New Iberia to a dance. Maw Maw's parents had come to town for supplies and brought her along. The dance was down near the bayou, so he saw her getting into the boat to go home. He said he fell in love with her that minute. She had long black hair and eyes just as dark, but he didn't know her name, and no one knew a thing about her. He could have been describing any girl in the state." She stopped and ate another piece of fish.

He waited.

"So a year passed. He went every week to the same place and looked for her, and she didn't come back. He almost didn't go that last time but he did, and that's when he found her. She and her father were just tying the boat to the dock when he realized she was the same girl."

"What happened?"

"He followed them to the store, where her father bought supplies and Maw Maw looked at fabric. She says she saw him watching her and put a little extra sashay into her step. I'm not sure how the courting business all went on, but it did. He made a lot of trips down the bayou to her part of the world, and they were married out there under the trees, when the azaleas were in full bloom that next spring. She went with him to the planta-tion to live in a one-room house. Same one she is in now, only they added another room for the kids."

"And they lived happy ever after?" he asked.

"No, sir! They fought like tigers. Her mother-in-law thought Paw Paw had married beneath himself. Her father told her when she left to be sure, because she wasn't running back home. Be-sides, if she did, her mother-in-law would win. So after the bloom of the honeymoon passed, and when the first baby was on the way, they had a sitdown. He made some vows, and she made some that night, and from then on they were a united front."

"And then came the happily-ever-after?"

"I didn't say that. Then came a marriage. She says that it was push and shove, but they kept it in the bedroom."

"What did they keep in the bedroom?"

"Their arguments and their making up."

They finished eating and worked together at the cleanup chore. It looked as if it might rain all day, but Kate couldn't sit still in the house that long. She dressed in loose-fitting shorts and T-shirt and flip-flops, and started out the door.

"You were serious about fishing in the rain?"

"It's either that or pace the floor. You stayin' or goin'?"

"I'm goin'," he said.

She nodded and stepped out of the screened porch into the rain, and he followed. They were soaked by the time they reached the old log, but it was a warm spring rain and not a cold winter one.

What if this t'ing with Hart didn't have a history? Maw Maw's voice was inside her head again.

Kate thought about that for a while but couldn't answer the question. No history would mean she'd not have had her heart broken. It would mean that she'd trust Hart because he was a good man from a good family.

When the opportunity comes knockin', invite it in and feed it some jambalaya. If I hadn't, there wouldn't be a Kate.

Kate tried to make sense of that, but nothing worked. Did Maw

Maw want her to move back to Texas? In her infinite wisdom, did she see happiness for Kate with Hart? The permanent kind?

Love is a big loaf of LeJeune's bread. Eat it all up by the end of the day, and make a new loaf the next mornin'.

Kate smiled. Maw Maw was a voodoo queen. Finally she made some sense. Kate was ready to go home. She was ready to put the past where it belonged and face the future with a clean slate.

"It's not so bad, being wet, is it?" Hart said.

"Actually feels better than the shower, doesn't it?" she said.

She heard the sound of the boat motor before he did, but she sat still. It might be Bubba or Claud, but then it might just be a shrimper. She'd only just figured out what she wanted to let go of and what she wanted to hang on to. She would have liked to think about it a while longer before she had to go home and actually do it.

When the boat motors stopped on the other side of the island, Hart looked at her with a question in his eyes. "Is that what I think it is?"

She pulled an empty line up out of the water. "Let's go get our things."

Hart followed her, but his heart wasn't in it. Two days ago he would have given half his ranch for that boat to arrive. Yesterday he would have considered giving a fourth of his ranch. Right then, he wanted one more day with Kate.

Claud was sitting on the porch when they reached the house. His rain slicker was draped over the back of a chair, and the umbrella was in the corner. "Y'all both still alive?"

"Barely. Where's Bubba?"

"He's layin' low. Said Hart might still kick his backside all over Louisiana and he wasn't comin' out here," Claud chuckled.

"Wasn't bringing me out here that I'd kick him across the state for. What made me maddest was you bringing Kate and puttin' her here with me," Hart said seriously.

"Guess then in that light I shoulda sent Bubba," Claud told him.

"What're you doing out of school this time of day? Aren't you supposed to be teaching?" Kate asked.

"Took a personal day. Maw Maw said you two was comin'

home today. Bubba, he said he wasn't goin' near Hart. Minnette
said we have to do what Maw Maw says, so here I am.

"Y'all are alive, all right, but did you get anything settled?"
He helped shut windows and rake ashes out of the stove.

"Ask Maw Maw. She's the one with all the answers," Kate said.

"Whew! Me, I'm just the delivery man. Don't be shootin' the
messenger," Claud said slowly.

The rain stopped and the sun came out as if on cue, as they
got into the boat. Hart found a seat and enjoyed the wordless
tour all the way back to the marina, where Claud docked his boat
and motioned toward his van. "I'll have you home in a little
while."

Kate didn't think so. It would take all day and part of the
night for her to get home, but she was on her way as soon as she
could load her belongings in the truck. If Hart wanted to spend
the rest of his vacation in Jeanerette, that was between him and
Maw Maw.

She chose a backseat, leaving the front passenger one for
Hart. He didn't take it, but crawled in beside her, making sure
they didn't touch. Something had happened out there in the
swamp. He wasn't sure what it was, and it might take several
weeks to figure it all out, but he was damn sure doing it in
Texas, not in Louisiana.

Claud started to help tote Kate's bag into the house but she
stopped him. "Put it in the pickup. I'm going home."

Hart was on the porch and thought his ears had surely only
heard what they wanted to hear. He jerked his head around to
look at her, but she avoided his eyes.

Maw Maw slung open the door and smiled. Her old eyes, set
in a bed of deep wrinkles, twinkled. "So y'all decided to come
on back, did you, no?"

"You're in a heap of trouble, Maw Maw," Kate said. "I'm going home right now. I might not come see you again until it's
time for me to put on my black suit, after the stunt you pulled on
me."

"*Chere*, I don't give care. It'll be your loss, you do a t'ing
like that." She reverted back to the deep Cajun accent that she

used only when she was angry or in the presence of her dearest friends.

Kate stopped in the middle of the living-room floor, popped her hands on her hips, and glared at her grandmother. "Why'd you let Minnette haul me off to the swamp?"

Maw Maw folded her hands under her breasts and glared right back at Kate. "*Mais*, was you takin' care of the matter? I helped you, yes. You don't like the way I helped take your scrawny hind end back to Texas."

Kate bit the inside of her lip to keep from smiling. "I'm half Cajun, so be careful."

"That's the half with some sense to it. Other half is *cooyon*," she said.

Hart waited in the doorway; Claud was on the porch.

"That means stupid," Claud whispered.

"You saying my momma is *cooyon*?" Kate asked.

"Your momma is a saint. She lived with my son, who was like his father, so she is a saint like me, yes. You got that stupid from your other grandparents. You get it settled. He's a good man, yes? He was a sorry boy, but sometimes they make good men," Maw Maw said.

"I'm not telling you one way or the other. After what y'all did, I'm keeping silent. And I'm taking my silence to Texas with me," Kate said.

"Then go get your stuff and get on out of here. Call me when the weddin' is set. I might come to Texas for that," Maw Maw said.

Kate blushed from her toenails to the tips of her hair.

"Hart Ducaine, you get your *cooyon* self in here," Maw Maw motioned.

"Yes, ma'am."

"I ain't trustin' her to go to Texas by herself in that big old truck. She's mad and she'll kill herself, yes. So you are goin' with her. Claud is takin' your car back to the airport, and Minnette can follow him."

The room went deadly silent.

Claud didn't mind a drive to the airport. He and Minnette

could have supper in that little restaurant down north of New Orleans that they seldom had time to frequent. But right then, he felt as if he'd walked into the eye of something bigger than Katrina.

"Yes, ma'am, I'd be glad to drive her home," Hart finally said.

"Do I get a say-so in this?" Kate raised her voice.

"Me, I don't think you do," Maw Maw said.

"I'm thirty-one years old, and it's my truck," she said.

"I'm thirty-three years old, and I agree with your grandmother. You've got a lead foot when you are upset," Hart said.

He could kiss the old Cajun woman. Kate thought the quarters were too close out there in the swamp. He'd see if she could survive ten or more hours in the cab of a truck with him without him throwing her out beside the road to hitchhike the rest of the way. It could be a very interesting trip, indeed.

"Then let's get our stuff and get out of here. I want to be in my own bed in Breckenridge by midnight," she said through clenched teeth. She turned and stormed down the hall with a big smile on her face. There she found all her things packed, sitting on the bed, and ready for travel. The smile faded and was replaced by a faint giggle. Maw Maw *had* to be part witch to figure out everything a step ahead of when it actually happened. Either that or something similar had happened between her and Paw Paw, and she was reliving history.

Maw Maw grabbed Hart's arm when he started toward the bedroom. "*Mais*, I did what I could to help you. Now you got to help yourself, son. You get her home by midnight, it's your fault, not mine."

He winked and kept going. It would never do for Kate to see them talking or catch the faintest syllable of a word. He had two days left before he had to be in Breckenridge, and he was driving.

Kate did hug her grandmother before she left, but she didn't thank her.

Maw Maw hugged Kate and whispered, "Call me when you get the date for the wedding, yes?"

Hart handed Claud the car keys to his rental and thanked him for taking care of it for him.

Kate hopped into the passenger's side of the truck, dug her cell phone out of her purse, and called Fancy.

Hart buckled up, started the engine, and waved at Maw Maw, who watched them leave from a straight-backed chair on the front porch.

"Hi, lady," Fancy answered. "So did you kiss or kill?"

"How did you know?"

"I called you, and your grandmother answered. Lovely little lady, but I had to listen really hard to make out some of her words. Spicy old girl, isn't she?"

"Homicide is still on the menu," Kate said.

"It serves you right, after the way you laughed at my predicament with Theron. I'm glad you got stuck out there on an island. Too bad it wasn't snowing and iced over."

"Don't give me grief, girl. I had an outdoor bathroom, no hot water, no electricity, one bed, and had to fish for my supper," Kate said.

Fancy's laughter was so loud that Kate held the phone away from her ear.

"What are you grinning about?" she turned on Hart.

"Compare disasters with your friend and leave me out of it," he said.

"Did you kiss him?" Fancy asked.

Kate hesitated.

"You did, didn't you?"

Kate didn't answer.

Hart looked across the cab at her.

"Keep your eyes on the road," she said.

"Sweeten up that tone or I'll get lost on purpose."

"You two need a couple more days. By the time Theron came to Florida and we started home, we weren't still fighting. Oh, I called your momma. She laughed so hard that she cried when I told her what Maw Maw did. She said you'd always wanted him; now you had him. She wondered what you'd do with him. I'm hanging up now. Sophie knows all about everything too."

"Some friends both of you are. You *could* commiserate with me," Kate pouted.

"Why? Did you commiserate with me?" Fancy asked.

"But you and Theron were in love and meant for each other. You just didn't know it." She wished she could take the words back the moment they were out in the air. Hart didn't need to hear that.

"So are you two. Have been a lot longer than me and Theron. So have fun on the trip home. Your grandmother told me Hart was driving."

"She's a witch," Kate moaned.

"If you don't want her, I'll take her. Oh, by the way, she says she's wearing a red dress to the wedding, so you might think about using that color just to make her happy," Fancy said.

Kate hung up on her.

Hart caught Highway 162 North out of Jeanerette and drove to New Iberia. He thought about stopping at Victor's place for dinner but decided to go on in spite of the hunger pains. If she was that close to the courthouse she might change her mind about going home to Texas, and he wasn't willing to take a chance. Not far up the highway from there, he caught Highway 90 toward Lafayette, where he'd catch I-49 all the way into Shreveport.

"You planning on letting me starve?" she asked, after they'd gone through Lafayette.

"No, ma'am. Name your poison and we'll stop."

"I want a steak. A big one with a baked potato the size of a watermelon. And I want dessert to go with it," she said.

"Where's the nearest Outback Steakhouse, then?"

"Up near Alexandria, and I'm willing to wait that long," she said.

By the time they followed the road signs and found the place, a plain old McDonald's burger sounded good. It was well after lunchtime, so they didn't have to wait for a table at Outback. The waitress brought Hart's sweet tea and Kate's beer right away, along with a plate of appetizers to keep them from eating the sugar right out of the little white packages.

Hart hadn't seen anything as beautiful as the T-bone the waitress set in front of him. He dug into it and shut his eyes, savoring every single bite. He liked fish and loved pork, but basically he was a steak-and-potatoes man. He'd never take it for granted again. It rated right along with hot water, flushable toilets, and air-conditioning.

Kate took a bite of the loaded baked potato and actually moaned. Sour cream and butter and bacon—all the things she had missed the past couple of days. When she cut off a chunk of rib eye and put it in her mouth, she knew she'd made the right decision. Louisiana cuisine was wonderful, and she loved it. But she was a Texan at heart and could never change. Give her Angus any day of the week, and she'd be happy.

"Missed it, did you?" Hart asked.

"More than I realized."

"You know I grow steaks on my ranch."

"You flirting with me, cowboy?"

"I might be."

"You don't have to if you've got a never-ending supply of this."

He raised an eyebrow. "Are we in agreement about something?"

"When it comes to food, we just might be."

"Want to see if we can agree on anything else?"

"Maybe."

"I'll pick you up on Saturday night for a real date, then?"

She stabbed a hot roll and buttered it. "They got one of these places close to Breckenridge?"

"You want steak? I can make it at the ranch even better than this one."

"Don't press your luck," she said and smiled.

Chapter Eighteen

Kate stole glances at Hart while he drove. The hair around the new scar looked less spiky, and with a little mousse, it might even lie down. Hart needed a haircut again but she liked the curls that formed on his shirt collar.

At one point he felt her gaze and turned her way. "What?"

"I didn't say anything."

"What were you thinking, then? I felt some kind of vibe coming from you."

"Probably that I like that song," she said.

"Me too."

He checked the clock on the dash when the sign said they were ten miles out of Alexandria. It was close enough to three o'clock for the check-in time at most motels, and he planned to find one as soon as possible. She might throw a fit, but he was the designated driver and he was tired and needed a real shower with hot water and a shave.

He took the motel row exit off I-49 and found a Baymont Inn. In his rodeo travels he'd stayed in everything from 1950s style motels to expensive five-star hotels. The Baymont was somewhere in the middle and pretty consistent with its offering of a decent room, plenty of hot water, and lots of air conditioning.

"I'm tired. We're getting a room and I'm going to refuel this gas hog." He pulled into a convenience store.

"Don't call my truck names. You've got one almost just like it."

"And it's a gas hog too. Been thinking about trading it in for a mule and wagon."

She smiled at that visual image. Hart Ducaine coming five

miles into town for lunch riding on a buckboard wagon pulled by a couple of ornery old mules.

He filled the tank and picked up a few motel supplies while he was in the store: a bag of corn chips and one of pretzels, a dozen candy bars, and three packages of chocolate cupcakes with those little squiggles of white on the icing. While he was waiting in line to pay, he added a newspaper to his stash.

When he set his purchases on the seat between them, she got a flashback of Maw Maw talking to him in the hallway. They'd cooked this up from the beginning. Had they also planned the swamp trip?

I did that all on my own, yes, Maw Maw's voice inside her head vowed.

He drove to the motel, and she followed him inside. He rented two rooms connected by an inner door and handed her a key. He carried both of their bags to the elevator and waited.

"Supper at six?" he said, when the doors opened.

"Sounds good to me," she said.

Kate tossed her bags on a chair and gasped. A king-size bed with white coverlet and extra pillows. She touched the sheets to find they were as soft as silk. A Jacuzzi in the corner, bathroom with bright yellow-striped wallpaper, and three-way mirrors. Hart did know the way to a woman's heart.

She started water running in the oversize tub and stripped off every stitch of clothing. She stuck a toe in, decided it was just right, and eased down into the warmth. When the water covered the jets, she flipped the switch and let it work magic on her muscles. A rolled-up towel worked as a neck pillow, and she turned off the water with her toes. As the tension eased out of her body, her eyes grew heavy and she dozed.

The cell phone ringtone woke her. She leaned over and fished the phone out of the pocket of her shorts and answered with a groggy, "Hello."

"Am I forgiven for everything in the past?"

"The jury is still out, but it's looking favorable," she said.

"Want to talk?"

"I'll be there in ten minutes. I want to talk."

He propped two pillows against the headboard and slung his long, muscular legs up onto the bed. "I'll be waiting right here. The connecting door is open on my side."

She crawled out of the tub with a sigh and applied lotion to her arms and legs before she got dressed. When she opened the door into his room, he handed her a Snickers bar and kissed her softly.

"My favorite." She tore into it.

"I remember," he said.

She looked over at him. "What? You remember what?"

"Snickers. I had one in my pocket the first time I met you. It was on the playground. You were there with Sophie and Fancy. Fancy went off with Chris Miller. I knew he was trouble in disguise, but it wasn't any of my business. Sophie had to go home, and we were there alone. Stephanie and I'd just broken up because I wouldn't give her an engagement ring. I gave you the candy bar when you said you were hungry."

She had to swallow around a lump in her throat. "I kept the wrapper. It's in my keepsake box."

It was his turn to be amazed. "Really. You've got a fifteen-year-old candy wrapper?"

"Five of them," she admitted.

"Who else gave you Snickers bars?" He frowned.

"No one. I've had roses by the dozens. Lots of boxes of candy. But no one else gave me Snickers."

"Been a busy girl," he grumbled.

"And you? How many roses have you paid for?"

He looked away.

"How many women did you give *my* Snickers to?"

"No one else has ever gotten Snickers. I swear it, Kate. Roses? Enough to buy a good stud Angus bull. Rings? One, and she didn't turn it down and got to keep it when I broke the engagement. Candy? Enough that I can't remember. Must have been at least twelve boxes or more, because there's been fifteen Valentine's Days since then."

"Sixteen," she corrected him.

He waved his hand. "Whatever."

Is he my knight in shining whatever?

"What are you thinking about that put a smile like that on your face? Keep thinking it. You are so beautiful when you smile," he said.

Is this a courtship dance? In a Baymont hotel with a Snickers in my hand?

"You going to tell me what went through your mind?" he asked.

"Good candy," she said. A woman didn't give away all her secrets; and it was a good candy bar, even more so after all those days on the island with no sweets.

"So talk about serious stuff?" he asked.

"Oh, that. You go first."

"Okay. If you laugh at me, I'll get a complex."

"Boys get complexes. Men don't."

He shook his head. "That's a myth. We're wired from birth with a fear of rejection. That's why we don't ask girls out, and why we don't talk about what's in our heart but about candy bars."

"Okay, then talk." Girls didn't like rejection a bit better than boys. The difference was that boys didn't have a network of friends to talk everything to death. She had always had Sophie and Fancy, and they had good broad shoulders when she needed to weep and moan.

He swallowed hard. "The reason I couldn't marry that girl had everything to do with you, not her. She was a good woman. A lawyer who loved rodeo and owned a ranch, so we had a lot in common. She was a good cook. A tall blond with crystal-clear blue eyes."

Kate looked across the room at her reflection in the mirror above the dresser. She was surprised that her skin wasn't leprechaun green.

"It was a month before the wedding. I was sitting on the edge of a motel bed after a bull ride one night and picked up a Snickers candy bar. Everything about you came back to mind. Your long dark hair. The way you made me feel like I was ten feet tall when you looked at me. All of it. I couldn't marry Gretchen, not feeling like that about you. I called her right then and told her the truth. She screamed and yelled and threatened to put out a contract on me."

Kate's mouth went as dry as if it had been swabbed out with freshly picked cotton balls. She was glad he hadn't asked her a question, because she couldn't have spoken if it had meant talk or die.

"For the next five years, every time I went to anything around Albany or Breckenridge, I looked for you. I even went into your aunt's café, but I never quite got the courage to ask her where you were. I think it was because I was afraid she'd say you were living in south Texas with your husband and had five or six kids already."

He went on. "So anyway, I didn't ask and finally just flat gave up. You'd gone your way and found happiness. I didn't deserve it. And then I looked across the room and there you were, of all places, at Theron's wedding reception. And you were a bridesmaid. God, you looked good in that red dress, but I didn't believe it could be you. After all, I'd been searching and thinking about you a long time. So I figured you were just a friend of Fancy's that looked like my Kate."

My Kate.

Her heart skipped a whole beat.

"You're not making this a bit easy. You could nod or comment every so often, so that I would have some inkling of an idea how this is coming across," he said.

She sat down on the edge of the bed and patted the place beside her. "Go on."

He slung an arm around her. "You were really Kate and I was almost tongue-tied. I'd played the scene so many times in my head about what I'd say when we met again, but nothing came to mind except to ask who you were. You couldn't be Kate, not right there in front of me," he said.

She snuggled in even tighter.

"Then we were in the motel room, and it was Kate all grown up and even more beautiful and desirable than she'd been all those years before, and we were laughing and talking. You know why I rented a room that night? Because I was afraid if you had to follow me all the way to my ranch to talk, you'd change your mind. So I pulled into the Ridge and rented a room so you wouldn't chicken out. You didn't have to save my skin and reputation, but you did. You didn't have to sit with me in the hospital, but you did. My life was going in the right direction. And then you disappeared."

"I was scared," she said.

"Rightly so, but you don't have to be. I'm not leaving you for someone else. I happen to be in love with you, have been for a long, long time. You do whatever you want with that information. I'm not rushing you. Just let me into your life."

Tears formed behind her lashes, but she kept them in check.

"Is that asking too much?" he whispered.

"No, it's not asking too much."

Chapter Nineteen

But Momma, I just got home and I need to unpack and do a million things. I haven't even talked to Sophie and Fancy yet," Kate said.

"Too bad. You've been gone a week. My other waitress just called in sick, and you are here just in time to take a shift. So get an apron."

"You are as mean as Maw Maw," Kate fussed.

"She let you fish for a week. I'm meaner than she is. Don't ever forget it. She might be more conniving, but I'm here to tell you, I'm the meaner. You are staying right here and working the supper rush, and then you are coming back to work at ten in the morning and helping out through the dinner rush. You thinking about a future with that man, then you'd best be saving up a bunch of money for a wedding," Mary said.

"There might not be a wedding."

Mary laughed and handed her an apron.

Kate sighed. She really thought if she put on a long face, her mother would send her home to unpack.

It didn't work.

Mary handed her an order pad.

She worked all evening and helped close up, then went home to a hot shower and fell into bed, where she dreamed of Hart taking her for a tour of a Snickers factory. She awoke to her mother's call the next morning.

"Hello," she answered, without opening her eyes.

"It's nine thirty. You got to be here at ten to make the tamales, which are the special. You better shake a leg, girl. And pick up a dozen donuts on your way in. Ilene has the coffee ready," Mary said.

"I'll be there," Kate said with a yawn. She pushed back the covers, got out of bed, brushed her teeth, dressed, and called Fancy on the way out the door. It went straight to voice mail. She left a message asking her to call as soon as possible, hung up, and called Sophie. It also went straight to voice mail. So much for her two best friends worrying about her.

She picked up a dozen and a half donuts because she was extra hungry, parked in the back of the café, and went inside. Ilene and Mary were sitting at the table in the cooking area with a pot of coffee between them. Kate set the donuts down and grabbed a canvas bibbed apron. She always made a mess when it was her turn to make tamales. When it was tied at the nape of her neck, the waist strings wrapped around her twice and tied in the front, she drew up a chair and joined her mother and aunt.

"Coffee is in the pot," Ilene said.

"I'd rather have milk this morning." Kate stood up, went to the refrigerator, and carried a half-gallon container along with a glass back to the table.

She ate four chocolate-glazed donuts and had two tall glasses of milk. It would be a long time before she had time to eat again—not until after the lunch rush, and sometimes that wasn't over until two o'clock. She had just finished the last of the tamales at eleven thirty when Slim and Bobby came through the front door. She barely had time to say hello to them when Fancy, Sophie, and Aunt Maud arrived.

"What are y'all doing in Breckenridge on a Monday?" she asked.

"You didn't call us, so we came to see if you were alive or if Hart Ducaine had killed you on the way home," Fancy said.

"I did call both of you. Left a message. Have a seat. What can I get you?" Kate talked fast. The place was filling up in a hurry, and she was the only waitress on the job.

"Hey, Kate," Cookie Mannford hollered from a table in the corner where she sat with Allie, the lawyer from across the street.

Kate waved at them and felt a touch on her shoulder.

"Need a little help?" Chrissy, the part-time waitress, asked.

"Thank God you are here. This place is a madhouse today," Kate said.

"Who're those people coming in here now?" Chrissy asked.

"Dear Lord." Kate rolled her eyes. "That would be Patrick and Elisa Ducaine, Hart's parents. What would they be doing over here?"

"Maybe they're meeting Hart for lunch. Your momma said he'd been gone a few days. They might just want to see him," Chrissy offered.

"Okay, you take the right side and I'll do the left," Kate said.

"Will do," Chrissy said.

Kate took half a dozen orders and was on her way back to the kitchen when she noticed Hart parking his big white truck out in front. She was amazed he'd found a vacant spot. So that's why Elisa and Patrick were in town after all. She wished she'd taken the right side of the café so she could at least show a little bit of cordiality. But she'd seen Sophie, Fancy, and Aunt Maud on the left and made a hasty decision so she could speak to them for a moment while they ordered.

It was entirely too warm for Hart to be wearing a windbreaker, but she didn't have time to ask him if he was sick or running a fever. She just waved and went on to the kitchen again. That time she found Alma, an older lady who worked part time, coming in the back door.

"I hope you are here to work," Kate said.

"Oh, do you need some help? I just stopped by for takeout, but if you need help I'll stay an hour or two," Alma said and smiled.

"Grab an apron. I'll give you my tips if you'll work," Kate said.

She carried Slim and Bobby's order out and nodded at Hart, who motioned her over to the table.

"Busy day?" he asked.

She nodded.

He stood up and held the chair. "Sit a minute and catch your breath."

"I can't. There's . . ."

The whole café went so silent, Kate was afraid to look behind her.

"Would you please sit down?" Hart's eyes were twinkling. She half-expected him to pull a Snickers bar from his windbreaker and offer it to her. If he did, she'd have a mountain of explaining to do.

She sat down, because in the deadly quiet she couldn't think of a single reason why she shouldn't. Hart peeled off his jacket and handed it to his mother. He dropped down on one knee and opened a red velvet box to reveal a square-cut diamond engagement ring. "Mary Katherine Miller, will you marry me?" he asked.

She stared at him as if he had three eyes and a dozen ears, then leaned back to see what in the hell was glittering on his T-shirt.

"I looked for a white horse and a suit of armor, but all I could find was my white truck. I did wash the mud off it, though." He leaned back so she could see the shirt. "I am your knight in shining whatever, so please say you will marry me."

Right there in glowing, glittery silver, written across the front of his T-shirt, was the word "Whatever."

He dropped back down on one knee again. "So I'm asking a third time and hoping this is the charm. Will you marry me?"

"Yes," she whispered.

He slipped the ring on her finger, kissed her long and hard, picked her up, and carried her out the front door to the applause of everyone in the restaurant.

Chapter Twenty

The sun set in an array of pinks, yellows, and oranges that matched the colors in Sophie's and Fancy's dresses perfectly. A white carriage pulled by six horses carried all three of them from the house where they'd gotten dressed to the barn where the wedding and reception were being held. Kate's mother, Mary, and Hart's mother, Elisa, had worked together overseeing the transformation from a barn into something medieval. Twelve-foot drapes of chiffon in the same colors as the sunset hung on the walls. Kate's three magic words were about to become reality.

"Nervous?" Sophie asked Kate.

"Yes, ma'am," Kate said. "I still can't believe y'all fixed up that engagement with Hart and didn't even tell me about it."

Fancy laughed. "He called me from the motel y'all stayed at on the way home and made me talk about your three magic words. He said he wanted to be your whatever and didn't know how. After we talked a few minutes, he laughed and declared that he'd figured it out. We were as surprised as you when he came in with that written on a T-shirt. He must've stayed up half the night gluing glitter to that shirt. What'd you do with it?"

"It's in my keepsake box."

She didn't tell them that it had joined a handful of Snickers wrappers and newspaper clippings of every time that Hart's name had been mentioned in the Breckenridge paper.

Fancy laughed. "Well, he's your *whatever*, and you look like a medieval bride who could knock a knight's armor off him with Ninja kicks."

Kate smiled. She wore an ivory silk gown styled with an empire waist and slim-fitting skirt. Her dark hair had been styled high on her head and was held with the pearl comb that Maw Maw had worn in her hair when she married. It was the white cowboy boots that didn't fit the rest of the look, but Kate had declared she was about to be a rancher's wife, so she would have cowboy boots.

"You are absolutely stunning. If you'd lived back in castle days, there'd be dead knights all over the land," Sophie said.

Kate cocked her head to one side quizzically.

"Hart would have killed every one of them that came for your hand," Sophie explained.

"I still can't believe I let you two and the mothers talk me into this. I didn't even want a reception," Kate said.

"This is not your wedding. It's your mother's. That's what Theron told me. When our daughters get married, then it's our turn. So grin and bear it," Fancy said.

"Hart is the knight. You are the lady. Here we are. Take a deep breath and be grateful the style wasn't corsets and eighteen-inch waists in that day," Sophie said.

"It might have been. Who knows? Momma just thought this was the perfect dress when we went shopping. She said it looked like the lady on the cover of a castle romance she read a few years ago. It's probably something from a different era altogether," Kate grumbled.

"How do you feel?" Fancy asked.

"Beautiful, and like the luckiest woman alive," Kate said honestly.

"Then go marry that man. You've waited almost sixteen years for this day. It's yours. Enjoy it," Fancy said.

Sophie adjusted the comb in Kate's upswept black hair and kissed her on the cheek. "Let's do this thing, girls. Let's go make the mommas proud."

"And the grandmas. Don't forget Maw Maw," Fancy said.

Theron waited by the carriage and took Fancy's arm, leading her into the barn. Patrick Ducaine escorted Sophie and served as his son's best man. Hart waited under a cast-iron arch, woven with roses of every color the mothers could find in a three-county area.

Carolyn Brown

Background music to "The Rose" began and Theron pushed back a layer of chiffon. He and Fancy strolled down the aisle on a five-foot section of pale green carpet. When they reached the arch, Theron gave Fancy a kiss on the cheek and went to stand on Hart's side. Then Patrick and Sophie came in and took their places.

When the curtains parted the third time, Hart's breath caught in his chest. Mary was on one side of her daughter, Maw Maw on the other. The traditional wedding march started, and the three women slowly made their way toward the groom. When they'd gone three or four steps, the music stopped.

Kate stifled a giggle. Something had to go wrong that day. Thank goodness it was a glitch in the music and not rain or a tornado. Hart took two steps forward, keeping his eyes on Kate. He had a microphone in his hand, and piano music began to tinkle from behind a curtain off to the left of the arch.

She recognized the song immediately.

It was "Lady" by Kenny Rogers, and Hart had the same throaty voice that made Kenny famous. From the moment he sang the first words that said he was her knight in shining armor, the rest of the world disappeared. Hart was singing to her, and she heard and saw nothing else.

Her mother and Maw Maw started walking with her again. Hart looked at no one else, as once he'd thought he'd never find her, and he'd waited for her so long. When she stood in front of him, he was singing that she was his lady and the love of his life.

The song ended, and he handed the microphone to Theron, and she gave her bouquet of multicolored roses to Sophie. Then he took her hand in his, and they turned to face the preacher.

"Dearly beloved, we are gathered here this evening . . ." he said, beginning the traditional ceremony.

When it came time for Hart to say his vows, he took both of Kate's hands in his and looked deeply into her eyes. "Mary Katherine Miller, you are the love of my life and my lady. I will always love you and I'll always be your knight in shining whatever. I promise to never, ever leave you."

She kissed him on the cheek when he'd finished. "Jethro

Hart Ducaine, I've been in love with you since grade school. I intend to love you, not unto death, but beyond that. When we are old and have loved for many years, if you should go first, wait for me outside the pearly gates, because I'll join you as soon as I can. I don't want to live a single day without you."

Mary sniffed into a lace-edged handkerchief.

Maw Maw wiped at a tear.

Elisa buried her face in a handkerchief and wept.

After they'd exchanged rings, the preacher pronounced them man and wife and told Hart he could kiss his bride.

He did the job justice.

"You are truly my lady," he whispered.

"And there's no doubt you are my whatever," she whispered back.

The preacher said, "I present to you for the first time, Mr. and Mrs. Jethro Hart Ducaine."

Hart led her to the back and out into the reception area. "How long do we have to stay?" he asked.

"Until Maw Maw says we can go."

"The bride and groom will dance their first dance together now," the lead singer of the band announced.

Kate melted into Hart's arms as the singer sang "Lady" again. To Kate's way of thinking, it didn't sound nearly as sexy as when Hart sang it.

The minute the last note floated out through the crowd, they were surrounded with well-wishing friends and family.

Patrick picked up a microphone and announced that food was being served and the band would be playing for the rest of the night. He thanked everyone for attending and welcomed Kate into their family.

"Rest of the night?" Hart moaned.

Theron clapped him on the back. "Take my advice and stay a long time. The mommas will love you."

Kate touched Hart's arm. "Let's eat. I'm starving."

Food was served Texas-style rather than by waiter. Several long tables were laden down with everything from jambalaya to barbecue. One table had been reserved for the wedding party, so when her plate was overflowing, Kate took her place beside her husband.

Aunt Maud hugged her from behind and whispered in her ear, "I'm so glad to see you settling down and happy like Fancy. This fall, when I die, Sophie is going to need your attention."

"We'll take care of her, Aunt Maud. She's liable to get her three magic words fulfilled too."

Maud moved around and sat in the chair reserved for Sophie. "I heard about that, and I sure hope she does. I'm doing everything I can to make it happen."

That got Kate's attention. "You're not looking at the preacher that keeps showing up in our circles, are you?"

"Good God, no! She doesn't need another preacher. She didn't need the first one. I need to tell you something so you'll be prepared, but you have to swear on your wedding vows that you won't tell Sophie. You can tell Fancy later, but never Sophie," Aunt Maud whispered.

Kate was all ears. "I swear."

"My late husband didn't leave his half of the ranch to his nephew, Elijah. He left the whole thing to me. It's me that's leaving half to Elijah. He's retired military and speaks his mind. He's rich as Sophie, and they're each going to try to buy out the other. It'll do her good to come up against Elijah. I just wish I could stick around to see the fireworks."

"Oh!" Kate said.

Aunt Maud shook a finger at her and giggled like a schoolgirl. "Just take care of her. She's going to need both of you. And remember, you swore."

She slipped away before Kate could say another word.

Hart leaned over and kissed her on the cheek. "Not regretting your decision about a honeymoon?"

"No, I am not. I just wish we could go to the ranch sooner," she whispered.

Hart kissed her, long and passionately. "I love you, Kate."

"And I love you, because you are my knight in shining whatever, and I'm your lady."